Sargie and the Scammers

A Doc and Daisy Mystery for Dog Lovers

Dr. Stacey Bonner, DVM

I0833665

This is a work of fiction.

 All names, places or incidents are products of the author's imagination or used fictitiously, and any resemblance to actual persons, living or dead, is entirely coincidental.

Contents

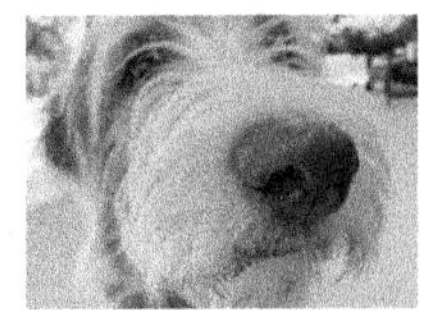

Chapter 1

Sue's House with Luke

My name is Daisy MacVety. I am a fluffy dog with a brown nose, red spots, and white fur. I enjoy walking everywhere with Sue, taking long naps, sniffing for tasty treats and clues, and slurping up greasy drippings that fall from the grill. I especially love running with my four-legged cousins after a car ride.

As everyone knows, Sue is my favorite person, playmate, and two-legged partner in crime-solving. After she retired from veterinary practice with her daughter in Haywood, she became a sleuth. Initially, she had no idea that crime would escalate in the idyllic riverside town she called home. Then, as times changed and Sweetwater Springs boomed, crime followed. Who would have thought? More people. More money. More crime.

According to Sue, there are over 300 springs on the river. Dogs have more interest in scents than Science, but she says the water filters through underground rocks, purifying it before it floods the river basin with 72-degree refreshment. People come from miles around to kayak and cool off from Spring until Fall.

Sue's friend, Luke, calls me the captain of the kayak. He paddles from the stern, Sue watches from the bow, and I captain from the middle. He paddles directly downriver with the current, avoiding swimmers, tubers, and other wildlife. It requires minimal directional navigation, but his compliments make me feel important.

Luke has a crush on Sue. I can smell love and believe it's mutual, but he has been away for work often. Sue doesn't want a long-distance relationship. Luke is a global hotelier, but his heart and philanthropy belong to Sweetwater Springs rather than development.

Luke sold his largest landholding to the one and only local billionaire, who plans to develop it for a hotel in the future. The billionaire wants a grande hotel and a Wild West theme park. He plans shootouts, cattle drives, rodeos, and attractions featuring cowboys and Indians.

His wife is Sue's two-legged partner in crime-solving. He names everything after Mia. Some people say that one day, he will change the name from Sweetwater Springs to Mia's Springs. A famous murder at her housewarming party brought them together.

When Sue gets nostalgic, she likes to imagine living in Sweetwater Springs before its development. Sue says it's been less than 150 years since the natives lived here. They had cool water year-round and plenty to hunt by land and river. It seems like a long time to me, but for Sue, it's just the blink of an eye.

Luke is coming for dinner tonight. He says he has something important to talk to Sue about. His brother has moved to Sweetwater Springs. He's not got the best reputation, but that's par for the course to have a black sheep in the best of families.

I can't wait to smell what Luke is cooking tonight and dabble into the spillage. The grill is something new. Luke bought it as a gift for Sue, but he cooks on it more often than she does. He used to be a sous chef in the kitchen, but now he's head chef in the backyard.

Luke thinks it's manly to cook outdoors. He cooks and splashes tasty meat grease behind the grill. He calls it cleaning when he scrapes the delicious liquid down the hole, but it's an everlasting feast for me.

I had no idea Luke's cooking would be so much fun. The grease soaks into the ground, making a blossom of enticing scents. I used to hurry to do my business in our small fenced yard. I could linger endlessly with my nose to the grassy patches and sandy yard.

Luke is one of my favorite people, second only to Sue. He has the most fantastic backyard where I can run with his dog. I have only a tiny backyard with no room for running, so I prefer Luke's house for a playdate. The grill is the second-best option for good times in the yard, but nothing matches a romp with my four-legged friends.

I raced to the door with Toby when Luke arrived. Although a bit annoying, Toby is Sue's cat and my best four-legged friend at home. He is a grey mackerel tabby who loves Luke's treats as much as I do. I like to be the center of attention, but I sometimes think Luke likes Toby more than me.

"Hi, Kids," Luke said as he marched through the front door and headed to the kitchen to give Toby some cat treats before passing a few miniature morsels to me.

"I have some dog treats under the counter for Daisy," Sue said, smiling and watching me bolt Toby's treats in my long mouth. "She probably didn't taste those little-bitty cat treats."

Luke reached under the counter and pulled out a long, jerky-style treat for me. "You're next," he said as I sat down for the jerky. It was delicious, and I lay on the floor, holding it between my paws to enjoy it.

"It's good to see you, Luke," Sue said. "I missed you this week."

Luke was often out of town working on something he rarely discussed unless Sue asked. "I missed you, too," he said, pecking her cheek, although he likely longed for her lips. "I'd love to hold you," he said, and Sue changed the subject.

"What did you bring for dinner?" she asked. "Daisy is looking forward to your cooking. She spent more time outside this week than ever."

"Bacon, barbecue, Swiss cheeseburgers," he said. "With corn on the cob."

When I heard the word "bacon," I envisioned my fate. It promised to be a good night for drippings.

The new grill was the most remarkable thing I had ever seen. Food was cooked twice as fast and was cleaned up even more swiftly. There was a container to store the grease, but Luke was such an authoritative cleaner that it often spilled past the bucket onto the ground. This was good news for me.

Sue was particular about my diet but overlooked the bacon. They used to recommend bacon grease for shiny dog coats before more appropriate products came with something Sue called balanced omega-3 and 6 EFAs. Bacon grease was fattening but delicious. I wasn't the most food-driven dog in the family, but I appreciated flavor as much as the next dog.

Luke cooked the bacon in less than five minutes, followed by generous beef patties. I'm not an expert on time, but I heard Sue mention it. This was dog heaven in the backyard for an only dog like me. For once, I didn't miss my four-legged cousins, who may have beaten me to it.

Despite the fabulous smells, Toby was uninterested in the bacon and stuck his nose in the air as he looked through the screen. This, unlike other things he did, was not annoying. I stayed outside to sample the drippings without his interruption while Sue and Luke ate burgers on the back porch.

"You're becoming an excellent chef," Sue said, wiping her lips with a napkin as they sat at the patio table.

"Thank you," Luke replied. "I've never been much of a cook at home, but this is fun."

"I'm glad you're enjoying it," Sue said.

It was a warm Spring evening with a gentle breeze, but not too hot. After licking the ground, I stood at the patio door and barked to join the others. Toby was staring at a tiny bird on the ground outside the screen. Luke and Sue watched the small alligator swimming across the cove.

"The alligators are back," Luke said as the long, narrow body slithered across the water. Sue agreed it was mating season when they were most active.

Luke was a cat man at heart. Toby was Sue's replacement for a kitten that Luke had discovered and generously shared with her ex-roommate's daughter. After the kitten moved to his new home upriver, Sue acquired Toby.

"Toby is a good cat," Sue said as he circled between her legs. "He's very affectionate," she added as I moved closer under the table.

"Do you think Daisy is jealous?" Luke asked.

"Maybe a little," Sue replied. "Siblings are like that, sometimes. They want our attention but love each other."

"Sometimes I wonder about my brother," Luke said. "I'd do anything for him, but I'm not entirely sure how he feels about me."

"Yes, tell me about him," Sue said. "You mentioned he just moved to Sweetwater Springs."

I snuggled in a curled-up ball under the porch table while they talked. Luke was the eldest sibling with a nearly impossible act to follow. He wasn't trying to beat everyone with his success in the hotel business; he just did. Some of them were more jealous than others.

"His name is Bill," Luke said. "He had two successful golf courses but lost money during the COVID-19 quarantine. He had to close both of them."

"I'm sorry to hear that," Sue said. "What is he doing now?"

"He wants to build a new golf course in Sweetwater Springs," Luke said. "He wants to buy the property on the Green Cove."

"It's expensive," Sue said. "That's a big piece. Over three hundred acres."

"With a massive waterfront on the bluff," Luke replied. "It has beautiful views."

"True, if the cove was clear," Sue said. "It's full of algae."

"Best time to buy," Luke said. "It will be worth a fortune after it's cleaned up."

I squirmed under the table as I recalled Green Cove, where the mayor and a murdered man had lived. I wouldn't drink the water there. Nope, nope, nope. Now, Luke's brother Bill had bought a nearby house.

"My brother is a gambler," Luke continued. "He was a whale in Las Vegas before he lost it big."

"Did you ever gamble?" Sue asked.

"A little," Luke replied. "Sometimes I made big bets but had the money to lose. My brother didn't."

"He took risks he shouldn't have."

"For me, it was fun. For Bill, it was a means to a living."

"That sounds like he has a gambling problem," Sue said.

"My brother is always in trouble," Luke said. "He gets attracted to the wrong people. He's a scam addict."

"I've never heard of a scam addict," Sue replied.

"Some people trust the wrong people. Most people learn from their mistakes. My brother doesn't."

Sweetwater Springs had its share of scammers, cons, and suspected mafia. They blended in and lived a small-town life with the rest of the residents. Everyone knew not to ask questions. They were nice to me, but a suspected Mafioso dog named Jelly Bean was a snob.

"I thought Thomas Baldwin would purchase that property," Sue said of the local billionaire. "Maybe he's not certain the algae will clear."

"Maybe he doesn't want to deal with the turtles," Luke replied.

"What turtles?" Sue asked.

"There are ten turtle nests on the property," Luke said. "They are protected species. Officials can legally relocate them, but Thomas doesn't need the controversial publicity."

"His hotel and Wild West theme park are more important to him than another development," Sue replied. "He has more than enough projects to keep him busy."

"That land could be perfect for a golf course," Luke said. "The turtles could dig their nests in the rough."

"Interesting," Sue replied. "Does your brother have the money for the land?"

"No," Luke replied bluntly, he doesn't."

The Green Cove brought back images I did not want to remember. Muck. Slime. Dead fish. A dead man. His pretty wife and his sweet daughter.

"My brother wants us to meet three friends to shoot archery on the property tomorrow," Luke said. "I should warn you—he doesn't choose his friends carefully."

"Anyone we know?" Sue asked, and Luke replied that two were out-of-town businessmen, and one was a local man, but he knew little more about them. "There's no telling what we may encounter."

"Is he married?" Sue asked.

"Yes, his wife's name is Lilly."

"Does your mother like his wife?" Sue asked, and Luke shrugged. His 94-year-old mother had an opinion about everyone and everything and didn't hesitate to share her thoughts.

"There have been a few problems between Bill and Lilly," Luke said. "Mostly, she talks about Bill."

"He sounds like a Black Sheep," Sue said, and Luke suggested he was more like a Bad Penny."

Finally, Sue asked the most critical question. "Does your brother have a dog?"

"Yes, his name is Sargent Stealth, but they call him Sargie. He is a Harlequin Great Dane."

"A big spotted guard dog named SS," Sue said, smiling at the initials. "Is he Stealth?"

"I don't know much about Sarge," Luke replied. "My brother only recently moved back to Sweetwater Springs." Looking at me, he added, "I told him about Daisy. She's welcome to come to the party."

"Will she be safe?" Sue asked,

"I hope so," Luke replied. "Whatever else he may be, my brother is a dog lover."

Luke went home early, and Sue prepared for bed with much on her mind. She tossed and turned much of the night as she imagined our new friends and acquaintances of questionable virtues and unknown motives.

Chapter 2

The Green Cove Property with Russ Johnson, Doug DeLeon, and Andy Lemar

I spent the night thinking about Sargie, except in my mind, he was Sargent Stealth, massive and spotted—a Harlequin Great Dane. Sue was concerned about my safety in meeting him, and Luke admitted he didn't know him. It was worrisome.

Whenever I fell back asleep, Sargent Stealth seemed larger than life. I liked most dogs except for the neighborhood fence jumper, who snapped and growled at me when he escaped his yard and charged at us while Sue and I walked past his house. I wasn't sure Sargie was my type— a friendly dog with good connections. I was afraid of the Fence Jumper, which was a Big, Dangerous Dog.

Don't get me wrong, I'm a brave Doodle with exceptional sniffing skills and a big heart. I'm not afraid of dogs. However, once a Fence Jumper has charged you, it changes you. You learn about aggressive dogs, and you lose trust in your tribe. I was fortunate that Sue could yell at him and make him go home. It was the loudest voice I'd ever heard from Sue when she told him to Go Home.

Sue was horrified when the local Animal Control took two months to investigate the Dangerous Dog's escape after he charged at me. Later, the dog escaped again and mutilated another dog. Sue was appalled when Animal Control allowed the owner to keep the dog. Sue says we need better laws to ensure dangerous dogs don't escape their yards and aren't returned to the same owner if they escape and attack another dog.

The fence jumper changed Sue, too. She changed our walking route and carried pepper gel. Sometimes, she drove to another neighborhood or a walking trail for our leashed walks. She worked towards implementing better laws to protect the dog walkers.

After the close call with a loose dog, I learned to take dangerous dogs seriously—hence my concerns about the Great Dane. I didn't know if Sargent Stealth was a friendly or dangerous dog, but he was big. This prompted Sue to ask Luke if it was safe for me to go to the party.

I still imagined the enormous Great Dane when we arrived at Bill's house for the archery party. Sarge was big, all right. But it didn't take long to see he wasn't dangerous.

He was big and old. Very old. Twelve years old, to be exact. Ancient for a giant dog, like a Great Dane.

"What a Sweet Boy!" Sue said, hopping out of the car to greet the tall dog with the lolling tongue. "Is this Sarge?"

"Yes, it is!" Lilly said, smiling at me. "Is this Daisy?"

I stepped closer to Lilly so she could massage my chest, which she seemed to want to do. "I love dogs," she said, and Sue agreed. "Dogs and cats are my life."

"I understand you're a veterinarian," she said.

"Retired," Sue corrected. "My daughter runs the clinic now."

"I've met your daughter," Lilly replied. "She prescribed something for Sargie's arthritis."

"Has it been helpful?"

"Yes, very much."

"You have to be gentle around Sargie," Sue told me, but I already knew it. I could smell old dogs and puppies and reacted accordingly. I would be gentle.

We walked closer to the bullseye archery targets where Bill awaited us. "Hi, Brother," he told Luke. "Glad you and your lovely lady could make it."

"This is Sue," Luke replied as we shook hands. "She's my best lady friend in Sweetwater Springs."

"If I were you, I would want her for my girlfriend," Bill said, and Luke agreed that he longed for it.

"Your brother is gone away frequently," Sue said. "I look forward to seeing more of him when he retires."

"Don't hold your breath," Bill said. "My brother may never retire."

"He has an amazing job building hotels worldwide," Lilly replied, without adding that it would have been nice if Bill had been so successful.

I could smell the tension between the brothers as we walked toward a turtle nest near the back of the property. Sue mentioned that Luke's success was tough for a younger brother to follow. One could find a different niche for extraordinary success—or give up and be a regular guy.

Bill had elected to build golf courses, but the COVID-19 pandemic had devastated his wealth. It was time for a new beginning.

"Did you hear about the tortoises?" Lil asked as we approached a ribboned-off section around a turtle dig.

"You wouldn't need to relocate the turtles to build a golf course," Luke said, and Lilly agreed that they were practically a blessing. They could nest in the rough.

A handsome middle-aged man fiddled with the demarcation ribbons as we approached the turtle nests. "This is Russel Johnson," Lilly said. "He's a stockbroker from Miami."

"Pleased to meet you," the dark-haired man with chiseled features said.

"Are you a Turtle man?" Luke asked.

"I'm a wildlife lover," he said. "I like nature," he added, and Bill suggested that his wife was obsessed with turtles.

"Oh, Honey, I'm not obsessed," Lilly disagreed. "I do like to protect them."

"Whoever knows why?" Bill said when I lay down beside Sargie, who continued to stand.

"Sargie rarely lies down," Lil said, ignoring the turtle question, and Sue suggested it was hard for him to get back up because of the arthritis. "Dogs are wise at adapting to their mobility issues."

"I should be so wise," Luke said, and everyone agreed he pushed himself harder than an older brother should.

A shorter man with a square face and slicked-back salt and pepper hair exited his yellow sports car and passed through a glorious bed of purple wildflowers that had just announced their spring bloom. Sarge barked a hoarse, older-dog bark as he approached the group while I sat beside Sue and watched.

"This property is fabulous!" he said. "My guests and colleagues would be delighted to spend a weekend of rest in this paradise."

"Wouldn't anyone?" Bill agreed, introducing the newcomer as Andy Lemar."

"I've never seen anything like it," Andy said, shaking hands. "I am impressed."

"Andy is a developer," Bill explained. "He's an entrepreneur from Miami."

"This paradise isn't right for a housing subdivision," Russ said, fiddling with the ribbon.

"I agree," Andy said. "But it is perfect for an Eco Retreat."

"An Eco Retreat?" Luke asked.

"Yes, a small retreat with farm-to-table food, massage, nature walks, and meditation."

"That sounds delightful," Sue said, and Luke suggested that the local billionaire, who was coming later, had his dreams set on a larger resort and theme park upriver.

"I'm no competition for Thomas Baldwin," Andy replied. I would love to create a beautiful retreat where guests can learn something about simple, healthy living on their vacation."

"That's an admirable suggestion," Sue said, and Lil suggested it could complement a golf course if there were enough land.

"There's not enough land for both," Bill said. "I'm sure of that."

"How did you find out about his property?" Luke asked, and Andy replied, "For sale signs, just like your brother."

"Would you consider lending me the money to buy it for a golf course?" Bill asked, and Luke instantly declined.

"I learned my lesson last time I lent you money," Luke said. "You never paid me back."

A gentle breeze swayed the tall purple wildflowers in various directions as a third man drove an Antique Green American Sports car onto the property. He parked next to the wildflowers and revved the engine.

"That's an old muscle car," Sue said, recalling she had driven her boyfriend's car in high school.

"There's nothing like them today," Luke said. "Nothing comes close to the power of those old engines."

"Listen to the engine rumble," Sue said as the man pushed the accelerator with the car in neutral."I enjoyed driving stick shift cars," she added.

A fit man with heavy muscling stepped out of the car and walked towards us, causing Sarge to initiate another round of hoarse barks. The old Dane's hoarse voice reminded me of a chicken learning to crow before his vocal cords were ready. Instead, he was an old dog trying to bark when his vocal cords were worn out.

I respected Sarge for not giving up his voice but empathized with him for the weak Arfs. Losing his voice was part of the circle of life for Sarge, but I had not noticed it in most older dogs. Maybe they quit trying to bark when the time came, but not Sarge. He just slowly said Woof, Woof, Woof.

Sue said the muscular man looked like he had eaten a lot of protein, but dogs aren't inclined to recognize such things. To me, he looked like a big man in the wildflowers. More muscular than most.

"Meet Doug Deleon," Bill said as the swaggering man approached.

"It's nice to meet you," Luke said, and Doug replied, "Likewise."

"Doug is a homegrown man," Bill said. "He is practically a Legend in Sweetwater Springs."

"I played a little football in high school," he replied.

"Lucky for you," Luke replied. "I was too small to play. My mother wouldn't let me."

"Your mama is a smart lady," Doug said, and Luke mentioned that she was sure of it.

"What do you do now?" Sue asked, and the man replied, "This and that. I got lucky with a few investments."

"You couldn't ask for a more beautiful place to invest," Bill said, and Sue agreed it was inspiring.

"I suppose you want to put a business on this property, too," Sue said, shaking his extended hand.

"Yes, ma'am," he agreed. "It's perfect for a steakhouse overlooking the cove from the bluff."

"Thomas Baldwin wants to build a steakhouse for the Wild West Theme Park at his hotel."

"No disrespect to Mr. Baldwin, ma'am," Doug replied. "A spectacular town like Sweetwater Springs could use more than one steakhouse.

Lilly photographed the three men who arrived for the archery target practice that brought them together. Doug DeLeon was tall, fit, and handsome; Russ Johnson was medium-built, chisel-faced, and attractive; and Andy Lemar was shorter, square-faced, rich, and good-looking.

"Are any of these men married?" Sue asked Lil while they walked toward the fabulous view of the cove. She replied that she had been told Russ and Andy were bachelors.

"They are a handsome crew, aren't they?" Sue said, and Lil agreed they were a sight for sore eyes before she walked away to join the men.

"I heard that," Luke said, teasing Sue after Lil was gone.

"I'm not asking for myself," she replied.

The ladies of Sweetwater Springs would have a field day with the good-looking men, and it seemed one of them had already been noticed. "I've seen Russ Johnson at Mia's Museum," Sue whispered to Luke. "The manager is Mia's daughter's best friend."

Chapter 3

Bill's house

I enjoyed the breeze with my red nose extended and nostrils twitching. It was a perfect spring day for a walk with Sue, Luke, and their new acquaintances at the Green Cove. I knew nothing about archery, but the targets seemed practical for something two-leggers enjoyed. I would learn more about the sport later on.

The tall grass was soft beneath my feet. We walked beneath tremendous grandfather oak trees that soared skyward with gnarly, long branches. Sue mentioned they were some of the grandest and oldest trees in Sweetwater Springs. Luke said they were several hundred years old.

"If only trees could talk," Sue said, and Luke agreed that there would be some interesting stories to tell.

"The phosphate miners dug this cove to make fertilizers over a hundred years ago," Sue said. "It was crystal clear less than fifty years ago."

"Now, it's green," Luke replied. "You can't see the bottom."

"There are no springs to replenish the fresh water on the cove," Sue mentioned, although Luke was familiar with the biology.

"Freshwater has to filter in from the headwaters upriver and the smaller springs along the river's route."

"It's remarkable how much times have changed since we've been guests on the planet," Luke said. "Now we know how much damage fertilizers do to the water supply and streams. Nobody knew back when they dug this cove."

"Creative and innovative minds will figure out how to fix it," Sue said, and Luke agreed it would likely happen sooner than we expected.

"Look at the brilliant green of the leaves," Luke said, pointing to the huge canopies of leaves, and Sue mentioned it was her favorite shade of the season.

It was a lovely walk on the sought-after property toward the tall bluff that led down to the cove. Sarge walked stiffly ahead of us, as older dogs do. His tall legs were more splayed than a younger dog's, but his spirit was uncompromised. He had the grit and determination of his younger years, but not the healthy body that accompanied youth.

Sarge was so nice that I began to feel guilty about having terrible thoughts about him. Still, I had reached the stage in life where a dog had to earn my trust. There were good and bad dogs in this world, just as good people and bad people. The worst-case scenario was when bad people, such as criminals, had bad dogs, such as the Dangerous Fence Jumper, who had charged me and nearly killed the little dog.

Nobody mentioned the pollen that was the downside of spring renewal. It covered the cars in a day and made people stuffy and sneeze. Some dogs got itchy from seasonal grasses, but I was fortunate not to be one of them. Sarge wasn't one of them, either.

Sue and Luke walked far behind the others. "My brother asked us to be here for a reason," Luke said. I doubt it has anything to do with archery."

"I figured as much," Sue replied, not mentioning they had joined two of the most eligible bachelors in Sweetwater Springs. "We'll find out soon enough."

When we reached the top of the bluff, Thomas Baldwin drove onto the property with his wife, Mia Baldwin, Sue's favorite crime-solving partner. Mia Baldwin was bright, beautiful, and generous with the local businesses where she purchased almost everything.

"We didn't expect to be invited to an archery meet," Mia said, and Luke suggested his brother must have wanted a reason to show off the property he wanted to purchase for a golf course.

"It is a fabulous property," Thomas agreed, pointing at the turtle nests. "Too much potential conflict for my tastes."

Luke agreed that some people wouldn't want the turtles moved, even if it were legal. "The turtles keep the price lower," he said.

"I want to make the locals happy," Thomas said. "It's hard enough to convince them my hotel and Wild West theme park are good for the community."

"Moving turtles is better for someone else," Sue agreed. "It's best not to rock the boat."

"You are about to meet three entrepreneurs who have a dream for this property," Luke explained. "One fellow is from Miami, one from Sweetwater Springs, and my brother, Bill, wants to build a golf course."

"The other two men want an Eco Lodge or a steakhouse," Sue added.

"There's room for everyone," Thomas said, with no hint of jealousy. "I hope my hotel and theme park will bring many new businesses to Sweetwater Springs."

"Would you be upset about the steak house?" Sue asked.

"Heavens, no," Thomas replied. "My hotel guests will want other dining options during their stays. I'd welcome a steakhouse, an Eco Lodge, or a golf course."

"Are we here to approve their projects?" Mia asked, and Luke said they'd find out shortly.

"Just to warn you, my brother is a bit of a schemer," Luke said. "I wouldn't be surprised if this is a setup."

I was lying on the soft grass beneath the canopy of the grandfather oaks when four men, Lilly and Sarge, walked away from the bluff overlooking the cove to greet us. After introductions, Thomas said, "What do you think of the property?"

"It's stunning," Russ said. "Perfect for many different projects."

"What is your project?" Thomas asked, and Russ replied that he wanted the right person for the project. "I'm here to support the right person for the task," he added, glancing at Lilly and Bill.

"I'm the golf course man," Bill said, taking his wife's hand and mentioning that Russ liked turtles.

"Oh, Honey, we've had golf courses," Lilly said. "I'd love a day spa."

Andy said, "The cove will be perfect for an Eco-Lodge when cleaned up. I wouldn't want to step on your toes," he told Thomas.

"If I had wanted it, I would have purchased it," Thomas replied. "It's still here."

"What would you do with it?" Thomas asked the local legend, Doug DeLeon.

"I'm the Steakhouse man," Doug said, looking strangely at Mia, who deflected her eyes, and Thomas replied that they would be honored to eat at his restaurant.

Everyone was separated into groups to shoot at the archery targets. I accompanied Sue, Luke, Mia, and Thomas, who were still perplexed at the purpose of drawing them together.

"Did you know that man named Doug?" Sue asked Mia before they stretched their bowstrings. "I saw you look away when he spoke about the steakhouse."

"He was a quarterback for the team in high school," Mia whispered. "Some strange things happened when he went to college. He got a football scholarship and lost it."

"That's odd," Thomas agreed. "Something bad must have happened."

"I don't know anything more about it," Mia replied. "I lost track of him long ago."

"We should talk about this later," Sue said as they stretched their bows and shot at the bullseyes. "I'm not very good at this," she said as Lilly and the men pursued their skills.

"Everyone else is an amazing shot, including Lilly," Mia said. "We should give up and watch what happens."

The six remaining people, including Lilly, Bill, and four guests, shot at six targets for the next hour. Sue and Mia sat in lounge chairs and watched the match while I lay on the grass nearby. They were all good archers, but Lilly and Russ got the most perfect shots in the center bullseye.

"That guy Russ has been seeing my daughter's best friend," Mia said. "Her name is Shameka."

"He's a good-looking man," Sue said. "I've seen him at the museum where she works."

"Do you think he's too good-looking for his own good?" Mia asked, and Sue replied that it took one to know one. "You're too beautiful for your own good," she reminded her. "You're doing just fine."

"Shameka is a very nice young lady," Mia said. "She's doing great work at the Sweetwater Springs Museum."

"You mean Mia's Museum," Sue countered because her friend was modest about the honors her husband bestowed on her.

"Do you know anything else about him?" Sue asked, and Mia replied she did not.

Sargie stood on the grass behind the archers, towering and occasionally wobbling. I admired his stamina and hoped I had as much at his age. He was a lovely and determined dog.

"That Dane looks like a nice dog," Mia said, and Sue agreed he was friendly and delightful. "He doesn't have a mean bone in his body."

"He must have come from a responsible breeder," Mia said.

"The best breeders choose both parents for temperament and health," Sue said, although her friend was aware of it.

"He's very old," Mia replied as the tournament ended with Lilly in first place, followed by Bill, Andy, and Doug.

"Congratulations!" Sue and Mia told Lilly as she approached them.

"Thanks! I get a lot of practice here. I don't know many people since we just moved to Sweetwater Springs. There's not much to do except turtles and archery."

"Your practice paid off," Sue said.

"I heard you talking about Sargie," Lilly told Mia. "He's twelve years old."

"That's practically a record for a Dane," Sue said. "They are prone to heart disease and other genetic problems. Many don't live past eight years old."

"His mother belonged to my daughter, and she found the perfect mate for him. Both of his parents were gentle dogs with no health problems."

"Your daughter knew what she was doing," Sue replied. "The world would be better for dogs with more breeders like her."

"You should be proud of yourself for taking such good care of him," Mia said.

"He's living on Love," Sue agreed. "It took your daughter's good sense to choose his parents and your good care for him to be a lovely dog."

I walked beside Sarge as he waddled toward the picnic table. He was indeed a sight to behold, with everything going for him from youth to old age. I longed to age as well as he did. I was fortunate to have Sue's care. I, too, had been bred for temperament and health.

The group assembled around the table for drinks of their choice, with most men choosing beer or sports drinks while the ladies chose wine or water.

"Thank you for coming to the archery match," Bill announced. "I'm sure some of you suspect an ulterior motive."

Luke cleared his throat. "Here it comes," he said.

"Several of us have dreams for this land," Bill continued. "Some of us need money to pursue them."

Sue looked at Luke and smiled at his foresight.

"It's probably not what you think," he continued. "You may have noticed that most of the guests are well-to-do from their given enterprises, whatever they may be. I want to propose a high-stakes poker match. Everyone here has the means to participate, including me. Winner takes All!"

Chapter 4

Loretta's House with Zeke

Dr. Loretta worked at her family's veterinary clinic in Haywood after Sue retired. Like Luke, she was one of my favorite people in the world. I couldn't choose between them. Luke fed me treats and showered me with affection, while Loretta nurtured me with a safe and happy home away from home and friendship with my four-legged cousins.

Lee was technically my full-blooded sister, while Luna and Stevie were my Doodle cousins. I am a medium-sized Doodle, but they are bigger than me. Toby hid under the bed when my furry friends came to my house. According to my two-legged friends, most cats have a beloved hiding place. Toby's is under the bed.

Despite my original misgivings about Sargie, the Giant, I am usually braver than Toby. He discovered the ripped interfacing under that mattress, squeezed inside the hole, and tiptoed across the wooden planks to find a place to disappear. He does this when most guests come over, including Luke, whom he adores, until he figures out it's him and snuggles up to him affectionately.

Toby knows when Sue comes home and meets her at the door. Indeed, he recognizes her car engine, as I do. We stand in the kitchen, waiting for her to enter and be happy to see us. We like it when she gets excited to see us.

Toby races off to the mattress escape room when my four-footed cousins arrive. He slips down the hall for a peak, bolting back into the bedroom if somebody moves. They are the gentlest dogs on the planet—just big and worrisome—like Sargie to me—before I got to know him.

One day, when Sue was dog-sitting for my sister Lee, Toby went nose to nose with her. I was so proud of him. This was a big step for Toby, who appreciated his solitude with Sue and me in his palace. Mostly, he likes to nap in the living room when it's just Sue and me at home.

Sue takes me to Loretta's house to see my cousins today, and Toby will stay home— where his heart is. Sue calls it guarding the fort, but we both know what he will do. Toby will nap on the back of the couch unless the doorbell rings. Then he'll race to the mattress hole, escape, and disappear to his cat dreams.

Loretta and Zeke's house is my favorite destination on the planet—even better than Luke's house on the river—a close second. It's impossible to control my excitement when we arrive. I can hardly wait for Sue to open the car door. I run fast as a Greyhound to reach the front door.

Today, Zeke opens it before Sue follows, much further behind me. Zeke is Loretta's husband. He is also an attorney, but I don't know much about his work as an attorney. Loretta had to find another attorney when she was arrested for the pub caper because he couldn't represent his wife.

Loretta is a fine, upstanding citizen and the best veterinarian in Haywood—some say the county, while others argue the state. No one could believe it when she was arrested, but the truth prevailed. Everyone was thrilled when she returned to Haywood, but none more than Zeke and her daughter.

My role in solving the pooches and pub murder interested Zeke in criminal law with crimes involving dogs. Now, he was on his mission to become the dog-lover's attorney. Sometimes, criminals use dogs to protect their loot. This illicit work gave all of Dogdom a black eye.

Sometimes, dangerous dogs escape and attack innocent dogs. Recently, a little dog had been mutilated and nearly killed by a drug dealer's dog. It was Zeke's first dog case, but a second was forthcoming. Dog DNA has solved more than a few crimes.

"Hi, Sue," Luke said as I thrust past him to greet my three cousins.

"Hi, Zeke," she replied as nearly three hundred pounds of fluff raced to the back door.

Anyone who has opened the door for four big dogs knows it's difficult to contain their excitement for a romp in the backyard. Holding the door from banging back into the house took a strong, steady arm when we plowed through toward the races. Sue had learned to use that arm.

"How's your dog case coming?" Sue asked of the dealer's dog, who had mutilated a Dachshund and broken her owner's leg, and Luke replied that it was finished and he had won.

"That's wonderful," Sue said. No respectable dog owner deserved the horror of that fate.

"Unfortunately, the owner will never trust dogs again," Loretta added, and Sue agreed that it was very sad.

"I wasn't expecting to enjoy crimes involving dogs," Zeke said, "but it's very gratifying when the right people win."

"You mean the innocent people," Loretta said, and Zeke agreed. "Some day, I'd like to improve the bad laws that allowed criminals to own dogs to use as weapons."

"We need stricter laws to protect the innocent," Loretta added, and Sue agreed that no dog should ever be used to guard stolen property or drugs.

"Where's Lucy?" Sue asked, and Loretta replied that her granddaughter and neighbor were out by the chicken coop.

When we finished the yard races, my cousins and I joined Zeke, Loretta, and the other two-legged friends near the chicken coop. Zeke and his friend from Sweetwater Springs were building the coop, which would soon house young chickens for the first time.

Loretta had raised the baby chicks with an incubator in an enclosed temporary pen in the house since they were one week old. The eight chicks had grown up together and bonded with the family. I had seen them briefly during their indoor weeks, but soon, I would see them more often.

Loretta and Zeke agreed that smaller farms were part of the solution to a safer food supply. Loretta had grown container gardens full of fresh vegetables, and now she was working toward raising chickens on her small farm.

"I love the chicken coop," Sue said of the gated area that led to an enclosure, coop, and outdoor run. "I'm impressed!"

"Hard work, but good work," Zeke replied. "I've been lucky to have Chris to help me."

Chris stopped pounding nails in the boards to attach the chicken wire and talked to Sue. "Good to see you, Sue," he said as Lucy hugged her grandmother. "I get to help put the chicks in the coop," Lucy said.

"How fun!" Sue replied, taking her granddaughter by the hand. "You'll be the first to know how much they love it!"

Two fences—one for the coop and one for the dog yard—separated the dog yard from the chicken coop. The coop had chicken wire, and the dog yard had non-climb wire. My cousins and I stood at the gate and watched our two-legged friends through the bars.

"I heard there was an archery tournament in Sweetwater Springs," Chris said, stopping his work to continue the conversation.

"I'm surprised you heard about it," Sue replied, raising her eyebrows. "It was a closed affair and not exactly news."

"It's a small town," Chris said. "I saw Tori at Cat Tails Pub, and she mentioned it. "She said only the wealthiest folks were invited."

"Somebody wants to buy that property on the Green Cove," Sue explained, and Zeke mentioned that only the wealthiest could afford it.

"Luke's brother Bill bought the property next door," Sue added, putting her arms on the fence to prop her chin. "He's got connections."

"Not sure if that's good or bad in Sweetwater Springs," Chris replied, and Sue suggested he was in good company to have the opinion.

"Who are these people who want to buy the land?" Zeke asked.

"Some men want to develop that beautiful property on the cove," Sue said, lifting her head off the rail. "Each of them has a different vision for the land. Luke's brother wants a golf course, and the others want a steakhouse or an Eco-Retreat."

Zeke was surprised. "Nobody wants a housing subdivision?" he asked.

"Nobody admits it if they do," Sue replied, because everyone knew Sweetwater Springs was busting at the seams with population. A housing subdivision would be mostly unpopular with the locals.

"What are their names?" Loretta asked.

"Bill Wilson," Sue said, and Loretta mentioned she remembered his Great Dane. "He's an adorable senior dog," she said, and Sue agreed. "Who else?"

"Russ Johnson," Sue said, and Loretta replied she had met him at Mia's Museum. "He and the new manager were all over each other," she said. "They look like lovebirds."

Sue declined to comment, although she had heard about it from Mia. "Andy Lemar wants an EcoRetreat," Sue continued, and Loretta said he had a delightful Golden Retriever. "He loves to kayak, like Daisy."

Sue smiled at the suggestion of another kayaking dog. "Doug DeLeon wants a Steakhouse," she continued, and Loretta mentioned she remembered his name from high school but couldn't place him.

"He was a Quarterback for Sweetwater Springs," Sue said, and Loretta recalled he had gotten into some trouble. "Haywood High School and Sweetwater Springs were rival teams," she explained. "I wasn't an aficionado of football, but his name rings a bell."

"I've heard about the trouble," Sue agreed, although she had yet to uncover the details.

"What happened?" Zeke asked, and Sue said she hadn't yet found out, but she'd keep them posted.

"How did you do at archery, Mom?" Loretta asked, and Sue admitted she didn't compete. "Mia Baldwin and I sat on the sidelines and enjoyed the lovely day," she said.

"I should have known the Baldwins were there," Zeke said, and everyone agreed the billionaire seemed the most likely to purchase the land, although he didn't seem to want it. "He has enough to do with his other projects," Sue said. "He doesn't want to develop anything else."

Everyone spent the next hour by the chicken coop while I played with my cousins in the yard. These days at Loretta's and Zeke's were the best days ever. Sue did not mention the high-stakes card game, but that would surface later. I was exhausted, in a good way, when Sue said it was time to go home. I couldn't wait for a long nap on the ride home.

Chapter 5

Mia's Museum With Shameka

Sue took me on a long walk at the Green Cove property the following morning. It was a glorious Spring day after a short heat wave. She opened the sliding glass door to give Toby and me some porch time before we left the house. The cool air poured through the opening and excited us to get outside.

Toby preferred watching for critters in the cove to just about anything. He was astute, street-smart, and had survived a tough start in the neighborhood. His younger ordeals gave him a quick sense of fear—a fight-or-flight reaction—but he did not have a mean bone in his body. Mostly, he appreciated having a loving home with Sue and me.

My favorite cat friend was a homebody. He purred frequently when snuggling with Sue and ran away from anything suspicious. If I barked at a bird, Toby found it suspicious. He could be focused on a grasshopper through the screened porch, and my bark would send him flying through the crack in the door to the back bedroom.

Toby didn't want to go outside; he just wanted to look outside. If Sue had opened the back door, he would have never tried to leave the house. He loved watching nature without participating in its endless possibilities of struggles. Unlike me, he was a spectator.

In contrast, I was an explorer. I loved taking long walks wherever Sue led me. I enjoyed hearing the jingle of my leash and collar when she was ready to go. I am an animated dog and quite excited about the things I love.

Sue called Toby inside from his porch duties and left him snoozing on the couch when we left. It was a short drive to the property on the Green Cove. Mia called just when we arrived. Sue talked to Mia while I was focused on the commotion at the tree line across the big lawn where they had the archery tournament.

"I see two deer at the edge of the property," Sue said while I focused on the animals I had never seen before. They looked the size of a big dog from a distance, not a giant dog like Sargie. They looked at us with curiosity but did not run away.

"Are they bucks?" Mia asked.

"They are a distance away, but I don't see horns," Sue said.

"They won't run away until you open the car door," Mia suggested as I focused sharply on the animals across Sue's lap.

"There are more than two," Sue replied. "Maybe three or four," she added. "They look like young females."

"I have heard there are deer in those woods," Mia said, and Sue mentioned they were caddy-corner across the river from Luke's house.

"Have you seen deer at your house?" Sue asked since Mia lived just upriver from Luke.

"Sometimes," Mia said. "I see them when I work in the yard."

"How nice for you!" Sue said. "I see deer on the trails, but this is the first time I've seen deer in Sweetwater Springs."

"That is a special property," Mia said. "Just on the edge of the wild, but still in town."

"It would be a shame for it to be developed," Sue said.

"That's why Thomas doesn't buy it," Mia agreed. "He's a developer at heart, but that piece deserves to be kept natural."

"I hope those men we met yesterday have the town's best interest in mind," Sue replied as one deer raised its head.

"How would you know?" Sue asked. "Two of them are from Miami, and the one from Sweetwater Springs has a flawed reputation."

"Agree."

"Luke has mixed feelings about his brother," Sue continued. "He thinks he's gullible and easily scammed."

"He must be a bit jealous of Luke," Mia said. "He is competitive, yet not as successful."

"I suppose we'll get an earful about her sons from their mother," Sue replied. "Luke wants to have the card party at his house so he can look out for Bill."

"I can imagine how Sophie will feel about that," Mia said, and Sue replied that Luke had assured her his mother would understand the importance of watching out for Bill.

"Daisy is excited for her walk," Sue said as one deer raised its head to eat leaves off the tree. "We should get going."

"Of course," Mia replied, remembering the reason for her call. "Could you meet my daughter and me at the museum later this morning?"

"Can Daisy come?" Sue asked.

"Absolutely," Mia replied. "I want you both to meet Shameka. She's my new museum manager."

"The one with a crush on Russ Johnson?" Sue asked, and Mia reaffirmed her suggestion.

When Sue opened the car door, the three deer scooted off into the woods as everyone thought they would. By then, I wasn't paying attention to the unfamiliar animals that looked like leaf-eating dogs. I caught a whiff of something fantastic in the grass where the targets had been yesterday. Sue might have called it stinky, but to me, it was dizzying.

She lifted my head from the grass, and we continued our walk through the meadow of giant trees. The trees saw everything past and present. Sue could easily imagine them as shade for the natives who preceded us. I could feel her nostalgia as a soft love for the earth and its people.

The meadow was recently mowed, leaving vast patches of wildflowers to attract butterflies, blowing in the gentle breeze. The spectacular beauty of spring was almost surreal in this fantastic place. There was nothing else like it in Sweetwater Springs. Who would want it developed and trampled?

We walked for a mile through a forest of bird songs. The cove glistened in the distance—big, round, and green, but not so green as last fall when Sue was investigating the pub caper. The algae had been reduced during the winter. It was a good sign that reducing the number of people on the river would improve the water quality in the cove.

Sue mentioned that the locals had lost their access to the river due to the influx of tourists during the summer. There wasn't enough parking for everyone in the public spaces. Eventually, you had to live—or rent—a house on the river to access the water. The locals without frontage were left out of the preferred guest list.

Sue believed every local deserves access to their cherished sparkling river, yet tourists who visit for a day, week, or month nearly take it away. I could sense Sue's wheels turning. The locals deserved their private entrance—an exclusive pass to access the river.

Sue knew the butterflies and bees needed a garden in the sun, the deer required trees to munch on, and the turtles needed space to dig. The town required green space to keep it from overheating from excessive pavement. Everyone loved the feel of grass under their feet. It was here in this miraculous space on the cove.

I followed Sue as she walked for an hour, breathing the clean air of the meadow. I enjoyed the soft grass under my four feet as Sue contemplated the evolving facts. Luke was a philanthropist and one of my favorite people. His rival brother had a big old dog who had been fuel for my imagination before I met him, and I discovered he was a sweet soul. He brought three men to the cove who likely cared less about the birds and the bees. Did they want an EcoRetreat, steakhouse, golf course, or something more sinister? What were they after? How far would they stoop to get it?

I sat in the back seat, gazing out the window while Sue drove to the tiny museum in the historic district. Technically, I wasn't allowed in the museum since I wasn't a service dog, but Mia had granted an exception for Sue. I was well-behaved around precious objects, friendly to people, and didn't bark without a reason.

The most precious object in the museum was a silver-plated handgun, mainly because it was nefarious. I had sniffed it a few times during the pub caper. It didn't have much smell, but it belonged to a notorious villain who had bequeathed the gun to his daughter, Sarah, upon his death. She didn't want it. Hence, she donated the silver-plated gun to the museum.

According to Sue, Sweetwater Springs has a long history of villains and heroes. It started with mining and land scams over a hundred years ago. The mining produced fertilizers that were distributed around the world. Years later, the fertilizers caused algae to grow in the rivers, limited sunshine, and killed fish.

Sweetwater Springs boomed with work, development, and money to spare. Land scammers sold properties that didn't exist to unsuspecting customers from other locales. They sold mineral rights for minerals that didn't exist on the land. Scammers cared more about the money they could make from the land than the land.

I don't know much about scamming and care nothing about money. However, I know that certain two-leggers are fond of the green. Some of them are villains. They have a peculiar smell. It isn't terrific. Some of them are heroes. They smell delightful.

Luke and Thomas smell good, like heroes. Some two-leggers think all developers are bad, but Sue and I disagree. The scammers are bad people—villains. They steal from the unsuspecting and pay the corrupt to look the other way.

Mia waited for us and held the door when we entered the museum. "Thanks for coming!" she said as I stood beside Sue.

"Thanks for letting me bring Daisy," Sue replied. "It was a lovely day for a walk at the Green Cove, and she loves riding in the car wherever we go."

A black girl with a sturdy body stepped over to pet Daisy. "What a cute dog," she said, smiling widely. "We're glad to have her any time."

"This is Shameka," Mia said as the museum's manager extended her hand for a firm handshake.

"I love dogs," Shameka said as I leaned on her body after the shake.

"She loves you, too," Sue said as Shameka massaged my chest precisely as I liked it. "Daisy rarely leans like that on anybody—especially when she first meets them."

A beautiful woman who looked like Mia stepped out of the back room where she had been working. "Shameka was my best friend in high school before I left Sweetwater Springs to live in Miami," Sarah said.

"Daisy is the best judge of character, and she loves Shameka," Sue said as I leaned on her bare leg. "You have good taste in friends."

Sue stepped over to a silver-plated gun in a glass case. "Is this the famous gun that put Sweetwater Springs on the map?" she asked.

"The one and only," Shameka replied as she continued my massage. "People come from miles away to see it."

"Has anyone tried to steal it?"

"Not yet," Shameka replied. "But, I did see one man peeping under the case to see how it was put together."

"Wouldn't it be easier just to break the case?" Sue asked, and Shameka said, "Yes, but it would be messy."

I followed Sue into the back room, where Sarah and Shameka worked on a full-scale three-dimensional river and town map. "This is amazing!" Sue said. "It shows every spring on the river."

"Russ helped me map the springs," Shameka said. "We take lots of photos on our kayaking journeys."

"Do you mean Russ Johnson?" Sue asked.

"Yes," Shameka replied with stars in her eyes. "How do you know him?"

"I met him at Bill Wilson's Green Cove archery meet this weekend," Sue replied. "He was placing ribbons around the turtle digs."

"He's such a dear man," Shameka replied, pointing to the digs on the map. "He loves nature just like I do."

I detected apprehension when Sue said, "It's nice when a man loves the birds and the bees."

Shameka frowned when she added, "We've been dating since Christmas."

"That sounds serious," Mia said.

"He lives at my house almost every weekend," Shameka said dreamily. "I'm falling in love."

"He's a gambler, Shammy," Mia said. "Be careful."

"How do you know he's a gambler?" Shameka asked, and Mia described the high-stakes poker match that his brother had arranged at Luke's house.

"A lot of men gamble," Shameka countered. "It doesn't mean anything."

"It means a lot when they are betting big money to win bigger money to buy three hundred acres on the cove."

"I've never seen him play cards or talk about playing cards," Shameka said, petting my side. "All we do is kayak and take pictures."

Mia stepped around the three-dimensional map to observe the details. Thomas Baldwin's glorious mansion, where she lived with her husband, was north of Luke's smaller but spectacular riverfront estate, where Luke lived with his mother and other family members. Both men had worked hard for their success in hotels, commercial development, and the power that accompanied it. Both were respected members of Sweetwater Springs.

Luke's brother Bill and the three men at the archery tournament were a different story. No one knew much about them. They were local and out-of-town entrepreneurs who played cards, the stock market, and land development.

"Luke is having the card party at his house next Friday night," Sue said, sensing Mia's concern as we prepared to leave. "We'd love you to join us for a ladies' party during the game."

Chapter 6
Cat Tails Pub with Cons

I jumped joyfully on my two hind legs when Sue mentioned we were going to Cat Tails Pub. Sue had my leash in her hand, which made me happy wherever we went, but the pub was the best dog-friendly restaurant in Sweetwater Springs. It made my day when Tori, who disappeared during the recent caper, brought me a bowl of ice water. She owned the pub.

Little things make a dog happy—grill drippings in the dog yard, a fallen French fry, a bowl of ice water served by a lovely person. Tori remembered me. She was happy to see Sue but happier to see me. Whatever I might scarf up from underneath the outdoor tables, she always remembered to serve my bowl of ice water.

Cat Tails Pub was the most popular hangout in town for two-leggers and four-leggers, local and otherwise. According to Sue, out-of-town customers came from miles around to dine at the riverside establishment. Some planned their weekends around a cold soak in the river and a long, leisurely meal-share at the pub.

As the town boomed from tourism, so did the pub. First, the locals dined at the pub. A few of them brought dogs. Then, the friendly tourists discovered the hidden gem and brought more dogs. Then the cons made a career of exploiting the locals and tourists.

A few criminals, villains, or cons brought dogs that didn't belong outside a six-foot fence in their yard. I was stealthily attacked from underneath the bar, alerting Tori to the need for a dog bouncer and Zeke to work toward better dog laws to protect us from the villains who were too stupid to watch over, know, or train their dogs before they brought them to a dog-friendly establishment.

Eventually, there were all kinds of scams in Sweetwater Springs, and most scammers had done time with their marks at Cat Tails Pub. Sue first met the man with the silver-plated handgun, which is currently displayed at Mia's Museum, at Cat Tails pub. I wasn't sure what to make of the piece on the first sniff, but it was odd. Sue didn't like it. She didn't want to see it.

Loretta was even less fond of the silver-plated gun for reasons substantiated in the Pooches and Pubs Mystery. Villains tried to make money on just about anything. Some found their way to Sweetwater Springs, bringing notoriety and a museum to the previously sleepy town, as the locals wanted it to remain forever.

Sue planned to meet Luke, Thomas, and Mia at Cat Tails Pub today. Toby was just as indifferent about the adventure as I was excited. I believe it's his limited vocabulary. Toby hears Cat Tails, and all he hears is the word cat. He knows the cat pertains to him but pretends he doesn't care about hearing it.

Toby gets attention by purring, rubbing, or pretending he doesn't want it. For now, he is curled up in an uncaring ball of fluff on the ottoman. Sue says he cares about us leaving but doesn't want us to know, so he ignores us when we go. It's like it never happened when he sleeps through the departure.

I love attention and am not ashamed of my desire for it. The best attention comes from Sue, but any attention from Sue's friends is also good. When Sue jingles my leash, I dance on two legs. Don't get me wrong; I enjoy snoozing as much as Toby, but dancing and getting excited is more fun than sleeping.

Today is an easy departure because Sue doesn't have to hunt for Toby before we go. "See you later, Toby," she says as we walk outside. "Take good care of the house while we're gone," she adds, although he doesn't stir.

"Hi, Homer," Sue greeted the local sheriff as we exited the car. I followed her to the entrance, where Homer was waiting for a table. The sheriff and his deputy never had to wait long because Tori had granted them priority seating and free food for life after they solved the first murder in twenty years that put Sweetwater Springs on the map.

"Good to see you, Sue," he said.

"I hope there's no problem at the pub," Sue replied.

"There's always something," Homer said, fluffing his feathers. "You know I'd do anything for Tori," he added without mentioning the free food.

"Of course, you would," Sue said, ignoring the self-importance that followed his somewhat bumbling yet correctly executed capture of the criminal. "She appreciates it, too."

"Catch you later," he said as the server guided him to a waterfront table.

"Enjoy your lunch," Sue called ahead, as Tori greeted us.

"I'm glad you brought Daisy," Tori said, leading us to a table with our friends. "It's been too long since I've seen my furry friend," she added, setting a bowl of ice water before me.

"Daisy says thank you, and I thank you," Sue said as I bobbed for ice cubes. "You always know what she wants."

"She's easy to please," Tori replied. "I wish all of my customers were so gracious."

"Is there a problem?" Sue asked.

"A couple of customers have been getting rambunctious," Tori said, nodding towards tables where two of Bill's friends from the archery party were seated in different locations.

"We've met them," Luke said. "My brother has unusual tastes in people," he added.

"That's putting it mildly," Tori replied. "They argued half the morning. I was ready to tell them to leave for disrupting the peace when they separated themselves."

"Is that why Homer is here?" Thomas teased, although everyone knew the answer, and Tori smiled. "I can take care of a few Bad Apples myself," she replied. "Homer is here for lunch."

"You certainly can," Thomas said, with evident confidence in Tori's abilities.

"What are their names?" Tori asked.

"The big man is Doug DeLeon," Mia said.

"He's been here before," Tori replied.

"He's a HomeGrown boy," Mia explained as a German Shepherd emerged from underneath the table.

"Is the Shepherd friendly?" Sue asked, since some villains used them as guards for their loot.

"So far, so good," Tori replied. "The dog bouncer would make him leave if Doug—or anyone else— was careless with a dog at my pub."

"You have a good bouncer," Luke said, and Sue agreed he didn't put up with the provokers, two-legged or four.

"He's settled a few fights among my customers," Tori said. "A few of the men are mean drunks."

Luke took a deep breath. "My dad was a mean drunk," he said, and Sue said he had never mentioned it before.

"It's not something I like to remember," Luke said. "It's better to move forward than dwell on the unpleasant."

"Are many of the men mean drunks?" Mia asked.

"Sweetwater Springs has its share of Thugs," Tori replied. "Lately, we see more of them at the pub than we used to."

"More boom, more crime," Luke said, and Thomas agreed crime needed to be addressed swiftly.

"What turns some people bad?" Mia asked. "We all have misfortune. Some people stay nice or at least stable, while others turn mean."

"Parenting. Church. Good Guidance. Moral lessons," Sue said.

"Genetics?" Luke suggested, and Sue agreed, that we were rooted in our DNA.

"Nature and Nurture," Thomas added, settling the tie with both answers.

Tori looked back towards the tables. "Who's the man with the thin nose and brown eyes?" she asked as he put his arm around a woman beside him.

"He's from Miami," Luke said. "His name is Russ Johnson."

"Who is the woman?" Mia asked as the woman promptly removed his arm.

"I don't know her," Tori said.

"Maybe just a random woman," Sue said. "She doesn't seem to like his attention."

"Keep an eye on him," Mia said as the man walked away. "He's dating my daughter's best friend."

"Is it serious?" Tori asked, and Mia replied, "Shameka seems to think so."

"Oh Geez," Thomas said because he was fond of Mia's Museum's new manager.

"Nothing has happened," Mia reminded him as they thought about the man who had helped Lilly with the turtles.

Sue suggested, "We should talk to Shameka about Russ." Mia agreed they should learn more about him. "We know he's a stockbroker and likes turtles," she said, but Mia disagreed. "We've been told he's a stockbroker," she said. "We don't know anything about him."

"We know he's invited to the high-stakes card game," Sue reminded her. "He must have a nest egg from something."

Doug DeLeon stood to leave with his German Shepherd. He went to the table, where Russ was again seated after the altercation with the woman. "You owe me $100,000.00," he screeched, loud enough for everyone to hear. "Win or Lose, I'll expect payment after the card game."

"What will you do if I don't feel like paying?" Russ asked.

"I've got people," Doug threatened as two thugs from a nearby table looked up at Russ with stone-cold eyes. "You know what they can do."

After the argument, both men left simultaneously. Each walked to their vehicles with confidence and authority. Doug left in his antique with the noisy, rumbling engine, while Russ left in his less assuming yet respectable truck.

The thugs watched with envy as they drove away. It was hard to say which they wanted more—the hot rod or the truck. Either vehicle would be the answer to their dreams and the envy of every other thug in Sweetwater Springs.

Sheriff Stone, aka Homer, stopped by the table where Sue relaxed with her friends after lunch. I was stretched out under the table, having given up on the falling crumbs, when his voice startled me back to reality.

"I'd like to stop by your house later," Homer told Luke. "There's something I want to talk to you about. Privately."

"No problem," Luke replied. "You're welcome anytime."

Luke and Sue drove to the mansion in companionable silence. I sat in the back seat on my haunches, looking out the rear window.

Thomas and Mia followed shortly behind them. Everyone was rattled by what we had seen and heard, but the news to come would be even more unsettling.

Chapter 7
Luke's House

Luke had a fine Hound dog named Artemis. Artemis was one of my closest friends along with my sister and cousins. We met at the park years ago when Sue was helping Luke with the neighborhood stray cats. One young kitten arrived at our house during a rainstorm and became part of the family. Later, Sue gave him to a child who temporarily lived with us, and we adopted Toby.

Sue was walking the neighborhood then with a group nicknamed the Dog Walkers. Luke sometimes joined the dog walkers with Artemis. Mostly, he used dog walking as an excuse to see Sue. Regardless, I got to know Artemis.

Artemis was the first hound dog I ever met. He had a strange voice, not a bark, but a bay, yet he was friendly, just like me. He liked to run. Sometimes, he got distracted by his nose and followed it wherever it led him. Luke says he'd follow his nose off a cliff, which worries me.

I have a splendid sense of smell, but don't get distracted by my nose, as Artemis does. When he's on a scent, nothing else matters. His whole brain seems preoccupied with the nasal component rather than assimilating the various senses. When that happens, I redirect him to a more wholehearted reality of sight, sound, taste, touch, and his overdeveloped strong suit, smell.

Sue says a considerable portion of his brain is devoted to smell. My brain is more evened out when it comes to interpreting the senses. I would rather be me than Artemis, but we can't help what we're born with. He is very good at being a hound dog.

That said, Artemis lives like a king at Luke's house. He has an enormous backyard that leads to the river. It's all fenced so that we can run free to our heart's content. It's nearly as big as the property on the Green Cove, where Luke's brother lives. Sue says it's big enough for a golf course, but Luke bought it with a forever-wild clause that he will never develop it.

Luke drove to his estate, followed by Thomas and Mia. He pushed a button, and the massive gate opened to let us inside. I jumped out of the car to join Artemis, who greeted me in the yard. We raced in great circles in the thick grass before we joined our families in the big house, Sue called a mansion.

Luke's 94-year-old mother served Artemis and me homemade dog biscuits while the friends settled on the back porch. He is very spoiled, but not fat, like Cousin Luna, who prefers counter-surfing to exercise. He runs it off when he follows his nose.

"We missed you at the archery match, Sophie," Sue said, warmly hugging the fiery old woman, who knew about everything, had an opinion about more, and talked a blue streak.

"I hear you're pretty good with a bow and arrow," Mia agreed. "Sue and I could use some lessons."

"I was good at archery back in my day," Sophie admitted, passing a plate of chocolate and caramel chip cookies. "I'm not much interested in shooting the deer that wander through the yard."

"I saw deer next to Bill's property when I walked yesterday," Sue said, accepting the home-baked treat. "Watching them at the edge of the bushes was fun."

"The deer come here every day," Sophie said.

"It must be old hat for you to see them," Mia offered.

"I still enjoy them every time they come," Sophie countered. "Artemis enjoys following their scent later on."

"I'll bet he does," Sue said, holding her glass for the lemonade Sophie offered her.

"We are blessed to have the animals," Sophie said. "We have deer, turkey, armadillos, turtles, and once I saw a bear."

"You saw a bear in your backyard?" Sue asked.

"Yes, but only once. I think the alligators took him."

"Can an alligator eat a bear?" Mia asked, and Thomas assured her it was possible. "The lawn workers caught an alligator capturing a wild boar on their motion cameras. He was bigger than most Florida bears."

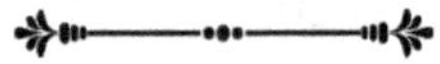

Thomas passed around the photo of the alligator capturing the wild boar, while Artemis and I lay on his king-sized dog bed. Although the boar was big and heavily tusked, it wasn't much of a match. The alligator easily captured the boar and drowned it for consumption.

"That's impressive," Luke said, and everyone agreed it was humbling to catch it on camera. "I wouldn't have believed it possible," Mia said.

"We are preserving hundreds of acres for future generations to learn about the daily life and hunting skills of the wildlife," Mia said. Thomas reminded her that they were private preserves.

"My Other son wants to make a golf course," Sophie grumbled, emphasizing Other. "No wildlife short of a squirrel or a turtle wants to live on a golf course.

I sensed that everyone felt uncomfortable by Sophie's description of Bill, the unfavored one. I was an only dog and never second-fiddled with anyone, not even Toby, whom Sue loved equally but differently because he was a cat. It couldn't be easy to be the less favored child of Sophie Wilson, Italian Mama to the tycoon Luke Wilson.

"Have you seen Bill?" Luke asked.

"He was here earlier," Sophie said. "It sounds like he's made some new friends."

"I was going to talk to you about that, Mama," Luke said.

"Let me guess. Are they shady?" Sophie asked.

"Possibly," Luke said, and Thomas agreed they didn't know them well.

"How come Bill never makes friends with regular people?" Sophie asked, and no one answered. She continued, "Why don't you build on the Green Cove Property, Thomas?"

"I fear I've rocked the boat with my future hotel and theme park in Sweetwater Springs," Thomas said. "I don't want to push the locals over the edge with another development project."

"I get it," Sophie said. "It could be a small project that uses all the land, but leaves most of it natural for guests to recall the wild Florida. Something that takes less land than a golf course."

"It will have to be someone else's project," Thomas said. "Not mine."

Artemis rose from the big bed where we had been comfortably lolling around when the sheriff called Luke to let him inside the estate. Sophie was unpleasantly surprised to hear from Homer Stone. She liked Homer, who had solved the recent murder with great help from Sue and Mia, but she worried about her Other son. "Is Bill in some kind of trouble?" she asked.

"Not yet," Luke replied formidably.

"Not that you know of," Sophie replied. "It won't take long. Trouble finds him."

"He's here to talk to us about the men we met at the Cat Tails Pub," Luke explained. "He wanted to talk to us privately."

"Two men we met at Bill's Archery Party argued at Cat Tails Pub," Sue told Sophie. "It was loud," Mia added. "One of them threatened the other man."

"I knew it, Bill's already made friends with the wrong people," Sophie said. "About what?"

"He didn't exactly say," Luke said. "He said he knew people who could care for it, if he didn't pay up."

"He knows People?" Sophie hollered, launching into a full-fledged review of her roots, which were known to all. "I'm from Sicily. I know what it means to know people. People in Sicily are connected—or not. Eventually, everyone knows someone who knows people."

"It seems Bill already knows people who know people," Luke offered, softly to calm her down.

"Did he say how much he owes him?" Sophie asked.

"$100,000.00," Luke replied, groaning because his mother would launch into a tirade at the large amount.

"$100,000.00? Are you kidding me? That's not like a broken finger or something. That's big potatoes," she screeched.

Mia was mortified by the sudden shift, which was more familiar to Sue, who knew Sophie better. Sue said Luke's father was part Irish, which made Sophie think about payment for services with potatoes rather than tomatoes or wine.

"People pay for it when people owe them big money, and they don't pay up!" Sophie said. "Where's this guy supposed to get $100,000 in Sweetwater Springs?"

"We don't know him that well, Mom. Maybe he has a big bank account," Luke said.

"He's a stockbroker from Miami," Sue added, hoping to console her, rather than fuel her.

"A Stock Broker! Miami!" Sophie groused. "Hell's Bells. Anyone can say they're a stockbroker from Miami. He probably never worked a day in his life!"

Sophie was still fuming when Homer Stone rang the doorbell. By now, Artemis seemed a bit nervous, which was entirely out of character for his laid-back self. I was also feeling her pain, but that was common for Doodles. I lay my head in Sue's lap when Homer Stone arrived for the consult.

"Good afternoon," Homer said, entering the big house and standing beside us. "It seems a bit chilly here," he added, regarding the general mood as everyone froze.

"We just told Mom about the $100,000.00 threat," Luke said.

"She's worried about Bill," Sue explained.

"The guy knows people," Mia added.

"Sophie's from Sicily," Thomas said, and everything became clear. Everyone knew that Sophie was a fiery yet well-informed woman and a protective Italian Mama.

"I see," Homer said, helping himself to a cookie. "What I'm about to tell you may not make it better."

Mia sighed while I snuggled up to Sue. Artemis stood on the Persian Rug in front of Luke and his mother, who was overcome with the increasing anxiety of the motives and means of her Other son's network of new friends.

"Get on with it, then!" Sophie cracked. "What's going on with these friends of Bill?"

Homer gulped a swallow of lemonade to wash down the cookie. "Well, ma'am," he said. "I'm not sure what it means, but I think I should tell you…."

"You can skip the formalities," Sophie said. "Tell us what?"

Homer took a deep breath and sighed. "Ever since these men came to town, we've seen an increase in accidents in Sweetwater Springs."

"Broken fingers?"

"No, broken legs," Homer replied.

"How?" Sophie asked.

"One resident got run over by a golf cart," Homer said, and Luke suggested that some of the older people didn't see as well anymore.

Sophie groaned. "What happened to the others?"

"Broken ribs, from a boat accident, and a fractured skull with a concussion from a farm accident," Homer said.

"How long has it been since you saw accidents like this?" Thomas asked, and Homer said never.

"One of the men is from Sweetwater Springs," Homer said. "His name is Doug Deleon. An ex-football star. He's a big man who could manage the threats, but claims he knows people to handle the dirty work."

"You mean Thugs?" Sophie insisted, and Homer didn't acknowledge her.

"The other two men, Andy Lemar and Russ Johnson, are from Miami," Homer said.

"I thought there were two men at the pub," Sophie called him out.

There were two men at the pub. However, accidents tend to follow those who interact unfavorably with all three men.

"Let me guess. All three of them were at Bill's archery party."

"You got it!" Homer said. "Andy Lemar and Russ Johnson."

"Russ Johnson," Sophie sputtered. "I've heard of him. A bad, bad man."

"Who is Andy Lemar?" she asked.

"A developer from Miami," Mis said, and everyone agreed the locals were fed up with development that increased the population, toxins, wastes, fertilizers that promoted algae growth, and destroyed their precious river.

"He claims he wants an Eco Retreat on the property, but he builds housing subdivisions in Miami," Sue said.

"We have to help Bill," Luke said. "He falls for the scammers every time!"

"He's my lost sheep," Sophie said. "We're the only people he has."

Artemis and I headed to the door to bid the sheriff farewell. Nobody mentioned the high-stakes card game Luke offered to host at his house. Sue gathered our belongings, and everyone left for home in their own directions. Tomorrow, we will walk on the green cove and, later on, travel to Loretta's to dissect the clues.

"What card game?" Sophie asked, and everyone froze since she didn't know Luke had offered to host the game at their house.

Chapter 8

Radcliffe Family History at Green Cove

The following morning, Toby was amusing himself with an impossible hunt for a critter under a low couch while I pretended to snooze on the floor. I was always on semi-alert when Toby was hunting because the action often transferred to an ambush on me when the hunt was unproductive. I was impressed that he could spend unlimited time on the task until the critter reappeared. However, if he was in full-hunt mode, he rotated between various prey, which might include pouncing on me for a playdate.

I slept with one eye open, in case he wanted to play. If so, I would rise to the occasion and play chase after a cat. Some dogs might consider it beneath them, but it was fun to run inside the house—or outside. Sue knew I was gentle with Toby, so she let us be as we embarked on a house chase.

When we finished our game, Sue prepared for the expedition to Loretta's house. She grabbed my leash, which always excited me. I suspected there would be an additional stopover because Sue never took my leash to Loretta's house. At Loretta's house, I got to run free in the backyard with my cousins.

"Load up, Daisy," Sue said, opening the car door. I jumped in the back seat for the ride.

My internal GPS kicked in when Sue turned left towards the Green Cove, driving past the mayor's house, and other familiar homes towards Bill's house and the archery match property where we had walked. According to Sue, no one had wanted it, and now everyone wanted it for different reasons.

Sue tugged my leash, and I jumped out of the back seat. "Let's go, Daisy!" she said, as I landed on the plush grass with four feet.

The groomed lawn was perfect for a dog walk under the grandiose trees. Although it was warmer than our previous walk, the shade was comfortable. We walked across the great lawn towards the homes on the cove. Sue said the air smelled like cut grass. I was more interested in sniffing the ground where the deer had been than smelling the grass.

A dog I had never met played fetch on the cut grass with his owner. I did not play fetch, but I had seen other dogs grasp the tossed ball and race towards their owners to return it. Depending on the dog, it was a happy interaction. Big dogs need to run off their energy, which took less than five minutes for some, like me, and much longer for others.

Later, I could enjoy three minutes of running with my cousins in Loretta's backyard, followed by a long nap in the afternoon. Still, I realized having an enormous fenced yard to run in was a privilege.

My dog yard was so tiny that I could barely manage a trot, let alone a gallop.

An off-leash dog park was a fabulous place for dogs to release energy. Sweetwater Springs did not have an off-leash park, but the Green Cove property was perfect for playing fetch since no one was there. Soon, that would change. Someone would purchase the estate and create a business on the cove.

A pretty young woman approached us with her Australian Shepherd. "It would be a shame if this property sold, wouldn't it?" she asked, as we crossed paths on the shady road.

"Yes, it is lovely," Sue agreed. "One of the few pristine estates left in Sweetwater Springs."

"It's been in my family for generations," the woman said. "My great-grandparents owned the plantation house on the river. This land was their summer sanctuary," she continued, extending her hand to Sue in friendship. "I'm Betsy Radcliffe."

"It's a pleasure to meet you, I'm Sue MacVety, and this is Daisy," Sue said.

"She's a Cute Dog," Betsy said. "This is Sammie," she said, stroking her dog, and Sue smiled. "She's a Sweetie."

"Why would you sell the land?" Sue asked, and the woman replied that life had taken her family in a new direction. "My great-grandparents owned six houses on the bluff and had eight houses near the wetlands. Most of them have sold."

"The property you're standing on was their horse pasture. They had a barn full of carriages for town and country tours and weekly dinner parties for their guests. Further down, they had a croquet field. Some guests paddled upriver to the headwaters to ride the glass-bottom boats."

According to Sue, the tax burden on riverfront homes kept people from buying them or forced family legacy properties into sales.

"Tori's parents bought the home with the magnificent yard," Sue said. "She owns Cat Tails Pub."

"Of course," Betsy replied. "Everyone knows Tori, and most have heard about her parents."

"They will be good neighbors," Sue said, without mentioning the suspected mafia ties, which were never proven and no one wanted to know.

"We don't want to sell the houses and land, but we have to," Betsy said. "It is expensive to maintain them, and the taxes are higher than the income they produce as rentals during the season."

"It must be difficult to part with a family legacy," Sue said, and the woman suggested she had never met her great-grandparents, but had spent many summers with her family in one of the guest houses. My brother will keep one of the houses."

"How nice for your family," Sue said. "You can revisit whenever you like."

"Yes," she replied. "It has many rooms, and my brother will rent some of them, but keep others for our family."

"He's a hardworking and generous man," Sue said.

"My brother is interested in finding a buyer who will purchase the land for a park," Betsy said. "My uncle spent his retirement maintaining this land," she added. "My brother doesn't want to do the same."

"I understand," Sue replied. "It's a lot of work for a nostalgic memory, but your great-grandparents' estate was spectacular."

"My great-grandpa would have rolled over in his grave to see his beloved cove turn green," Betsy said.

"It's a terrible shame," Sue agreed, "But people are working hard to correct it."

"My uncle watched it happen. The cove was sparkling clear when he maintained the lawns. Then, when my brother took over, it had already turned green."

"I believe they will find a solution to the algae problem," Sue said, and Betsy agreed it was a matter of time.

"What did your great-grandfather do?" Sue asked.

"He was a road builder," Betsy said. "Some people liked him. Not others."

"Sounds like most wealthy people," Sue said. "Maintaining this estate must have required a multitude of workers."

"My grandfather built the smaller houses for the groundskeepers and security guards," Betsy said. "Their grandkids kept two of them. They still live in them."

"Interesting," Sue said. "Their families must love Sweetwater Springs."

"They never went anywhere else. Never wanted to," Betsy replied. "They want this land made into a park more than anyone."

"I'll bet they do," Sue replied, and I could sense her mind working. Sue was deep in thought.

"I'll bet they don't want a golf course here," Sue said.

"Nope. They don't want a steakhouse or an Eco Lodge either," Betsy added, and Sue seemed quizzical. "How do they know about that?" she asked, but the woman ignored the question.

"Mostly, they don't want a subdivision," Betsy continued. "Andy Lemar better keep his nose clean, or he'll meet his match with the Boggs brothers."

"Are the Boggs brothers the descendants of the original security guards at your great-grandparents' estate?" Sue asked.

"Yes, Frankie and Butch," Betsy said. "They are brawny men with an axe to grind."

"Do they have a golf cart?" Sue asked, and the woman replied, "I wouldn't know…but I've heard they beat people up for a price."

"I hope they're not upset with me," Sue stammered.

"Just a heads up," Betsy said. "They get upset easily."

"Why do they want a park so badly?" Sue asked.

"They like to hunt the deer in season, they're not social types, they want a park for their children, and they and their friends used to float this river when it was clear and clean."

"Before the tourists came," Sue said, and Betsy agreed it was a problem.

"They are angry that their kids can't access the river for the float," Betsy said. "There is no place to launch floats on the river without paying a steep fee."

"The locals should have a local float pass," Sue suggested.

Betsy agreed. "It isn't fair that the tourists have access to the river at their riverfront lodging and the locals lost their launches."

"No, it isn't fair," Sue said.

"Butch and Frankie want to even the score for the locals," Betsy called as she walked away. She tugged Sammie's leash as she strolled toward Bill's house.

"It's nice to meet you, Sue," she said, without elaboration on the float plan or the parks.

"Likewise," Sue agreed. "I hope we meet again."

Sue walked back to the car with me in tow. It had been a fruitful discussion with a historical landowner's offspring, and she had begun to mumble the details of the conversation in her mind. I launched into the back seat for the ride, suspecting she would still be mumbling when we reached Loretta's house. When Sue had something big on her mind, she talked to herself.

Chapter 9

Loretta and Zeke's House

When we approached Bill's house, I stood in the back seat on all fours, looking out the window. Sue grunted answers to her internal questions and mumbled something about thugs. She had not mentioned them before, but I detected they were a source of concern. Thugs were new for me, but whatever they were, they worried her.

Lilly bent over in the flower garden, picking weeds, and Sargie rested nearby. He looked much smaller lying down than when I met him at the archery party. Sargie was a sweet old man who followed his two-legged mama everywhere, like I followed Sue. I had been wrong to succumb to my fevered imagination about Sargie before I met him, but he was huge when he stood tall to his Harlequin Great Dane self.

I am not in the habit of barking at dogs bigger than me for obvious reasons, but seeing Sargie raised my voice.

"Woof, woof, woof…" I barked, and he stood up to his full wobbly black and white spotted height.

"Arrrrrrffff, Arrrfff..." he returned in his hoarse old dog voice that creaked, croaked, and prolonged the syllables.

I admired his effort, but selfishly hoped it didn't happen to me as a senior dog. Still, he seemed unfazed by his dramatic voice that had surely been clear and strong in his prime. The dog exchange brought Sue back from her mumbling question-and-answer session, and she noticed Lilly crouched in the garden.

"Hi Lilly," she said, stopping the car for a chat.

"Good morning, Sue," she replied, walking towards the car.

"I almost didn't see you crouched in your garden," Sue continued. "Daisy saw Sargie, and they've been having a bark party."

"So I've heard," Lilly replied, smiling. "They should be friends."

"Daisy loves to play," Sue said. "She's good with my cat but might be too rough for Sargie."

"Would you like to come inside for a cup of tea?" Lil asked. "I've just purchased a new loose-leaf tea from Nella at the tea house."

"I'd love to, but I'm on my way to Loretta's house," Sue said. "You'll love her tea house," she said. "Nella has the best teas from around the world."

"A tea tasting would be delightful," Lilly said, and Sue agreed it would be fun.

"I'd rather put a tea house on the property than a golf course," Lilly said. "That big, beautiful property deserves something more refined and enriching than chasing golf balls."

"I'm sure Ms. Radcliffe would agree with you," Sue replied. "It's been in her family for three generations."

"I saw you talking to her," Lilly said. "Why do they want to sell it?"

"Taxes, moving forward in different directions, too much work to maintain…"

"The usual reasons for rich folks when the first generation wealth passes on," Lilly replied. "I wish Bill could settle for being the ordinary brother, but he just can't stop competing with his brother."

"Luke and Sophie worry about him," Sue replied.

"I like Sophie, but she's an odd duck," Lilly said. "She says she cares, but did nothing to keep her boys from being overly competitive."

"People are who they are," Sue said. "There's only so much you can do to shape your children."

"Your daughter turned out well," Lilly said, and Sue agreed she was proud of Loretta. "She's a kind and devoted daughter, mother, wife, and veterinarian," she said. "She's had her share of ups and downs," she added.

"Bill is a jealous brother and a gambler," Lilly said. "He's not exactly a doting husband, either."

"You sound angry at him," Sue said, and Lilly didn't argue. "He used to be a better husband before he lost the golf course during COVID," she said. "I can't believe he wants to turn that magnificent property into another course."

"What do you think it should be?" Sue asked.

"Anything but a golf course," Lil said. "It would take most of the land and benefit the elite more than the locals."

"I can think of a few people who would agree with you," Sue replied. "Some people want a forever park for the locals."

"That could be interesting," Lilly said. "I like it."

"Are you coming to the card game?" Sue asked.

"I wouldn't miss it. Bill connects with unsavory people and gambles away our money," Lilly said. "I can't stop him from his get-rich-quick schemes, but I need to keep up with them—and do what I can to help."

"That's why Luke wants to protect him," Sue replied. "He doesn't want Bill to get scammed by cons or hurt by thugs."

"Thugs?"

"Yes," Sue replied, and I could feel her tension as it surfaced when she said too much. "According to a reliable source, Sweetwater Springs is experiencing a rash of unexplained accidents."

"That's scary," Lilly said. "It could mean many things."

"Yes, it could," Sue agreed, tugging my leash. "I should be moving along," she added. "Loretta is expecting me."

It was the second time that day that I heard about thugs. Sue mumbled about thugs and argued about her conversation with Lilly on the drive to Loretta's house. "Why did I say so much?" she asked herself, recalling that it poured out. "She has a friendly dog, but I barely know the woman," she muttered. "She hasn't earned insider information from trusted sources."

I jumped from the back seat when we reached Loretta's house and raced to the door. My three cousins awaited me inside the front door. Loretta quickly escorted us to the backyard, where we could get three minutes of fast-paced exercise before we conked out near the evolving chicken coop.

Zeke and Chris had joined forces to build the coop of Loretta's dreams. Chris lived in the house Sue called the best buy on the river with one of her best friends. She was also a previous roommate, a health geek, and the ex-wife of a hot-tempered husband. Chris had many skills and lent a hand wherever help was needed. The chicken coop had been his design for Loretta's coop.

"The coop looks fabulous," Sue said, admiring the indoor-outdoor run made of chicken wire, fence posts, and wooden planks. "You've been busy."

"Zeke has been a big help," Chris replied, about Loretta's husband, who was a better attorney than a builder. "It was good to have him working with me."

Chris could build almost anything, mostly projects he engineered or tackled from others' descriptions. He was handy with power saws and nail guns. He was mentoring Zeke in his fields of expertise.

"The chickens will love it," Sue said.

"We'll bring them outside soon," Loretta replied. "They've been indoors with the heating element long enough. They're ready for the real world."

"That will be an exciting day!" Sue said. "I can't wait to hear about it!"

"What's going on at the Green Cove?" Chris asked, and Sue updated him about those who wanted to purchase the land and those who didn't like it developed. "The list is growing," Sue said. "Some of the naysayers don't have the best reputations."

"What do you mean?" Chris asked.

"I mean, they resort to threats, scare tactics, and violence to get their way," Sue said. "Sweetwater Springs is increasing in unusual accidents, including broken fingers and legs."

"Are any of them using dogs to threaten people?" Zeke asked because he had become enthralled with lawsuits against people who used dogs as weapons.

"Not yet," Sue said.

"They met the wrong attorney when that happens," Zeke said. "I will fight them, and there will be consequences for anyone who uses dogs as weapons to guard stolen products or hurt people."

"It's animal abuse to use dogs as weapons," Loretta said, and Sue agreed. "It gives dogs a bad reputation when some are used maliciously."

Loretta continued, "Doug DeLeon brought his dog to the clinic for a wellness checkup yesterday. He seems like a friendly German Shepherd, but I'm not sure about the ethics of Doug Deleon."

"After he left, another client, who saw Doug Deleon, told me he lends money for mortgages at two to three times the normal rate. Someone else said he'll lend money for about anything at an exorbitant price."

"He's a loan shark," Chris said, and Sue took a deep breath. Chris had been the first person to tell Loretta that Thomas Baldwin wanted to buy her clinic to launder money. It was false, but it led her astray for a while.

"Some loan sharks will use thugs to scare debtors to encourage them to pay," Zeke said.

"That means they break fingers and legs," Chris said, but everyone knew it.

My cousins and I watched with interest as Sue used a nail gun to pound a nail from a cross rail into a post. The nail gun was loud and made a cracking sound. Luna didn't like it and roamed to rest with Stevie in another part of the huge fenced yard.

Lee and I watched the process on the grass opposite the chicken coop.

"Luke is planning a high-stakes poker game," Sue said.

"Why would he do that?" Zeke asked, and Sue explained that Bill needed money to buy the property and would play the game whether or not Luke was there. "Luke doesn't trust the players," she said. "He wants to participate so he can referee the game."

"That sounds dangerous," Zeke said.

Sue replied. "He wants you to play."

"We don't have that kind of money for poker," Loretta said. "We don't have that kind of money for anything."

"Luke will finance your game," Sue said. "None of the players know you're an attorney, and he wants a fresh set of eyes to oversee the game."

"I'm not a card player," Zeke said, and Chris offered to help him learn the game. "I'm an expert card shuffler and a decent player," he said, "but I'm not playing high-stakes poker with untrustworthy men. People die over big money."

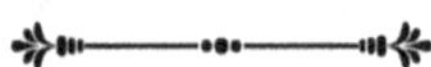

When they finished talking, Sue gathered her belongings for the drive home. I lay down on the back seat for the ride. It had been a busy day, and I was tired. I wanted to be rested for tomorrow's adventures.

Chapter 10

Mia's Museum

The following morning, Sue woke so late that I rubbed my paw on her arm to ensure she was okay. It was unlike Sue to sleep late, and my internal clock was ticking. She opened her eyes and looked at me with trepidation. I had never woken her up before.

"Wow, it's almost 6:30," Sue said, glancing at her watch. "You must need to go outside."

I didn't have to go outside, but was concerned about Sue. She looked tired, so I lay back down, stretched out on the big bed beside her. If Sue needed rest, I could wait for her to get out of bed.

Twenty minutes later, Mia called, and Sue rose to answer her cell phone, which she kept on the dresser a short walk from the bed.

"Hi Mia," she said, putting her phone on speaker before Toby could shift his foot under the door for his first morning attention. "I just woke up."

"Wow, you must have needed the sleep," Mia replied, knowing I was usually an early riser. "I've been up for an hour."

"I've been awake for twenty minutes, but was resting with Daisy," Sue said, following me outside, while she chatted with Mia.

"Do you want to walk the cove with me before we go to the museum today?" Mia asked.

"I'd love to," Sue replied. "I've met someone there. Her name is Betsy Radcliffe."

"Awwwww, the Radcliffe family," Mia replied, as she had lived here most of her life. "There is a street in Sweetwater Springs named after their family."

"It amazes me to think that only a few families started this town," Sue said.

"Most of the first miners have streets named after them," Mia added. "It amazes me that the first mining was only slightly over a century ago."

"The Radcliffe family were road builders," Sue reminded her, and Mia replied she didn't recall.

"Our families weren't close," Mia said. "I remember the grandsons of their security guards from school, but the Radcliffe children went to boarding school."

"Interesting," Sue replied. "The great-grandsons of their security guards still live at the property."

"They must have inherited the guardhouse," Mia said. "It's worth a lot of money now."

"I believe they did," Sue said. "And unlike most of the family, they want to keep it."

"They could make enough money to live in a house on the river as groundskeepers," Mia said.

"I can't imagine a more beautiful place to be a groundskeeper," Sue said. "Except your place, of course."

Mia laughed. "No wonder they want to keep it," she said. "It's a million-dollar view of the river and a means to pay the taxes. Our place is lovely, but it's on a creek."

"It's on a lovely spring that feeds a creek," Sue corrected her. "A half-century from now, everything will be named after you," Sue said, as her two-legged crime-solving partner already had a museum and a spring-fed creek named after her.

"Thomas wants to preserve our love rather than his last name for history," Mia said, and Sue mentioned it was very sweet. Mia added, "It's doubtful his children from his first wife will move back to Sweetwater Springs. A guard or groundskeeper may save our legacy, too."

"Your daughter is still here," Sue said, and Mia agreed that Sarah would most likely stay in Sweetwater Springs forever. "Thomas is growing very fond of Sarah," Mia said. "He loves her like I do."

When we returned from my potty break, Toby was resting on the back of the couch, looking smug. I felt certain his biological clock wasn't as fine-tuned as mine, but he must have noticed it was light outside. It had been an unusual morning. Sue was running late, he didn't get to stick his feet under the bedroom door, and it was past time for breakfast.

Sue poured food into our dishes before making coffee and a bagel for breakfast. She picked up the remains of a tortured palmetto bug from Toby's night activities and shook her head. She could not convince Luke to shut the patio door when he let Toby outside to play on the back porch.

Toby joined Sue on the ottoman beside her chair while she ate her bagel. I lay on the floor beside them, awaiting our walk. She grabbed my leash when she finished, which excited me, but Toby took it in stride. He would wait for us to come home, as he always did, despite the unusual morning activities.

"Bye, Toby," Sue said, as she often did when she left the house. "Take care of the house, while we're gone."

I sat in the back seat, observing the cars, while Sue drove to Green Cove. The short drive was becoming very familiar, but the cars were different. There were more of them. Sue said that some were very expensive, as the carriages must have been in the peak of the Radcliffes' Golden Age.

When we drove past Bill and Lilly's house, Sargie was still indoors. I missed my oversized friend, but my thoughts were short-lived. We found Sargie accompanying Mia, Lilly, and Russ Johnson at a turtle dig.

"She has eggs," Lilly called, as they replaced the ribbon that guarded the nest.

"I can see why you don't want a golf course here," Sue said, and Russ agreed the land was essential to them.

"You don't seem the turtle-loving type," Mia said, and Russ said he had a soft spot.

"We're going to see Shameka later," Sue added, as Lilly tied the ribbon to a post.

"I love that museum," Russ replied. "Tell her hello from me," he said. "I'll be there later."

Sue tugged my leash, and we walked through the meadow for a view of the cove. "It would be spectacular without the algae," Mia mentioned.

"You're lucky to live on a spring," Sue said. "The water will be sparkling clear forever."

"I hope you're right," Mia said. "Thomas has some ideas to fix this problem."

"He's one of the few people who have the ideas, money, and political pull to make a difference," Sue said. "I hope he finds the solution."

Lilly and Russ had left the nest with Sargie when we returned from the walk on the cove. "Oddly, they're together, don't you think?" Mia asked, and Sue mentioned that stranger things had happened. "What do we know about Russ?" she asked.

"He's a stockbroker from Miami, and he likes women and turtles," Mia said.

"He borrowed money from Doug DeLeon and didn't pay it back," Sue said.

"He likes to gamble," Mia added.

"All of them like to gamble," Sue said, "including Bill."

"I don't like to pry, but we must find out how serious their relationship is…for Shameka's sake."

Sue tugged my leash, and we walked toward the river. A man was stepping out of his yellow sports car. He carried a tripod with a device attached to it. From a distance, Sue watched him set up the tripod and look through the device, which I had never seen before.

"He's surveying the property," Sue declared, as we walked closer.

"Isn't that Andy Lemar's car?" Mia asked.

"Yes," Sue replied. "And that's Andy Lemar doing the survey."

"I thought he wanted to build an Eco Retreat," Mia said. "Why would he need a survey for an EcoRetreat?"

"I don't know," Sue replied.

"Maybe he's more interested in building a subdivision than he admitted," Sue said.

I sat beside Sue and Mia, looking towards the road that passed through the property. While they were talking, an old two-tone yellow and brown truck roared past. Inside were two middle-aged men, both unshaven and rugged-looking.

"The Boggs brothers," Mia whispered, although no one could have heard her, except Sue.

"Betsy Radcliffe told me about them," Sue replied.

"They must have seen Andy doing the survey," Mia said.

"They may have seen Lilly and Russ, too," Sue added. "They know about the golf course; their greatest fear is a subdivision."

The heavier driver revved the engine as the truck slowed beside us. "I suggest you Ladies be careful," the passenger man shouted, while the driver thumbed his nose. "You don't want to be messing with the Bogg's brothers."

Sue and Mia had been threatened before, but never so poignantly. "I'm not going to tell Luke about this," Sue said, and Mia agreed, "I'm not going to tell Thomas about it, either."

"Do you think they'll say something to Andy Lemar?" Sue asked.

"I don't know," Mia replied. "I guess we've been seen with all the bad guys and we're an easier target."

I barked at the men to shoo them away, but it made no difference. They didn't plan to stay. They were gone as quickly as they arrived and disappeared down the street into the wetlands.

"We've got our hands full," Sue said, and Mia agreed it was true.

"Let's go talk to Shameka," she said.

I sat in the back seat of Sue's car while Mia drove separately to the museum. Having been threatened, it wasn't wise to leave a vehicle behind. It was a short drive, with little time for Sue to think. She didn't mumble about the altercation with the Boggs brothers.

Sue grabbed my leash and we walked inside the museum. Shameka was bubbling when we found her standing beside the case with the silver-plated gun. "Russ told me he saw you at the Green Cove," she squealed. "He's such a nice man," she said. "I know you're going to love him!"

Sue and Mia exchanged glances as Sarah joined us from the back room.

"What?" Shameka said.

"What do you mean what?" Mia asked.

"Why did you look at each other like that?"

"It's good to see you so happy!" Sue finally said.

"You are happier than I've seen you in a long time," Mia said.

"I've never seen you so happy!" Sarah agreed.

"As you know, Russ and I have been living together on weekends," Shameka said. "I think he may be "The One."

I sensed Sue's distress over Shameka's proclamation, but the words could come later. She had no proof of anything regarding Russ, just some strange overtones and suspicious behaviors. This was not the right moment to break the news to Shameka.

Chapter 11

Jessie's House with Chris

The following morning, Toby was in rare form. He had spent the night jumping between tables and chairs in a frenzied attempt to capture something. Perhaps it was something in his imagination. Sue found no remnants of an insect or critter on the floor, but the carved wooden pelican statue had moved from its previous location.

The pelican had lived in the house for as long as Toby, but it only occasionally grabbed his attention. When it did, the statue moved from place to place. Last night, it faced the river. This morning, it faced the fireplace.

It was a heavy statue—too heavy for a small cat to move. But it had a rope around its base that gave Toby some leverage. When he pawed the rope, it moved the pelican in a new direction.

After such a wild night, Toby often slept in the guest room. Sue called it Toby's room because it was his favorite resting location after his rambunctious adventures. Who knew what started it, but Sue was convinced he'd be a kitten forever, just as I would always be puppyish. When she called him, he followed her down the hall toward the living room.

Toby was having breakfast on the counter when Sue let me back inside from my romp in the dog yard, to eat dog kibble. We relaxed in the living room while she had coffee and her usual half-bagel. Sue caught up with the local news while she ate. A local man had been struck by a car while walking his dog, and he was recovering in the hospital.

Sue planned a busy day for us at one of my favorite places. We were joining Mia for lunch at Chris and Jessie's house. They had a big yard, where I enjoyed jumping off the seawall into the river. I loved it when Loretta brought my cousin Luna for a playdate at Jessie's house, but today it would be just me and Jessie's senior dog, a Doberman named Redman, who was too old to play in the river.

I took a nap with Toby on the couch while Sue cleaned her house and did a laundry load while waiting for Jessie's call. Neither of us liked the robotic vacuum, but it was a necessary evil that we avoided by sleeping on the furniture. When it wasn't running, Toby went nose-to-nose with the black box where the robot slept, as we did. He quickly backed away after he touched it and stared at the foreboding box, which occupied a wall opposite the pelican.

I suspected the robot's box might become part of his nightly endeavors, but it was something to touch with his nose. For now, Toby napped on the couch with one eye open, as the robot sucked up his shedded fur. I was a non-shedder, but the robot also found some of my fur. It was light. Toby's fur was dark.

It was late morning when Jessie called. "Lunch is ready. Are you coming over?" she asked, and Sue replied she was looking forward to it.

"Mia is on her way," Jessie said. "It's been too long. I can't wait to see you."

Sue grabbed my leash, signaling the end of my vacuum-distracted nap, and I happily jumped in the car for the drive upriver. I missed Jessie and her daughter, Beth, who had adopted the alley cat, Boomer. I had not fallen in love with Boomer, as I had with Toby, but he had opened my heart to the feline species.

Jessie worked as a nurse and cooked as a hobby. She firmly believed in the importance of a healthy diet and was writing a cookbook that included recipes from her creations and those of her friends, who loved to contribute. Sue contributed easy recipes for the CHEWS COOKBOOK: Cheap, Healthy, Easy, Wholesome, Spicy Recipes for Healthy Living.

Jessie's boyfriend, Chris, had been working on the chicken coop for Loretta. He was Zeke's friend and building mentor. Everyone knew that Zeke had mastered the law books better than the building mechanics. The chicken coop was a prize endeavor.

When we arrived at our destination, I jumped out of the car and raced across the yard. Chris and Jessie were outside with Jessie's daughter, Beth, and Mia, seated at the picnic table near the river.

Chris was the first to shower me with loving affection, rubbing behind my ears and making me groan. "We should get a Doodle," he told Jessie. "They love to swim."

"Maybe someday," Jessie said as Beth passed me a homemade dog cookie. "Redman is enjoying his senior years as an only dog for now." Sue agreed that although I loved to swim, my high energy might be too much for Redman as a live-in.

I devoured the dog cookie, making a path of crumbs in the yard. "We made the dog cookies outside," Beth said. "Mom said they stunk too much to cook them in the house."

"How smart of your mother," Sue replied, looking at Chris. "You have the perfect outdoor kitchen for baking dog cookies."

"I didn't help make the dog cookies," Chris said, and Jessie mentioned he did build the kitchen.

"It takes a village," Mia said. "Everyone does their part to make it work."

Jessie poured icy peach tea from a fat pitcher for all. "This is the perfect day for a picnic," she said. "It's finally warm enough to eat outside, but not too hot."

"The breeze is delightful," Sue replied, as a gust of wind blew off the sparkling river.

"Mia tells us you have been walking on the property at the Green Cove," Jessie said. "It's quite a hot topic at work. All of our patients are talking about it."

"It's been for sale for a long time," Sue replied.

"Suddenly, three out-of-towners want to buy it," Sue added.

“Three out-of-towners and a local,” Mia corrected her. “Doug DeLeon is from Sweetwater Springs.”

“Technically, Russ Johnson never said he wanted to buy the property,” Sue said. “He just keeps showing up there to help with turtle nests.”

“It’s odd, isn’t it?” Chris said, and Mia agreed that Russ was odd. “My instincts tell me something isn’t right with him.”

“Instincts are often right,” Sue said, and Mia added that she wished Shameka hadn’t gotten so close to him before she met him.

“Andy Lemar says Russ Johnson is a Card Shark,” Chris declared.

“When did you talk to Andy Lemar?” Sue asked, and Jessie said he had kayaked past their house with his Golden Retriever.

“Card Sharks cheat at cards,” Mia said. “I will mention it to Thomas.”

“I’ll tell Luke,” Sue said. “Both of them have agreed to play poker at the match.”

“Why would the two wealthiest residents of Sweetwater Springs play poker with unsavory people?” Chris asked, and Sue explained that his brother had buddied up with them and that he wanted to protect Bill.

“Bill wants to buy the land for a golf course,” Sue said, but his wife Lilly didn’t seem enamoured with the plan.

“The Radcliffes are ready to sell their family’s inheritance after three generations of taxes and maintenance,” Mia said.

“Who are the Radcliffes?” Chris asked, and Sue explained they were among the first families to develop Sweetwater Springs and owned much land on and near the river.

"The Boggs brothers have a different opinion about selling the property," Mia explained. "They want to keep the property as a park and preserve."

"Interesting," Chris replied. "They don't own it."

"They are the descendants of the Radcliffes' security guards," Sue said. "They inherited a riverfront house."

Neither woman mentioned that they had threatened them after they saw them with Russ Johnson and Andy Lemar on their walk at the cove. "Have you seen more accident victims than usual at the clinic?" Sue asked.

"No, not necessarily," Jessie said. "There are more people in Sweetwater Springs than there used to be."

"I suppose you're right," Sue said. "I'll keep that in mind."

Chris jumped into the river and called me to join him. It didn't take much to get me to fly off the seawall and dog-paddle towards his arms. Beth was soon to follow, as the three of us splashed in the shallows.

I was glad to have a man and a child in my life, as they were more likely to join me at play. Don't get me wrong; I loved Sue, the detective work, and dog walks. But I also loved any outdoor play.

"Andy Lemar was excited to see my container garden," Jessie said, as we assembled at the picnic table to build our lettuce wraps. "My Bibb lettuce and Kale are in full bloom," she added.

"Andy says he wants to build an EcoRetreat," Chris said. "He wants guests to leave with better life skills than when they arrived.

"So he says," Sue agreed, as Chris cooked teriyaki chicken strips with fried coconut rice and vegetables on the outdoor grill.

"You don't sound convinced," Chris said, and Sue reminded him that Luke wanted Zeke to attend the poker match for a reason. "We're sure we need to be careful," Mia added. "We don't know these men well, but they have an angle."

Jessie served a variety of homemade dips in tiny bowls set in a long boat to accompany the wraps. Nothing fell under the table, but Beth fed me two dog cookies during the luncheon. It was a fun day, just as I expected—full of food, games, and water play.

Tomorrow we will meet Zeke and Loretta for dinner at Luke's house. I am excited to see Artemis, who still loves to run and play. Sue says it's about time somebody told Sophie that Luke is hosting the card game at their estate. It's a bit scary to think about, but I like Sophie. She's a good lady, and it will be alright.

Chapter 12

Luke's House with Zeke and Loretta

"If you play with fire, you're going to get burned!" the fat man yelled across the river.

When the shouting started, I played chase around Luke's enormous yard with Artemis and my three cousins. We could hear the man clearly because the sound was amplified over water. He had a deep, gruff voice that rang familiar. I had met him, but where?

"Who do you think you are coming near my family with a threat?" Sophie shouted at the two men standing in a camouflaged color fishing boat with a shallow draft engine. "You boys best get outta here before I get something to make you run that peanut roaster boat of yours back where you came from–and then some."

"Shut up, you old….." the skinny man yelled, stopping short when he saw Luke, who chastised the fisherman.

"Be careful what you say to my mama!" Luke shouted, and Sue looked at Mia, who recognized them as the two men in the truck at the Green Cove.

"It's the Boggs Brothers," Mia grunted.

"In the flesh," the fatter man said. "I'm Frankie. And this is Butch."

"My mother is 94," Luke exclaimed. "I'll expect you to show her some respect."

The skinny man tipped his ball cap, "My family has been in Sweetwater Springs longer than you are old…ma'am," he grunted.

"Did you say I was OLD!" Sophie spat, marching towards the river before Luke stopped her, and held her firmly and lovingly under his right arm. "I'll show YOU what OLD can do!"

"Let's find out what they want, Mama," Luke said.

"These two boys have been coming here daily for a week," Sophie groused. "Fishing and grunting on the river in front of my backyard…" I don't care what they want!"

Zeke looked at Loretta, who sighed. Sophie was unfiltered on the attack.

"I know what I want….for those two to be banned from fishing forever!" Sophie was on a crusade. "Come to think of it, I'm going to get fishing banned on the whole river!" she shouted. "Just to make sure those two NEVER come back!"

"If we can't fish, we'll swim!" Butch goaded, and Frankie added, "We'll play music real loud, too!"

"Calm down, Mama," Luke said. "We should find out what these fellows want before we have a war." As a premier hotelier who developed resorts outside Sweetwater Springs, Luke was versed in deals and diplomacy.

"Maybe something will benefit everyone," Thomas, who wanted a Wild West Theme Park and hotel in Sweetwater Springs, agreed.

We were visiting Luke's estate for the dinner party when the shouting match occurred. Sophie had planned the party outside because of the lovely spring weather. Soon it would be hot, but for now, it was delightful. I especially liked the soft wind that blew the fur around my face.

Zeke and Loretta brought my three cousins. After the lawn races, Luna watched a fish and dunked her snout at the water's edge. Stevie sat beside Loretta with her head resting on her thigh. And Lee, my sister, watched for crumbs to fall from the snacks Sophie had served.

Artemis and I watched the men in the boat, who were quieter after the shouting match. "Would you like to come ashore for antipasto and bruschetta?" Luke asked. "Mama makes them the best."

"We have deer jerky and chips," Butch replied, and Frank agreed they didn't care for fancy snacks, but they would join them for beer if they had some.

"I'll get it," Sophie said, and returned shortly with a stout from Holland. "I've never seen that beer before," Frankie snarled, rejecting the import. "I'll wait to get home to drink my brand."

Butch furled his lip after sipping the bitter brew and set the dark bottle on the table for the remainder of the conversation. "Bad news?" Frankie asked, and his brother agreed. "Worst beer I ever had."

"Where did you get the deer jerky?" Sue asked, seeking a connection that fell short.

"Made it ourselves," Frankie said. "Butch shot one of them deer that came out of the woods last year, and we butchered it for sausage and jerky. Do you want to try it?"

"No thanks," Sue said, although I might have enjoyed sampling it with my four-legged cousins.

"I'll bet you eat alligator," Mia added, and Frankie agreed it was a rare treat since they didn't give many permits for alligator hunting.

Sophie got to the point. "Why have you been fishing behind my house for a week?" she asked, and Frank launched into a dissertation regarding the Radcliffe family roots and his family's role as their security guards.

"Your women are hanging out with the wrong people," Butch said, referring to Sue and Mia. "You don't know it yet, but those men who have been scrounging around the Green Cove with your brother, Bill— your son, ma'am— are big trouble.

Sophie appreciated his respectful behavior and offered the men peach tea, while Luna, the counter-surfer, scarfed a piece of deer jerky off the table. I wanted to try the deer jerky, but Luna didn't share. She downed it in an instant.

"I played football with Doug DeLeon in high school," Frankie said. "The man is a scum bag."

"Go on," Sophie said. "I've known plenty of them during my 94 years on the planet. Nothing shocks me."

"He'll lend anybody money," Frankie said. "He has just as much fun beating the tar out of the deadbeats as getting a big return on his investment from the high-risk takers."

"We've heard he is a loan shark," Luke said, and everyone but Sophie agreed because no one told her.

"He beat up one of our friends," Butch explained. "He and that card shark, Russ Johnson, set up a poker game, then duped him.

"Where did they play?"

"Our friend has a farm," Frankie said. "They played at his house."

"Doug lent him the money for the game, then Russ Johnson and he rigged the game."

"Do you mean they work together?" Zeke asked.

"Sometimes. They work together at the card games," Butch said. "They use signals for the most seasoned players and rig decks with the least suspicious players."

Luke took a deep breath, and Sophie shook her head. "Leave it to Bill to make friends with a card shark and a loan shark," she grumbled.

"We heard about a farm accident," Luke said. "Your friend must be the one."

"They locked him in a stall with a bull," Frankie said. "He was going to pay up the next day."

"That's awful," Sue said, and Mia mentioned that Doug claimed to want the steakhouse.

Butch watched Luna scarf another piece of deer jerky off the table and offered me a piece of the meat. Sue said one small piece would be okay for me, but declined a further offer. I bolted the jerky and hoped she changed her mind about the quantity. She didn't.

"What do you know about Andy Lemar?" Sue asked.

"Not much," Frankie said.

"He looks like a surveyor with the equipment he uses," Butch added.

"He was a developer in Miami," Mia suggested, and everyone agreed he could be lying about plans for an EcoRetreat.

"How stupid does he think we are?" Frankie asked, and no one commented.

"I don't think you're stupid," Mia said, and Sue added, "What do you want from the Green Cove property?"

"A park," Butch said. "A place for local kids to play."

"Why do you keep fishing near my house?" Sophie asked.

"We have our eye on the property across the river," Butch said. "We want a launch for the local kids to float."

"The local kids?" Mia asked. "What about the tourists?"

"We'll see," Butch said. "They've taken most of our access, already. It's easier for them to get on the river than the locals."

"Thanks for the tea, ma'am," Frankie said. "I hope you'll be cordial next time."

After they were gone, Luna jumped off the bluff into the river with Artemis. I stayed behind with Sue and the others. There were fewer food crumbs without the two men, but Luke offered me a bite of bread.

"People are not always what they seem," Sue said, and Mia agreed that her first impression was less favorable.

"I want to host the card party at our house," Luke told his mother. "We can spot a cheat."

"Bill needs our help," Sophie agreed. "I'll help with the food for the poker game," she added, and Sue and Mia offered to help her.

"It sounds like we need to encourage these scammers to leave Sweetwater Springs," Zeke said.

"Forever," everyone agreed.

"I'll give you the money to join the poker game," Luke told Zeke. "We could use a fresh set of eyes."

"Chris offered to teach me to play," Zeke said. "I don't know how much help I'll be."

"You may be more help than you know," Luke said. "My brother needs all the help he can get."

"Has Bill borrowed money from the Scum Bag already?" Sophie asked, and Luke replied that he didn't know how his brother planned to finance the game.

After dinner, Loretta and Zeke departed for home with my cousins. Artemis looked forlorn when I jumped into Luke's car for the home ride. It had been a fun afternoon for him and my cousins, his four-legged friends. Artemis had everything a dog could want, but best of all, he loved to play with his friends.

Chapter 13

Peter and Stanley's house

I was tired from a big day at Luke's house the following morning. Running with Artemis and my cousins was fun, but also exhausting. After many days without rain, it was warmer than usual for spring. My curly fur coat was long enough to keep me from sunburn, but soon, Sue would take me to the groomer for my second cut of the season. Yuck for me to itch, but Sue kept my fur shorter for summer.

I relished a nap on the cool tile in the long-dog configuration this morning while Sue drank coffee. I could do the long dog on my side or on my belly, but I preferred side naps for sleeping. My legs were fully stretched in both directions, and my head was on the floor. Still, I kept one eye open in case Toby launched into action.

Toby had been on guard all night, with little evidence of his activity. Frankly, Sue overstated his guard duty commission. Although I was mostly a connector dog, I was the alarm of the house. My job was to be the alarm that barked away the boogie man—and I was good at my day job.

I slept so deeply at night that Sue didn't think I'd wake up for anything or anyone. For that reason, she gave Toby credit as guard cat for resting on his laurels on the couch most nights. I suppose he might have roamed down the hall chirping if something had happened.

Sue and Mia faced threats concerning their evolving ties with Bill's unsavory friends. The Boggs brothers had warned them to avoid trouble, but they were sure to stick their noses where they didn't belong. Sooner or later, Sue might need our help. Hence, she commissioned Toby as a night guard.

Toby's favorite activity, when not chasing lizards, bugs, or dust bunnies, was to be a stay-at-home lounging cat. He had no shame in doing nothing, while Sue and I marched off into the forces of the unknown. I will admit he was quicker to wake up at night. Some nights, there was so much raucousness, I wondered if he slept.

Last night was a quiet one, without a peep from Toby. Still, sometime during the night, someone had slipped a note into Sue's mailbox. Now, she sipped coffee while she read it aloud—"Choose your friends carefully," she said, stroking Toby, who had jumped into her lap and purred loudly. Who would write such a note? she muttered, as if she had not chosen her friends carefully. Mia was, after all, her best girlfriend and partner in crime solving in Sweetwater Springs.

Luke was her favorite male friend, protector, and community philanthropist. His brother, Bill, had started a dilemma for the community: What should be done with the property that some people wanted and nobody wanted to sell?

"I have the best friends on the planet," Sue said, as Toby crawled on her chest, purring and making bread.

"Technically, it should have said, choose sides carefully," she added. "Or maybe, back off and stay out of this!"

"There is no backing out of this now," Sue said, setting Toby on the floor beside me. "Sophie has approved the card game, which a card shark, a loan shark, a gambler, and a developer will attend."

I was lying long on my belly with my legs stretched out when Mia knocked on the door. Sue was talking to herself. "What's up, Sue?" she asked when she let her inside. "You're white as a sheep."

"I think you should have a seat," Sue said, leading her friend to the couch and passing her the note.

"That's weird," Mia said, digesting the strange words. "Where did you get it?"

"It came in my mailbox," Sue replied, and Mia suggested she should have checked her mailbox before she left home. "I wouldn't want Thomas to find a note like this," she said. "It sounds like a threat."

"It's not the first time," Sue said, reminding her of the private eye Luke hired to follow them during the previous caper. "You don't have to be involved," she added.

"I wouldn't leave you alone with this," Mia said, and Sue suggested it was Luke's brother who started the trouble, and Thomas had nothing to do with it.

"Shameka is my daughter's best friend, and she manages the museum. She's in trouble, too," Mia said. "I'm already involved."

"I suppose you're right," Sue said. "Is Thomas up for the poker game?" she asked.

"He doesn't want to play high-stakes poker anymore, but knows Luke needs his help. He wants to be there for him."

Toby was startled and raced down the hall when Sue's phone rang. He wasn't usually jumpy about a phone call, but having Mia at the house was exciting. I took it in stride, as dogs do about everyday things.

"That was Peter," Sue told Mia when she finished talking. "He wants us to join him and Stanley for tea and homemade scones."

"That would be lovely," Mia said of Sue's neighbors who lived on her street. "It's been a long time since I've seen them."

Peter was the head chef at Cat Tails Pub, where Sue and Mia met up with some of Sweetwater Springs' notorious characters. He loved to cook, rescue cats, and was willing to listen for valuable and interesting local information from the pub. While he specialized in pub grub at Cat Tails, he loved all kinds of cooking.

Stanley was his life partner and an attorney from Miami. He mainly worked from home but drove his hot rod car to Miami as needed. The car's roaring twang stirred the neighbors, some more than others, who were unequivocally perturbed, settling for upscale Caribbean treats as penance for his obnoxiously loud engine. Mia's husband had used Stanley's services, with excellent results.

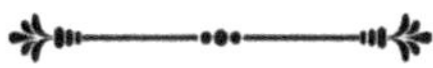

Sue grabbed my collar and leash for the short walk to the neighbors' house with Mia. "Let's go see Uncle Peter," she announced, as I was fond of him. I liked Stanley, who gave me too many treats to compensate for his lack of affection.

"I don't want anyone to miss me too much," Stanley had declared regarding his affection problem, but everyone knew he was less amiable than Peter's warmth.

"Hi Daisy!" Peter shrieked, opening the door. "It's good to see everyone," he added, massaging my chest. "Please come in! Stanley is waiting for us in the living room."

Sue removed my leash, and we followed Peter to the living room, where the large man sat with an orange cat on his lap. "I'm sorry not to greet you at the door," he said. "I simply couldn't disturb O.C."

"Of course not," Sue said, and Mia agreed. "I wouldn't expect you to disrupt his catnap."

Peter passed the scones and served Chai tea in tiny Japanese cups. "These cups are adorable," Mia said. "Thomas and I may have to follow in your footsteps for a Japanese holiday."

"I hope you do," Stanley said. "I'll give you a list of places to visit when you go." Mia thanked him for his upcoming advice and added, "Thomas appreciates your law services," she said. "He thinks highly of you."

"I learned to make scones during our Great Britain trip," Peter said. "I hope you like them." Mia replied, "You are certainly an expert at bringing back the best of every country in your travels."

I sniffed the cat in Stanley's lap while they talked. He wasn't impressed, giving me an evil eye for the nose treatment. A cat's evil eye is much more apparent than most people, who use words for less effect.

"I have so much to tell you," Peter said. "The pub has been busy with Russ Johnson and Doug DeLeon having spats," he said.

"I've heard them argue," Sue admitted.

"Sheriff Stone can't keep up with it," Peter replied. "They cause trouble wherever they go."

"They have a scam going on," Mia said. "Doug offers someone money for a loan, but they don't pay up, and then he or one of his cronies goes after them."

"When the scam is poker, Russ Johnson is a card shark," Sue added, showing Peter and Stanley the photo of everyone from the archery match at Bill's house. "Have you seen this man?" she asked, pointing at Andy.

Stanley pored over the picture that included Andy Lemar. "He looks familiar," he said, "but I'm not sure where I know him from."

"His name is Andy Lemar," Sue explained. "He's a developer from Miami, turned self-proclaimed Eco-Retreat aficionado for Sweetwater Springs."

"I've seen Russ Johnson in Miami," he said. "He says he's a stockbroker but dabbles in many things. He likes to be admired by many women."

"He flirts with women at Cat Tails," Peter added. "I don't know how women don't see through his transparent facade."

"Russ is too good-looking for his good," Stanley said. "Women swoon over him in Miami."

"Shameka is swooning over him in Sweetwater Springs," Mia said, and Sue added she hated to hear about his philandering with women. "She's the new museum manager," Sue said.

"Shameka is a nice girl," Mia said. "She is a lifelong friend of my daughter."

"I'd hate to see her hurt," Sue added. "She thinks she's in love with him."

"Someone should warn her about his reputation," Peter said, and Stanley added, "He's not a good boyfriend for a small town girl."

The orange cat stared at me from his hefty perch on Stanley's lap when Sue and Mia finished eating their scones. A few crumbs had fallen on the floor, but his watchful eye kept me from moving to consume them. I kept a safe distance from the cat for the sake of peace over the joy of a nibble of food.

Sue and her friends kept talking, ignoring the cat that held me at bay. They were deep in conversation when he finally decided I wasn't worth the trouble. He closed both eyes to a formidable squint. I quietly scooched on my belly to sample a crumb, but he opened his eyes, and I gave up on the tidbit.

"What's with Luke's brother?" Peter asked. "He's sort of quiet at the pub."

"It must be impossible to compete with Luke," Stanley said. "He doesn't stand a chance in Sophie's eyes."

"He's not quiet when you get to know him," Mia said. "But I agree about Bill and Luke. Bill must find his direction in life and forget about competing with Luke."

"Bill wants to buy the property for a golf course," Sue said. "His wife doesn't seem so thrilled about it."

"Where will he get the money to buy the land?" Stanley asked.

Sue replied, “He plans to host a high-stakes poker game at Luke’s house.”

“Where will he get the money for the game?” Peter asked, and Mia replied, “That's a good question.”

It finally rained that afternoon, leaving a shimmer of green on the trees. Patches of brown grass turned green overnight after the drought. Mia called Sarah and Shameka to join us on a walk at the Green Cove. I looked forward to a dog walk after the rain.

Chapter 14

The Green Cove with Girlfriends

I'll be honest. I don't like thunderstorms. They make me anxious, like Chicken Little. I don't know why the sky is falling, but I know it makes the grass feel softer beneath my feet when it's over.

The rain wasn't very comforting for a dog like me. Toby and I were alone inside the house when it started. Sue had gone on an errand where dogs weren't allowed. We had the house to ourselves for a long time. With the rainfall, it seemed like forever.

It lasted into the evening, with tiny droplets dimpling the cove. I felt better when Sue got home, but I was still nervous, staying close by. She seemed happier about it than I did. I snuggled beside her for the evening until it stopped.

Toby is not afraid of a falling sky like I am. He takes it in stride, which makes me feel better. A moving blade of grass sends him bolting down the hallway, but he cares little about rain or thunder. We are a good match for comforting each other, especially when Sue is away.

Toby is afraid of little things. I'm afraid of bigger things. It's an odd arrangement, but it works. I can't imagine if we both got the zoomies together.

The following morning, Toby was his usual lovable self with Sue. He followed her into the kitchen, rubbing against her and purring. When I returned from my little dog yard, he enjoyed a hefty breakfast on the countertop. I felt relieved that the sky hadn't smashed my new, improved dog yard, while he had forgotten it rained.

Sue grabbed my leash and drove to the Green Cove to meet Mia, Sarah, and her museum manager, Shameka. She found Mia parked on the berm of the coveted property, where Andy Lemar had appeared to be surveying the parcel.

I jumped out of the backseat and tugged the leash to greet Mia. "It's hard to believe this parcel is causing so much unrest," Mia said, massaging my chest.

"It's hard to believe, but understandable," Sue sighed. "The locals will have no river access if someone doesn't stand up for preserving the last remaining properties in Sweetwater Springs."

"Thomas has donated a lot of wetlands already," Mia said. "Most people don't know that."

"Unfortunately, the wetlands have no river access," Sue replied. "The locals need a street, parking, and a launch."

"There are several parks with ramps," Mia said, and Sue countered that most of the parking was taken by the tourists early in the morning. "There simply isn't enough parking for everyone."

“If Andy Lemar builds an Eco-Retreat, he could donate land for public access,” Mia suggested, and Sue replied that all of the projects could involve donated land for ramps.

“The locals don’t want public access, they want local access,” Sue replied. “They need a local pass—Free or reduced price for the residents of Sweetwater Springs.”

“Good idea,” Mia said, and Sue mentioned that Luke had talked about it.

At first, I didn’t recognize Bill when he rode his bicycle down the shady street. “Hi, Ladies,” he said, hopping off the two-wheeler and petting me behind the ears. “It’s a glorious day after the rain,” he added, looking through the tree tops.

“We needed it,” Sue replied, grimacing at Luke’s brother.

“You must wonder why I picked Sweetwater Springs to build a golf course,” he said. “Would you believe I wanted to be closer to my mother?”

Mia grumbled, and Sue sighed.

“Haven’t you heard my mother is Sicilian?” he asked, knowing the answer. “Italian families are very close. We help each other no matter what.”

“Some people think you’re jealous of your brother,” Mia said.

“I can be jealous of Luke and still love him,” Bill said. “He should have lent me the money for it.”

“Luke says he’s lent you money before,” Sue replied. “You didn’t pay it back.”

"More power to him," Bill said. "If he won't lend it to me, I'm forced to look elsewhere."

"Where did you find these players?" Mia asked.

"They were looking at the parcel before I was," Bill said. "It was a logical step in the right direction for me to purchase it, but I needed more money."

"Let me guess," Mia said. "The bank won't lend it to you."

"Not that much," Bill said. "I have bad credit."

"Great!" Sue replied, and Mia said she suspected as much. "Surprise, surprise," she added.

"If I don't buy it, somebody will," Bill said in defense. "I'm doing Sweetwater Springs a favor by buying it before they do. "Who knows what they'll pitch on this property?"

"Do you know their true motives and goals?" Sue asked.

"Nobody knows anybody's true goals," Bill said. "We know what they say, and these guys aren't known for their honesty."

"True," Sue said, breathing deeply. "Just for the record, someone put a threat note in my mailbox," she added. "I'm not so sure you did me a favor by dragging Luke into this."

"I didn't drag him into this," Bill groused. "He offered to have the poker match at his house.'

"To support you," Sue countered. "He thinks you're an easy mark for scammers."

"What did the note say?" Bill asked.

It said, "Choose your friends carefully," Sue replied, and Bill said it was good advice. You can't exactly call that a threat," he added.

"Maybe not," Sue said. "Under the circumstances, it doesn't seem like friendly advice."

After Bill left, Sue tugged my leash and marched towards his house with Mia. Shortly after, Sarah and Shameka joined us for the walk around Green Cove. I enjoyed the smells of the wet earth and fresh grass in the shade of the enormous oak trees while they talked.

"Isn't it a lovely day?" Shameka said, bubbling with delight as she had in the museum. "It feels like love is in the air."

"It's dandy," Mia replied, and Shameka caught her sarcastic drift.

"You don't sound like you mean that, Mom," Sarah said, frowning at Mia. "Is something wrong?"

"Everything is wrong," Mia replied, without further elaboration on the many ills befalling Sweetwater Springs.

"Your mother is afraid Shameka is falling in love with the wrong man," Sue said, to open the difficult conversation.

"He's so nice to me," Shameka replied. "How could he be the wrong man?"

"He's nice to everyone," Sue explained, and Mia said, "It's part of his act."

"I don't believe it," Shameka replied. "He's kind and sincere and most of all, loving."

"He has the reputation of being a lady's man," Sue explained. "Do you know what that means?"

"He used to be a Lady's man," Shameka said. "That was before me."

I felt my dog instincts kick in while they talked. The tension suggested that Sue and Mia were getting nowhere with the conversation. Shameka seemed tense and frustrated. Her shrill voice was unusual, as if she might cry.

Sarah shifted the conversation to offset her friend's emotions. "The display at the museum is coming along beautifully," she said. "Shameka is a mastermind and an artist."

"Yes, she is," Mia said. "That's why I hired her to manage the museum."

"We're stressed because of the card game," Sue suggested, and decided not to offer more information about the integrity of the players.

"Whoever wins the game will have the money to buy the property," Sarah suggested. "It could be Bill, Andy, Doug, Russ…or anyone."

"Some people already have the money to buy it," Shameka grunted, "Maybe they should."

Sue and Mia glowered at her. "I'm sorry I said that," Shameka said. "It's none of my business."

"It's more complicated than it seems," Sue said.

"I'm sure it is," Shameka agreed. "Thank you for asking me to come today. The cove is awesome!"

I heard Sargie's hoarse bark when we rounded the curve beside the pine tree. He sounded like an old, old dog, just as always. I felt the familiar twang of embarrassment for my preconceived notions about him. Sargie was a good dog.

"Hi Lilly," Sue said when we got closer.

"This is my daughter, Sarah, and her friend, Shameka," Mia added. "It's good to see you."

"Shameka manages the museum," Sue said.

"Russ loves the silver-plated handgun you have on display in the case," Lilly said.

"Russ talked to you about the silver-plated gun?" Shameka asked, surprised.

"Many times," Lilly said. "He helps me with the turtles," she explained.

"I've heard about that," Shameka said, although Russ had not mentioned it.

"Will you be coming to the card game?" Sue asked.

"Honey, you better believe I'll be at that game," Lilly said. "Bill hawked my diamond ring to get the money to play."

Sue was stunned. "He hawked your ring?" she asked.

"Yep, that's what he did. Bill hawked my ring. Got $100,000 for that beauty," Lilly growled.

Shameka gasped. "That's a lot of money," she said. "I had no idea rings cost that much."

"It's not the first time he hawked my precious things to play in a high-stakes card game," Lilly said. "When no one lends him money, my precious things become his bank."

Before we walked away, I sniffed at Sargie's nose. It was good to get close to him. I wished he could talk, but he couldn't. He might have more to say than the trees on the parcel.

"Lilly was mad," Shameka said, out of earshot.

"Can you blame her?" Sarah asked.

"Nope, I don't blame her," Shameka replied. "You don't give your wife a diamond and pawn it for a card game."

"I wonder who he pawned it to," Sue said, although it wouldn't be hard to find out. There weren't many shops in Sweetwater Springs that handled that kind of money.

I had never been to a pawn shop before, but suspected that destination might be on Sue's list. For now, I was thirsty. Sue poured water for me in a collapsible bowl and headed home before planning our next endeavor.

Chapter 15

Val and Giovanni's House with Couples

By afternoon, the rain had cleared, and Sue said the sky was blue and cloudless. I don't know colors, but I knew it was preferable to a falling sky. Sue opened the back door so Toby could go outside on the patio. He found his favorite perch under the grill and sat in the corner watching a family of ducks who made the cove part of their repertoire.

From a distance, the ducks in a row looked like an alligator, rippling through the water with a mother duck, followed by nine baby ducks, and a straggler, perhaps from a different species.

"Wow, that's a big alligator," Sue said aloud as she watched Toby watching the procession through the safety of the screen. "I haven't seen one that big in the cove for a long time. Sue said gators were more active when searching for their mates in spring.

Soon, the family swam sideways across the cove in a perfect line, and it became obvious they were birds. Toby watched with fascination as the raft separated, ducks waddled onto the grass, and walked across the yard. The cove was fascinating if one didn't get too close to the action. It was remarkable how much happened if you paid attention.

"It's those ducks," Sue chuckled aloud, as the family marched across the yard on their daily route. The straggler who joined them followed shortly thereafter. "He must have lost his family," Sue said, mentioning he was safer with the raft of ducks, if they would have him.

Toby watched the ducks with interest until they waddled out of sight. He moved toward the sound of grass rustling behind the patio and focused on the noise. Sue walked over to see what Toby could see, but she saw nothing. "I'm sorry to disturb your porch duty," she said, carrying our little cat friend inside. "Daisy and I have a date this afternoon."

I was excited to see my leash and collar, as always. It didn't matter where we were going. Sue took me to interesting places at any time of day. I hopped into the back seat wherever she took me. Sue talked to me, as she often did, along the drive.

"We're going to Gio and Val's house," Sue said, but I hadn't been there. "They just bought a new home on the river."

I remembered Gio and Val. Gio gave me forbidden treats when we saw them in the street near my house. I got so excited that I jumped on him and got in trouble. Once, they had come to Luke's house for a gathering, where I could run free with my four-footed friends. Val's dog was friendly, but Gio's dog, Jelly Bean, couldn't be bothered.

"Jelly Bean will be there," Sue said, and I remembered his name. I had never met a more aloof fellow in my life. My only hope for a play date was Val's dog.

"Luke is coming, too," she announced, and I perked up because he might bring my friend, but he quickly let me down. "Artemis is staying home this time."

I would have a good time at a gathering, with or without my furry friend. People could pet me on the head and call me "Cute Dog." I would miss Artemis, but I could make a new friend.

"Mia and Thomas are coming," Sue said. "So is Tori."

Tori was the daughter of Val and Gio. She owned Cat Tails Pub and gave me ice water, which I loved. Her parents' obscure reputation led her to Sweetwater Springs to start a new life. They followed her from Miami after she went missing on a kayak trip.

Gio had many friends. Sue said some folks believed Gio was a mob boss, but no one knew if it was true. His connections, from various careers, helped solve the first caper. Whatever he did for a living, Gio knew people.

My internal GPS was familiar with most sights along the short drive. We passed through Green Cove and the houses of people I remembered. Most recently, I had been to most of them, including Bill's house. Today, Sue drove past his house and through the groomed jungle where we had walked, and we had come for the archery match.

Sue parked at a house on the river we had never been to. I could smell freshly cut grass when I hopped out of the car. From the front, it looked about the size of Sue's house. Inside was different.

"Hi, Sue," Val said, petting me on the head and leading us to an enormous living room that faced the river.

"Your home is lovely," Sue gasped, as we followed her to the floor-to-ceiling windows overlooking the main river. "Your view is spectacular," she said.

"We are very fortunate," Val said. "Gio has given us a good life."

Tori brought me an ice cube from the freezer, which I crunched into pieces that fell on the floor. "It will clean up," she said, mopping the mess with a napkin. "Everyone who lives here likes to get dirty."

"That's Daisy's favorite thing to do," Sue smiled, looking at the backyard for me to run and play with Val's dog. "She'll have the best day ever running with her friends."

"Jelly Bean doesn't run," Val reminded her, but I already knew. The dog preferred looking down his nose at me to all else.

We walked into the backyard, where the men stood around an unlit fire pit. Gio and Luke were chuckling about something. Gio was holding Jelly Bean, giving him ample opportunity to look down his nose, since I was taller than he was on the ground. When he set him down, he ignored me.

"It's good to see you, Sue," Gio said, hugging her, and Sue concurred, as Luke squeezed her hand. "It's been too long."

"I didn't know you bought a house," Sue replied. "I thought you were renting."

"We were, but we couldn't pass this beauty up," he said. "When it came up for sale, we jumped on it."

The house sat between the Radcliffes' estate and the Boggs Brothers' house. "Have you met your neighbors?" Sue asked.

"Yes," Gio replied. "They're good people," he added.

"The first time I met the Boggs brothers, I wasn't sure, but they grew on me," Sue said.

"They have legitimate concerns for the locals of Sweetwater Springs," Gio said, and Luke agreed. "Places are destroyed, and the tourists leave," he said. "The locals will still be here."

Thomas and Mia walked back from the river. "Thanks for coming," Mia said, and Sue replied that she wouldn't miss it.

Tori and Val served sweet tea and home-baked cookies, which the men devoured. Tori offered me tiny dog biscuits while Sue and Mia picked some fresh mango and sipped the tea. I wondered where Val's dog was, but didn't see her, so I stayed with Sue.

"Luke asked us to attend a high-stakes card game at his house," Gio told Val, and Sue added that there would be a separate party for the ladies.

"Whatever you would like, Dear," Val said. "I'll be happy to join these lovely ladies."

"My brother is a sucker for scammers," Luke explained. "A few of them have caught up with him again."

"Two of them are from Miami," Sue said, exposing a photo of the three men who would be at the card game.

"Do you recognize them, Honey?" Gio asked Val.

"Of course I do," Val said. "How could I forget them?" She looked at Sue. "Russ Johnson calls himself a stockbroker, but he's set up some bad investments for people."

"He took a few of my friends for lots of money," Gio added.

"Andy Lemar is a developer," Val said. "He builds nice homes, but he's shady."

"He says he wants to build an eco-retreat on the property next door," Mia said, and Gio replied that he wouldn't trust him. "He'll tell you he's putting in an Eco-Retreat building forty houses on that property, instead."

"Russ Johnson is a card shark," Gio said. "He's well known around Miami, but people in Sweetwater Springs are naive to his cons."

"The sheriff says he's bamboozled some locals already," Luke said. "The big guy, Doug Deleon, is from Sweetwater Springs. He takes care of the marks who don't pay."

"The sheriff wants all three of them gone," Thomas added, and Mia suggested they weren't good for Sweetwater Springs.

"Sometimes they dine at Cat Tails," Tori said. "Doug and Russ argued over a debt last week."

Jelly Bean dined on cookie crumbs while they talked. Sometimes he stopped to glare at me, and I stayed out of his way. It was his house. He didn't like me. And, there was no one else to play with. I stretched out on the grass on my belly to avoid him.

"What is the sheriff willing to do to remove these cons?" Gio asked.

"Whatever it takes," Luke replied. "We don't want scammers in Sweetwater Springs."

"He's not a detective," Mia said. "We may have to help him with logistics."

"He'll need marked bills to follow a money trail after the game," Gio said. "I've got friends in Miami who know who they are, what they've done, and where they shop. How high are the stakes?"

Luke said. "$100,000 per player should suffice."

Sue added, "My son-in-law has agreed to play. His name is Zeke, and he is an attorney."

"Can Zeke play cards?" Gio asked.

"No," Sue said. "He's building a chicken coop. His friend, and building partner, plans to teach him to play."

Gio shook his head. "Zeke and I will need $50,000 in marked bills each. We can watch the game when we lose it to the scammers."

"Zeke is a great observer," Sue said.

"Thomas and Luke will need $100,000 in marked bills each," Gio continued. "They can play to the bitter end."

"The four players, who are out to catch the scammers—Thomas, Luke, Zeke, and me— will need $300,000 in marked bills," Gio said. "The rest of the players will play with their own money—Doug, Russ, Andy, and Bill— will play with unmarked bills. The winner will take home $700,000.00, including their investment."

"Will the sheriff get the money back?" Sue asked, and Gio said, "Maybe. It's a risk to take down this level of cheaters," he said. "Best to get them out of Sweetwater Springs."

When they finished talking, the women separated for a house tour while the men chatted about the plan.

"Russ is still flirting with women at the pub," Tori said during the kitchen tour. "I know you're worried about him and Shameka."

"I'll talk to Sophie about it," Val said. "Maybe she can get through to Shameka."

"Russ is no good for her," Mia said, and Sue agreed they hadn't made progress to convince Shameka that Russ was trouble."

Mia said. "Shameka says she's in love with him."

"She has people to console her when the relationship sours," Sue suggested.

"Sophie has a way with words," Val said. "She's the right person to talk to Shameka, before it gets more serious."

I stayed beside Sue most of the afternoon, following the ladies and avoiding the evil eye of Jelly Bean. Val's dog was at the groomer, so there was no chance to run with a playmate. Sue and her friends will meet at Luke's house tomorrow to plan the card party. I was done with dirty looks from Jelly Bean and looked forward to a romp in Luke's yard.

Chapter 16

Luke's House with Girlfriends

"If it's not Bill, it's Lilly," Sophie was screeching when we arrived at her house to plan the card party. "One of them is always in trouble."

Sophie seemed to be in rare form, but then again, she was pithy with her opinions. She stood at the gate when Sue and Mia drove to the estate. Today, she was loud, but probably no more audible than usual. It was just earlier than she usually started her rants.

I was happy to see Artemis at her side. Yesterday had been a long day with Jelly Bean's cold stares, but today I was joining a friend. Artemis wagged his tail and popped into the car with me in the back seat.

"Artemis! Get out of Sue's car," Sophie exclaimed. "Daisy is here to play at your house. You aren't going anywhere!"

Artemis ignored her orders, as he often did. Sophie's loud voice got her nowhere with Artemis, who preferred Luke's calmer suggestions. Finally, we both jumped out of the car, raced around the enormous yard three times, and followed them into the house.

Running calmed our nerves and released our energy. Dogs need to run. Artemis preferred running to Sophie's yelling. I wasn't sure why Sophie was so loud, but she enjoyed listening to herself.

Sarah and Shemeka looked out the window towards the river and the dog races. We walked inside to join them, with Artemis leading the way and me at his side. The friends greeted, sat on two couches facing each other, while the eldest, Sophie, stood, as they continued the conversation.

"I know why Bill is in trouble," Sue said. "What's going on with Lilly?"

"She told Bill he's out of the house for good if he loses the card game," Sophie replied.

"Maybe that's what Bill needs to hear," Sue said, not mentioning the hawked ring at the pawn shop because Lilly could tell her, if she wanted her to know. "He needs to stop gambling with money he may or may not have."

"He doesn't have money!" Sophie said. "He lost his money and the golf courses during COVID."

"That's a good reason Lilly wants a different business," Sue said. "She's been through golf courses already."

"There's not enough land for a golf course on that property," Mia said, and Shameka agreed the turtles needed land for their nests. "I had no idea Russ was helping her save the turtles," she said. "I guess that's good? Right?"

Everyone agreed that saving turtles did not seem like something Russ Johnson would do. Sarah replied. "It makes me think Russ is up to something we don't know about."

"I'll tell you what he's up to," Sophie declared. "He's up to buttering up Lilly."

"Why would he want to do that?" Sarah asked.

"That's what I don't know—yet," Sophie said. "He wants something."

"He owes Doug Deleon some money," Sue said. "Russ must want to win that card game awfully bad, too."

"Lilly is tired of putting up with Bill's gambling," Mia said. "It's none of my business, but Bill needs to get a real life before he loses his edge."

"You and I both know it!" Sophie agreed.

I lay beside Artemis on the big dog bed in the living room. Artemis lived like a king, but he acted like a hound dog. I liked that about him. Artemis wasn't a snob about anything.

Sophie tossed two dog biscuits from her pocket and was talking again.

"According to Lilly, Russ talks about your silver-plated gun at the museum but never mentions you," Sophie told Shameka. "Your friends have been trying to spare your feelings, but I will be straightforward. Russ Johnson is bad news. He's a bad boyfriend, if I ever saw one—and believe me, I have seen a few of them."

"I love him," Shameka said, and Sophie mentioned that most women had at least one bad boyfriend during their lifetimes.

"He doesn't love you," Sophie said. "If he loved you, he'd talk about you. He doesn't mention you at all."

"You don't know that," Shameka said. "He doesn't talk about me to Lilly, but he might talk about me to other people."

"He's not talking about you when he flirts with other women at the Cat Tails Pub," Sophie said. "Val called me last night. Tori says he flirts with anyone who will listen to him. "He talks about those turtles more than he talks about you."

"He's fascinated by the silver-plated gun," Sarah said. "He's probably looking for a way to steal it."

"What would he want it for?" Shameka asked.

"I don't know. A conversation piece. To shoot someone. To use it in a heist."

"He's using you to get close to that gun," Sarah declared.

"You're making me mad," Shameka replied. "He's not using me."

"I'd rather make you mad now than see you hurt later," Sarah said. "I'd be a terrible best friend if I didn't warn you about men like Russ."

Sarah had worked as a call girl in Miami after a rough start in Sweetwater Springs. I didn't know what a call girl was, but it didn't seem glamorous. It had been a dark period in her life that ended with her return to Sweetwater Springs. I shifted on the dog bed with Artemis, while I pondered my memories.

I first met Sarah at the Baldwins' housewarming party. Later, her family tree and dark secrets were revealed, leading her to

Miami, where she met Tori's parents, Gio and Val. She returned to Sweetwater Springs for a fresh start and a better life.

"I know men better than most people would want to," Sarah said.

Shameka knew that many men had shared the secrets of their troubled relationships with Sarah. She frowned and said nothing.

"Russ Johnson is not a good catch." Sarah declared.

"He's a liar, a con, and a womanizer," Sophie said.

"I'll think about what you are saying," Shameka replied. "But I love Russ."

I walked over to Sue and lay at her feet. The conversation shifted to the upcoming card party. The friends had done all they could to warn Shameka about Russ, but it was up to her to decide what to do.

"We'll have a ladies' night while the men play cards," Sophie said, and everyone said she was an exceptional hostess. "I've had more parties than I care to remember."

"I'll make sangria," Sue said, and Mia offered Guacamole and crackers.

"What shall we do for fun?" Shameka asked, and Sarah suggested target practice with the crossbow. "I always wanted to learn, but never got the chance."

"Why not?" Mia replied. "Sue and I aren't good at archery, but it gets us outside."

"We can have a dog party in the yard," Sue said, and Mia agreed it could be fun. "Loretta can bring Leela, Luna, and Stevie."

"Four Doodles and a Hound Dog," Sarah said. "I love it!"

"We can watch chick flicks," Shameka said. "Everyone can put their favorite movie in a hat and we'll pick them out one at a time."

"I'll serve the card players drinks and return with the updates," Sophie said, and everyone agreed it could be a lively party. "We can take turns with that job," Mia said. "When it's over, we can vote on the best revelation."

Sophie let Artemis and me go outside before our departure. It was fun to run with my friend again. We chased butterflies toward the river and ran circles around a rock. When we returned, Mia and Sue were talking.

"Do Sarah and Shameka know how much money is at stake for this card game?" Sue asked.

"I didn't tell them," Mia replied.

"Does Lilly know?"

"She could make an accurate guess."

"This is going to be some night," Sue said.

"It's making me nervous," Mia replied. "I'll be glad when it's over."

The Boggs brothers passed by in their boat while we played chase in the yard. I recalled the plight of the locals who didn't want to lose their land to a developer. So far, they were happy with our progress. Still, they had no idea how much there was to come.

When we returned home, Toby awaited us at the kitchen door. He was happy to see us, stretching his front paws and arching his back when Sue petted him. For a moment, I wondered what it was like to sleep all day when there was so much to see and do on our daily rounds. Still, Toby seemed quite content with the arrangement. He slept on the bed while we were away, and waited at the door when we got home. It was a good life for my favorite cat in the world.

Chapter 17

Loretta's house with Chickens

"Mom, I worry about you," Loretta said as a baby chick ran out of the chicken coop. "How do you uncover the shadiest people in Sweetwater Springs?"

"Luke's brother found them," Sue reminded her. "Or somehow they found him."

"Zeke is looking forward to putting them behind bars," Loretta said, and Sue mentioned he was the right attorney for the job.

It was the chicken's first day in the coop that Zeke and Chris had built. My four-footed cousins and I were in the dog yard watching the activities. We had been allowed to sniff the chickens while Loretta held them before they left the heated pen inside the house, but we were not allowed near the coop.

Sue and Loretta were inside the coop with eight two-month-old chickens. The door was as big as the one on my home screen porch, where Toby likes to watch nature. The enclosure was almost as big as my porch. Today, the chicks were quick to explore their new home.

Loretta was quick to retrieve the chicken that had bolted through the door. She had spent much time indoors with the chicks, and they trusted her. "If you want your chickens to be friendly, you have to bond with them while they're babies," Loretta said, replacing the chicken inside the enclosure. "These chicks think of me as the food lady because I let them eat from my hand while they were growing."

Loretta and Zeke brought the chicks home when they were a week old. Now, they were the size of the crows that roamed through my backyard. "They grow up so quickly," Sue said.

"This one is an olive egger," Loretta said, of the brownish-green egg-laying chicken. "They are a bit smaller than the Easter Eggers, mostly black."

"I think the black one with the white feathers is a rooster," she said. "The rest are egg-laying hens."

My sister, Leela, and I were more interested in the chickens than Luna, who pushed a red ball around with her nose. We stood beside each other inside the fenced dog yard, watching Sue and Loretta watch the chickens. Stevie was off somewhere by herself, most likely rolling in mulch from the lawnmower.

"It will be fun to listen to the rooster learn to crow," Sue said, making a long gurgling sound to imitate the process. "It takes a while for that to happen."

"Zeke and I will watch them in the morning while we drink our coffee," Loretta replied. "At night, we can watch them with cocktails."

"That sounds like fun," Sue said, smiling. "I hope Luke and I can join you."

"Chris says he refuses to retire to drink beer and watch chickens," Loretta said, and Sue said he would change his mind when he realizes how much fun it is.

"How is Chris coming along to teach Zeke to play poker?" Sue asked, and Loretta said he looked like a professional shuffler and knew the rankings of the hands. "He's an attorney, so he has a poker face when he wants to."

"How's he at betting?" Sue asked.

"He's getting better," Loretta replied. "A lot of it is luck," she added.

"It's less about luck when you're playing with a card shark," Sue said, reminding her that Russ Johnson and Doug DeLeon had a reputation for conning the locals.

"Did I tell you that I got a note in my mailbox to choose my friends carefully?" Sue asked.

"No, you did not," Loretta replied. "Do you know who sent it?"

"No—I do not know who sent it," Sue said. "It sounded like a threat."

"That's exactly why I worry about you," Loretta said, shaking her head. "They are shady people—or as Sophie would say, Scum Bags."

"Some of them may be criminals," Sue replied.

"Interestingly, one of Sophie's sons collects criminals and the other collects sleuths and an attorney to protect him."

Leela and I watched the chickens collect in a corner of the pen. When one of them led, everyone else followed. Sue and Loretta said they looked forward to learning the hierarchy, but Lee and I just liked to watch them scoot about.

Sue's horse, KP, watched the horse pasture from the other side of the fence. He seemed disturbed that Sue and Loretta gave the birds so much attention, but Lee and I didn't care. "I think KP is jealous," Sue announced, and Loretta agreed it was true.

"I think Bill is jealous of Luke's success," Loretta announced, and Sue agreed he needed a new direction.

"Luke has $50,000.00 in marked bills for Zeke to play poker with," Sue continued. "It doesn't matter how long he plays, as long as he can convince the scammers that he is a legitimate player, not a plant to spy on them."

"They must have wreaked some havoc for the sheriff to want them out of town this bad," Loretta said, and Sue reiterated the information they had so far.

"One of the Boggs brothers played football with Doug Deleon in high school," Sue said. "He's known him for a long time."

"Go on," Loretta said.

"Russ Johnson and Doug Deleon set up a poker game in his barn at one of their friends' houses. "They took his friend for $10,000. When he accused them of cheating, it was too late. They left him to be kicked by a bull in his barn."

"Did he survive?" Loretta asked.

"Barely, but he couldn't prove anything."

"No wonder Sheriff Stone wants them out of town," Loretta said, and Sue replied that there had been other local cons.

"Doug brings his German Shepherd to the clinic, and Andy Lemar brings his Golden Retriever," Loretta replied. "I'd gladly help follow the money trail from the marked bills."

"How they spend the money could alert us to the next scam," Sue said. "Eventually, they'll get caught."

Leela and I watched the horse lean down to rest his nose on the ground, near the chickens. He looked like he wanted to sniff them, but a board got in the way of the pasture and pen. The chickens were unafraid of the big horse and went about their merry business of scuttling about the pen.

"What else do you have on the players?" Loretta asked, and Sue replied that Russ had a history of cheating his customers with bad investments as a stockbroker.

"Russ Johnson has scammed some of Gio's friends with housing funds. The funds are set up so the clients never get their principal back. They can collect dividends, but the money is gone forever."

"That's wrong," Loretta said.

"It's unethical and gives the providers a black eye," Sue said. "He worked for a legitimate company and used its reputation to gain trust. Most customers listened to his charming spiel and never read the fine print."

"He can be charming," Loretta agreed. "Now he uses his charm on women."

"Probably always did," Sue replied. "Something is up with Lilly and the turtles, too."

"Once a con, always a con," Loretta said.

"Let's just say, Gio's friends aren't thrilled to be on his list of the duped customers. Gio was eager to help the sheriff devise a scheme to catch him and the other cons. The marked bills were his idea."

Luna pushed her ball towards Lee and me, but no one wanted to play. We watched Loretta feed the chickens some stalks of something, but they weren't interested. It would take time to get to know them and discover their quirks.

"What have you learned about Andy Lemar?" Loretta asked.

"He's slick, like the others," Sue said. "No one trusts him, but he has a good line."

"What does he want?" Loretta asked.

"The Radcliffes and the Boggs brothers think he wants a subdivision of houses on the property. He claims he wants an Eco-Park to teach people about nature."

"What do you think he wants?"

"It's hard to believe a developer from Miami suddenly shifts directions from development to conserving nature in Sweetwater Springs," Sue replied.

"Why would he play cards with a broken stockbroker and a loan shark?"

"Maybe he likes to play cards," Sue replied. "We should look into it."

"Anything else we should know before the game?" Loretta asked.

"Lilly threatened to leave Bill if he lost the game," Sue said. "I don't think he has much chance of winning."

"That's a stiff ultimatum," Loretta replied. "Do you think she'll do it?"

"Bill hawked her ring, and this isn't the first time he sold her jewelry for a card game," Sue said. "She's tired of his gambling."

"I don't blame her," Loretta said. "Do you think he knows he could lose Lilly if he loses the game?"

"She's warned him before," Sue said. "She's ready to draw the line."

Zeke and Chris emerged from the house and walked to the chicken coop while Sue and Loretta talked. Before they got there, they stopped to pet Lee and me. By now, we had inched our noses closer to the fence, so it was easy to pet us.

"I love your chicken coop," Sue said. "You did a fantastic job building it."

"Chris is a good teacher," Zeke said. "I hope I make him proud at the card game."

"Are you ready for the game?" Sue asked.

"Ready as I'll ever be," Zeke said, and Chris said he was a good learner. "Zeke is a smart man," Chris said. "He catches on quickly."

"He wants to be the dog lover's attorney," Loretta said, and Chris insisted he'd make it at whatever he put his mind to."

"Thanks for helping him," Loretta replied. "He couldn't do it without you."

Sue left early for the drive back to Sweetwater Springs. She had much to do before the card game. I hopped into the car for the familiar ride that took us to and fro to visit my best furry friends. Everyone was excited for the party, which meant much to the future of Sweetwater Springs.

Chapter 18
The Card Game

Sue was nervous and excited on the day of the card game. I lay on the bed, stretched out on my belly with two legs stretched backward and two in front, my favorite prone position for watching rather than sleeping, which I preferred on my back, or flat out on my side. I could sense when Sue was nervous; today was one of those days.

I watched her change her clothes again as she decided what to wear. Everything looked the same to me, but Sue kept changing her mind. Finally, she called Loretta and asked what she was wearing.

"How long will it take to play the game?" Loretta asked, and Sue replied that it could be an all-nighter with eight players, most of whom had $100,000 worth of chips to bid. "The game is a Freeze Out," she said. "It could take a long time for seven people to lose all their chips, and one person to win all of them."

"Gio says to use $50, $100, $500, $1000, and $5000.00 chips," Sue said, and Loretta agreed it could be a long game.

"Can they take breaks?"

"Yes," Sue replied. "They can take a fifteen-minute break every three hours."

"That's a marathon," Loretta said. "I hope Zeke is prepared for a long game."

"He should be," Sue replied. "Chris is a good teacher."

"They can make the game take longer with smaller bids," Loretta said. "Who will watch the cash drawer?"

"Luke has a safe," Sue replied. "Everyone will put their money in the safe before the game."

"Someone will take all the money when it's over," Loretta said. "It will be a good start towards a down payment on the Green Cove property for the winner."

"Russ doesn't want the property," Sue reminded her. "He just likes to play cards and save turtles."

"It sounds like he likes to cheat people out of their money at cards," Loretta said. "I hope he doesn't cheat Bill out of the money the pawn shop paid for Lilly's ring."

"What kind of man hawks his wife's wedding ring?" Loretta asked, and Sue replied, "A compulsive gambler."

Toby joined me on the bed and we both watched Sue change clothes. He wasn't a great observer, like I was, but he enjoyed looking over things when he felt like it. That was the key with Toby—he had to feel like doing something. I followed Sue like a shadow because I always wanted to be with her.

"How does a card shark cheat?" Loretta asked, and Sue replied, "That's what Gio intends to discover. He wants to confirm Russ is a cheat, and if so, his methods."

"Sounds like a plan," Loretta said. "Go on."

"Sheriff Stone will follow Russ and his cronies with the marked money trail if he knows they cheat. It will keep his local targets from losing money and getting hurt if they don't pay up."

"Not to be rude," Loretta interjected, "but Sheriff Stone isn't the brightest bulb in the box regarding detective work. How did he think of this?"

"Gio helped him with the marked money plan," Sue said. "Mia and I will help him with following the money trail. He will need some private investigators for stake-outs and such."

"You're sleuths, Mom," Loretta said, and Sue agreed they weren't professionals. "We're pretty good at whatever we put our minds to," Sue replied.

"Did Sheriff Stone get the warrant for the marked money?" Loretta asked, and Sue confirmed. Everyone getting marked money will have it for the game tonight. Everyone else will play with their money so the marked money can be hidden in the stash."

Toby was lying beside me on the bed, like a twin, although he was much smaller than I was. He loved lying on the bed, mainly because it was off-limits for him. He spent a few minutes every morning relaxing in bed, simply because he enjoyed spending time in the bedroom. Today was different. He was watching Sue dress and redress, like I was.

"What are you wearing to the card game?" Sue asked again.

"Something comfortable," Loretta replied. "With layers, since it can get chilly at night."

Sue chose stretch pants, a camp shirt over a tank top, and a sweater, and sent her a photo. "Looks nice, Mom," Loretta said, returning a photo of herself in a jean jacket with a tank top over black jeans. "Very cute," Sue said. "I like it."

"Are you bringing one of your dogs?" Sue asked. "Daisy and Artemis would love to have another friend."

Loretta replied, "Not tonight. It's a big night. I'm not sure what to expect with this crowd."

"Daisy will miss her cousin, but I don't blame you," Sue said. "Anything could happen."

Later that afternoon, Sue loaded the car with wine and fruit for sangria. She also filled Toby's bowl with extra cat food and two bowls with water. It would be a long night alone for the little cat, but he was a homebody. He'd sleep most of the night and never miss us.

I launched into the back seat for the drive to Luke's house. When we arrived, the guests arrived, and most players were already there for the card game. I took two big romps around the yard with Artemis and went inside to find our niche with the guests.

Eight men filed into the sunroom for the card game, which was played at a large round table. They seemed nervous, as Sue had this morning. I wasn't sure if it was the excitement of a high-stakes match or something more sinister. I can sense evil, but didn't feel it—yet.

I could hear the clanking of plastic on the wooden table. Sue had called the plastic object chips and mentioned they were white, red, green, yellow, and gold. She said each chip stood for a value of money in the safe. The money was in the safe, and the men were ready to start the game.

Zeke patted me on the head, as if he wanted me to join the ladies' party. Since he was usually very affectionate, I was not accustomed to being snubbed in such a way. He appeared to be breathing heavier than usual, but didn't want the others to notice. Luke, who loved me dearly, was as standoffish as Zeke.

The six other men ignored me with varying degrees of indifference. This was a serious affair, more suited to gambling men than silly, perceptive dogs. I decided to join the ladies, who were no doubt more fun.

I trotted into the living room, where Sue and Loretta giggled and chatted with their friends. Women seemed to have more fun than men. I was lucky to be a protective and nurturing girl dog, rather than a stronger, serious, loner, and potentially deceptive boy dog. Artemis was not deceptive, but stronger, serious, and alone.

The younger women, Sarah and Shameka, sat together on the couch across from the elders, including Sophie, the oldest.

"I would love to learn to shoot your crossbow," Shameka said to Lilly, who, like Loretta, was in the middle of the group.

"By the time I was your age, I could shoot the eyes off a snake," Sophie bragged, as she lacked the humility of youth.

Sarah groaned. "That's an atrocious comparison," she said, and Sophie neglected to improve it. "I'm from Sicily.....she ranted... .we are strong women, not babies, like some Americans—present company excepted. We hunt, fish, skin, and cook over an open fire."

"The crossbow is in Bill's truck," Lilly said, getting Sophie off the hook for her infamous rants. "Let's check it out."

Sue and Loretta admitted they weren't skilled with the weapon and had little desire to learn. "We can watch," they agreed.

I lay beside Sue and Mia, while the two younger women and the most elderly shot the crossbow. They worked with the weapon for over two hours, and when the first man appeared outside, it was during the break from the card game.

"How's it going?" Shameka asked Russ, who took the crossbow from her, for a shot at the target. "Not bad," he replied. "I'll be cleaning their clocks before too long."

Lilly was not impressed. "To remind you, you're playing against my husband. He hawked my wedding ring for this card game."

"I'm sorry to hear that, my turtle-loving friend," Russ said. "Bill doesn't stand much chance against the masters."

"What do you mean, masters?" Shameka asked.

"Doug and Andy are experts at the game," Russ said, shooting a bullseye and passing the crossbow to Doug. "How about some target practice competition, my friends?" he asked.

Doug shot the crossbow and shot slightly east of the bullseye, then passed it to Andy, who shot barely south of the center.

Lilly matched their skills with a perfect shot and passed the crossbow to Shameka, who had beginner's luck and hit the center. The other women passed up the opportunity to compete with the cockeye group.

Artemis and I sat with Sue and Mia while the others boasted and bragged. We could feel the tension, almost burning. Finally, the men left the target practice to return to the card game indoors.

"How do you stand him?" Shameka asked Lilly when Russ was out of earshot.

"He's your boyfriend," Lilly spat.

"He's your turtle-loving monster," Shameka said, and Lilly agreed she didn't think she had sized him up very well.

"Me neither," Shameka said. "I thought he loved me; he only wants to use me to see that silver-plated pistol at the museum."

"He wants to figure out how to steal it!" Sarah insisted, and Shameka was so mad she growled.

"I thought he cared about turtles," Lilly screeched. "He cared about using me to set up a high-stakes game with Bill and his brother to buy the property."

"I'm glad you finally get it," Sophie said. "We've been warning you for weeks! And, Lilly, my daughter-in-law—you should have known better."

"You raised him, Sophie!" Lilly stammered. "I can't help who Bill is. He's a jealous brother. He wants to gamble. I have to go along—or leave him."

Artemis and I had never felt such anger among the women before. It was hard to say who was angrier, Shameka or Lilly. But one thing was certain. They were both mad at Russ, who had used them both.

Chapter 19

The Girl's Party at Luke's House

After shooting the crossbow, Artemis and I followed the ladies back inside the house. The men had separated back to the sunroom to resume the card game. Gio sat with his back to the living room, where Sue and her friends were enjoying a pitcher of sangria.

"This sangria is delicious," Val told Sue. "Not too sweet, but plenty of flavor."

"How do you make it?" Lilly asked.

"I add cinnamon to the sangria," Sue said. "Lots of fruit, wine, sparkling water, and some brandy, too."

"It's the best I've had," Val said, noting Sue had used white wine.

"Sometimes I make it with red wine, other times, white wine."

Sophie carried a tray of antipasto back from the kitchen and set it on the coffee table. She followed it with a giant bowl of mussels steeped in wine and fresh bread. She offered plates and tiny forks to all who wanted to partake in the feast.

"This is lovely, Sophie," Loretta said. "You've outdone yourself," she added, dipping the bread into the mussel broth. "Zeke would love this."

"I'll take the men something to munch on later," Sophie said. "This is too messy for a card game."

"They seem very focused," Loretta said. "It's quiet in the sunroom."

"Almost too quiet," Mia said. "Any news from the players?"

"Russ said he was going to clean everyone's clock," Shameka said.

"He's playing against some experts," Val replied. "Anything could happen."

"Thomas doesn't like to play cards anymore, but he's an excellent player," Mia said.

"I wish Bill didn't like to play," Lilly said. "I can't stop him."

"Have you asked him to quit?" Mia asked, and Lilly replied, "I've done everything short of divorce papers. That's next."

Artemis nibbled at a crumb of crackers that had fallen off Sophie's plate. I sat beside Sue, where nothing fell. Fortunately, I wasn't a chowhound, like my cousins, since Sue was strict about my diet.

Shameka picked a chunk of cheese off the tray and spread jam on a slice of fresh bread. "Does anyone know if Russ is still a stockbroker?" she asked.

"He used to be a stockbroker," Val said. "He dabbles in this and that, now."

"What exactly is this and that?" Shameka asked, and Val replied that it could be anything. "Whatever is trending," she said. "It doesn't have to be legal."

"Drugs?"

"More likely gambling, shopping centers, development, and investment scams."

"I feel so stupid to have fallen in love with a man like that," Shameka said. "Why didn't anyone warn me about Russ?"

"We tried to warn you," Sarah said. "You wouldn't listen to anyone."

"Love is blind," Mia said, and Shameka admitted it was true. "Russ is a cagey piece of garbage."

"Did you meet Russ when you worked in Miami?" Shameka asked Sarah.

"Oh, Honey, it's a big city. I've never seen that man, or his Cronies, before in my life."

"Did Gio know Russ?" Shameka asked, and Val replied that Gio had heard some things about him. "Not good."

"Is that why Gio agreed to play cards tonight?" Shameka asked, and Val said she had shared as much as she knew.

Artemis and I stayed out of the card room while the men played. We listened to the slaps of cards on the table, sighs, and grunts. Now and then, we heard something that sounded like a conversation, and the angry end of a phone call. Mostly, I napped with my eyes and ears open.

"Excuse me for asking, but why doesn't Thomas buy the Green Cove Property?" Shameka asked Mia.

"He's got enough on his plate for now," Mia replied.

"Is he working on the hotel and theme park?"

"He's trying to get the locals to accept the projects, too," Mia said. "Big development stirs controversy, especially in small towns. People will be upset if he buys more land."

"I understand," Shameka said. "That makes sense."

"The turtles make Green Cove a controversial piece," Mia said, looking at Lilly. "Russ knows that."

Lilly blushed. "The turtle nests keep some buyers away," she admitted.

"Did Russ suggest the ribbons to make the nests more obvious?" Shameka asked Lilly, but she didn't answer right away. "Maybe—or maybe I did. I'm not sure."

"Are you protecting Russ?" Mia asked, and Lilly didn't answer for a long time. "Why would I do that?" she finally asked.

"For starters, he's a fine-looking man, you don't want another golf course, and you're sick of Bill's gambling," Mia said, and Lilly seemed like she could explode.

"He hawked my wedding ring," Lilly shouted. "Do you have any idea what that feels like?"

"For the record," Sophie exclaimed, "Bill promised Luke that, win or lose, he'd quit gambling after this card game."

The game continued for an hour before the next break. By now, the room was tense, and Sue kept peeking at her watch. I sat at her feet, listening to her count off the minutes until they might hear more about the game. Sometimes, I leaned on her legs so hard that I was sitting on her feet.

"Daisy, Sweetie, please move over," she said, pushing me slightly so that I edged off her feet.

"Bill has promised to quit gambling before," Lilly told Sophie. "It isn't the first time."

"He means it this time," Sophie said. "He's my son, I know him."

"He's my husband. I know him better than you," Lilly insisted. "You haven't lived with Bill for twenty years."

"He's a good boy," Sophie said. "He's confused."

"He's confused because you loved Luke more than him," Lilly said. "You confused him."

"It's about time you gave him a child," Sophie said. "It's not so simple as you think it is."

"He hawked my jewelry, my car, and my house to gamble," Lilly replied. "I've had enough of your good boy!"

I leaned tighter against Sue's leg. The room was as tense as any I could remember. Everyone seemed agitated or ashamed to be listening to the erupting conversations. Sophie was always tense and unfiltered, as Sue liked to say. She was getting to know Lilly, and this was no way to learn about her.

Finally, the card session came to a break, and Zeke returned to the living room. "Can I talk to you two outside?" he asked.

"Of course," Loretta said, as I trotted beside Sue to join them.

"It sounds like some of you have been arguing," Zeke said when we stopped walking near the river. "We can hear you in the sunroom."

"I'll say," Loretta replied. "Can you hear what anyone is saying?"

"Bits and pieces," Zeke replied. "Nothing completely."

"Most of it revolves around Russ and Bill," Sue said, and Zeke mentioned he'd heard both of their names.

"There's something you should know about Russ," Zeke said. "His wife called three times during this card game. His son is sick. He won't come home. And he's mad-very mad—at her for calling during the game.

"I'm surprised he didn't turn off his phone," Loretta said, and Zeke replied, "He did."

Loretta and Sue gasped. "Can we tell the others he's married?" Loretta asked, and Zeke replied. "Be my guest. This guy, Russ, is as low as they go."

I followed Sue and Loretta back inside the house. Artemis was lying on his big bed, the one I liked so much, and avoiding Sophie altogether. I stayed beside Sue while she relayed the messages from the card game.

"How's the game coming?" Shameka asked after she poured a glass of peach tea.

"Zeke didn't say anything about the game," Loretta said. "He talked about Russ."

"What about Russ?" Shameka asked, and Lilly frowned to hear the revelations.

Loretta continued. "As everyone knows, Russ has been a voracious flirt at Cat Tails Pub while he's been dating Shameka. But what no one knew is that....he's married."

"He's married?" Lilly gasped, and Val said she wasn't surprised.

"He's a cheater and a creep!" Sophie said. "I knew it!"

"I'm sorry, Shameka," Sarah said. "Every woman has at least one bad man on her date list."

"He's worse than bad!" Shameka spat. "Russ is evil!"

The game continued for three more hours until the next break. By then, it was daybreak, and the birds were singing in the trees. Artemis and I couldn't wait to get outside for a romp and release. The tensions of the night had been far more than anyone predicted.

Chapter 20

Luke's house after the Game

Shortly after daybreak, the card game came to an end. I was tired from a long night spent both inside and outside with my furry friend, Artemis, as we accompanied our two-legged companions. We hadn't done much running in the big yard, but we hadn't done much sleeping, either. If I had been at home with Sue, I would have spent most of the night sleeping on the bed.

Instead, I'd spent most of the night listening to the tensions of the players' wives and girlfriends. They had never seemed more anxious. Some were angry or nervous about the card game, but Shameka, Lilly, and Sophie were the loudest of all.

I was more than ready to go home and join Toby in a peaceful slumber on the couch when the fighting started.

"Pay up!" Doug Deleon shouted at Russ. "You owe me $100,000. You have the money!"

Russ Johnson won the card game, as he had insisted he would. Shortly thereafter, the arguing erupted in the sunroom where the men had played cards at the round table. The voices were loud, deep, and filled with anger. Naturally, Artemis and I would join our two-legged friends to oversee the hustle.

We followed Sue into the sunroom, accompanied by her friends. Six men sat at the card table while Russ and Doug stood by the safe, engaged in a heated battle. I could sense their anger and disgust. No one was happy, while everyone had their reasons.

Russ looked down his nose at Doug. "I'll pay you later," he said, holding a briefcase full of cash. "The money isn't going anywhere."

"You're darn right it isn't going anywhere. It's not going anywhere until you pay off your debt."

"Do you think I'm going to count your money right now?" Russ asked, flinging the case on his shoulder. "I'm going home and to bed. I'll catch you later."

"You'll pay now!" Doug yelled, glaring at the card shark. "Don't leave this house with the money you owe me!"

"I'll pay now—or you'll do what?" Russ asked. "Throw me in a stall with a bull?"

"I'll take care of you, myself," Doug said, shaking his head. "I could smash you with my bare hands!"

Russ fled out the door, ignoring the warning, briefcase in hand. "Get a life, Doug," he said. "I'll catch you later."

Doug Deleon left through the front door, followed by Andy Lemar, shortly thereafter.

"Thanks for the game, Gentlemen," Andy said, as he closed the door behind him. "Just for the record, I'll never play cards with those two men again."

Andy was out the door when Gio, still seated at the card table, started talking in a controlled, disgusted voice.

"Russ and Doug are cheats," Gio calmly said, causing Bill to grind his teeth and Lilly to gasp. "Doug peeks at cards and passes clues to Russ by scratching his head, tapping his fingers, or clearing his throat."

"I saw it, too," Luke said, regarding Bill's poker buddies.

Lilly was livid. "Why would you let them cheat?" she screamed. "Why didn't you call them out?"

Gio glared at her with indifference while the rest of the men said nothing, making Lilly angrier. "He's your brother," she said to Luke. "He pawned my wedding ring to have money for the game!"

"Whose problem is that?" Gio asked because he had known many gamblers and had no sympathy for their wives.

"It's my problem!" Lilly screamed. "It was my problem, but not anymore. I want a divorce," she screeched, and Bill cringed.

"I'm sorry, Baby," he said, and Lilly growled. "I'll give you one week to get my ring back," she said. "I don't care what you have to do to get it!"

"I'll do whatever it takes," Bill replied, and Lilly blurted, "Don't come home without it!"

"Yes, ma'am," Bill said, sighing deeply. "I love you," he said.

Lilly didn't soften. "I'll get the ring myself, if I have to."

"How are you going to do that?" Bill asked.

"I'll get that money, somehow," Lilly said. "Just watch me!"

Bill took a deep breath. "Be Careful," he said, and she growled.

"I'm going home," Lilly spat as she marched out the door. "You can stay here with Sophie, if she'll have you!"

"Of course, Bill can stay here," Sophie said, without Luke's approval.

Luke took a deep breath. It was his house, nobody asked him, and he always locked horns with his brother. "You can have the front guest room," he said, and Sophie offered to get it ready for him.

"Sorry, Bro," Bill said. "Looks like you're stuck with me."

"Don't go getting in any more trouble," Luke said. "You're in too deep already."

"Thanks for the advice," Bill said. "I need to clear my head. I'm going for a walk."

"Do you want company?" Sophie asked, and Bill replied, "Thanks, Mom. I'd rather go alone."

I leaned against Sue's leg, as I often did when life was tense. People said I protected Sue, but she protected me. I had lived through high spirits before, but this took the doggie prize.

Shameka erupted next. "How can you men be so calm?" she blurted. "Lilly just lost her man over the money for a card game. This is not a calm moment."

"Not my problem," Gio said again. "You've been dating a married man, haven't you, Young Lady?" he asked. "That's your problem."

"I didn't know he was married," Shameka replied, hanging her head.

"You knew he was flirting with other women at Cat Tails Pub," Val said. "That should have been enough of a red flag to move on."

"It should have been," Shameka said. "I thought I loved him."

"He didn't love you, or he wouldn't have been messing around with other women," Val said. "You just met him. This is the HoneyMoon phase, not the seven-year itch," she persisted.

"He's a Jerk," Shameka said. "The world would be better off without him."

"The world is full of men like him," Sophie said. "Just when you think there's progress towards elimination, another one comes along."

"I'm going home," Shameka said. "I feel like I could sleep for a week."

"Do you want me to drive you?" Sarah asked.

"Thanks, but I'd rather be alone," Shameka replied. "I'll see you at the museum."

After they were gone, Sophie prepared the bedroom for Bill. Everyone else talked about the card game, while Artemis and I sat on our haunches by the sunroom windows. It was a warm morning, without relief from the recent cooler air. Summer would come quickly and hard. We had a few good romps before, but soon there would be no relief in sight except for jumping in the river.

"Did you see Russ and Doug cheating?" Loretta asked Zeke.

"It would have been hard to miss," he replied, and he mentioned seeing Russ pull a card from the deck. "Of course, I knew what to look for," he added. "Chris was a good teacher."

"You held up long enough," Gio said, and Luke and Thomas agreed he didn't look like a Rookie.

"Unless I miss my guess, Russ will invest in some new scams soon enough," Luke said.

"We can watch the money flow when he does," Gio said. "Russ has scamming in his blood."

"You had a good idea to suggest marked money to Sheriff Stone," Sue said, and Mia agreed he wouldn't have thought of it.

"Glad to be of service, Ladies," Gio said. "Now, if you don't mind, it's been a long night. I'd love an Irish Coffee."

"Thanks for your help," Mia said, hugging Val after Sue. "Thank you both for coming."

It was a long night, and would soon turn into an even longer morning. The worst was yet to come. Artemis and I would be the scouts who discovered the latest evidence of the ongoing troubles plaguing the community. Our next romp in the yard would prove deadly.

Chapter 21
The Murder

Artemis and I had been cooped up long enough in the house. Staring out the window could be fun, but sometimes dogs have to stretch their legs. We both knew what we wanted. I pawed at Sue to let us outside for a race around the yard.

We flew in three great circles around the yard, with me in the lead. I was a flyer, while Artemis was a slow runner. By the third circle, he was far behind and ready to walk. He stopped by the river for a break from the chase.

The Boggs brothers were fishing across the river in their boat as they often did. I recognized them from walks with Sue at the Green Cove property and the argument with Sophie. I wasn't sure what to expect of their volatile nature today. Sometimes they were friendlier than other times.

"Isn't that the dog that belongs to that veterinarian?" Frankie asked Butch, as we lingered at the river's edge.

"Yes, I think it is," Butch replied, as I stood erect looking at them. "Her name is Daisy."

"Why would she be at Luke's house this early in the morning?" Frankie asked and Butch replied, "None of my business, yours neither."

"I heard they were having an all-night party last night," Frankie said, looking at Artemis and me.

"Where did you hear that?" Butch asked as he threaded a worm on his hook.

"I saw Doug Deleon at Cat Tails Pub yesterday. He said he had been invited to Luke's house for a card party. He figured it might last all night."

"No good comes from having Doug DeLeon at a party," Butch said, and Frankie, who had played football with him in high school, mentioned it seemed that way. "Trouble follows him. Always did."

"I hope nobody died," Butch murmured, and they both returned to fishing.

Bill meandered out of the wetlands towards the lush grass of Luke's backyard, where Artemis and I were standing. He was looking down and walking slowly, like his mind was somewhere else. I had seen Sue look like this on occasion when she was deep in thought. It was during these times that she could be startled.

The Boggs brothers saw him looking strange, as we did. Artemis had only just met Bill, but I had seen him more often. His present condition was no way for a man to appear as he emerged from the woods.

"You look like you just saw a ghost," Frankie said, startling him, and he jumped.

"Are you all right?" Butch asked, and Bill answered that he got some bad news, but he didn't want to talk about it.

"Sorry to startle you," Frankie said, then asked if he was Luke's brother.

Bill said, "Yes, I'm his brother, but my mother would say I'm from the dark side."

"Ain't that interesting?" Butch said. "My mama used to say Frankie got the darker side, and I got the brighter side."

"Do you think that can happen?" Bill asked.

"My daddy used to say we're all good and bad wrapped up in one," Butch replied. "I suppose one child can get the good genes, and the other gets the bad genes, but most children get some of each."

"I ain't no double bad seed and that land ain't no place for a golf course," Frankie said, and Bill mentioned he probably didn't have to worry about it after last night. "Lilly doesn't want another golf course, and I don't have the money to buy that land."

"Good," Frankie said. "That land belongs to the Radcliffe family, but the locals should have it."

"Have you caught anything?" Bill asked, changing the subject.

"A couple of pan fish," Butch said, pointing to a sandy hole between the grasses in the crystal clear river. "There's a big bass right down here with my name on it."

"I hope you catch it," Bill said, and Frankie mentioned that Bill might feel better after breakfast. "You should eat something," he said. "It always works for me."

"I wish it were that easy," Bill said. "I'm afraid it's more complicated than that."

"Good luck with your troubles," Frankie said, and Bill wandered off towards his brother's big house with Artemis and me trotting beside him.

"Look what the cat dragged in!" Sophie announced when Bill returned home. The three of us, including Artemis and me, walked into the sunroom to join the remaining guests from the poker party. I stayed close to Bill, who seemed to need some help.

"Mama, for once, could you say something nice to me?" Bill asked, frowning at Sophie. "It's been a rough morning."

"It wouldn't be so rough if you'd behave yourself and quit your gambling," she replied with authority. "Luke never was a menace, even when you two were little."

Sue and Mia looked at each other and shook their heads in unison. "Why do you always have to compare me to Luke?" Bill asked.

"You compare yourself to Luke," Sophie reprimanded. "He's not your measuring stick."

"You compare me to Luke," Bill said. "Just like you compare everything that happens to your childhood in Sicily."

"I'll work on not comparing you to Luke," Sophie agreed. "But, I'm never going to stop talking about my childhood in Sicily."

The remaining guests from the party were seated at the card table in the sunroom. Loretta grabbed Zeke's hand under the table while Mia and Thomas sipped cappuccinos with Sarah. Gio and

Val drank Irish coffee, while Sophie served bacon and ham quiche and muffins.

It was uncomfortably quiet when Luke and Sue petted me underneath the table. I felt grateful to be able to give them comfort. Something was wrong. Wrong. Dogs can sense this kind of thing, but no one was talking.

"I'm sorry about Lilly," Loretta finally said, breaking the ice.

"It's my fault," Bill replied, after he swallowed a bite of quiche. "I had it coming. I should never have hawked her ring."

"I'll say," Sophie said, then bit her tongue to stay quiet.

"I don't know how you found those people," Luke said. "They're trouble."

"Big trouble," Gio agreed. "More than you know. Russ Johnson is under the radar in Miami for the scams he devised in Miami."

"Now, he's here, in Sweetwater Springs, cheating people at cards," Val said.

"In my house," Sophie declared.

"Russ Johnson is dead," Bill uttered under his breath.

"What did you say?" Sophie asked.

"I said, Russ Johnson is dead," Bill reiterated more audibly.

Sarah grabbed her heart. "Holy Cow," she said. "Poor Shameka!"

"What do you mean, 'Poor Shameka'?" Mia asked. "She lost a bad boyfriend."

"Yes, and she said the world would be better off without him," Sarah replied, recalling her best friend's state of mind when she left the party. "She was angry when she left the house."

"Shameka will be under investigation because of her words," Zeke agreed, and Loretta said, "She may need your help."

"I'd be glad to represent Shameka if she needs an attorney," Zeke said. "She's young and naive. She fell in love with the wrong man."

"What about Lilly?" Luke asked, remembering her anger and the promise to retrieve the ring at any cost. "She said she'd get the money somehow if Bill didn't bring home the ring. Just watch me!"

"I'll keep an eye out for Lilly," Sue said, and Mia agreed to help her. "We don't know Bill's wife well, but it's obvious he loves her."

"I'm an idiot for hawking her ring and losing all that money," Bill said, sighing deeply. "I don't know how Lilly puts up with me. Can you help her?" he asked Zeke.

"I'll be there for Lilly if she needs an attorney," Zeke promised. "She wanted her ring back and issued a warning that she intended to find the funds to retrieve it if Bill didn't bring it home. The sheriff will question her as well."

Mia added, "Doug DeLeon also had some harsh words for Russ. "He referred to Russ as a runt and said 'he'd smash him with his bare hands," she reminded them.

"Doug DeLeon can find his attorney," Zeke said. "I don't represent Scammers and thugs."

Sue held me close to her leg, under the table. Artemis sat behind Luke's chair. The bacon quiche smelled delicious, and it made us hungry. Finally, a morsel fell from somewhere, and we pounced on it together, but I was faster and more agile in retrieving it.

"I said I'll do whatever it takes to get the money to repurchase Lilly's ring from the pawn shop," Bill reminded them. "Lilly kicked me out of the house and threatened to divorce me if I didn't get her ring back."

"You're a strong suspect," Zeke agreed, and everyone remembered the question no one had asked. "How did Russ Johnson die?"

Bill took a deep breath before he spoke. "He was shot in the back with my Crossbow," he replied. "I kept it in my truck."

"Where was the money?" Zeke asked, and Bill replied that it was missing. "Whoever killed Russ must have taken it."

"Where is the crossbow?" Zeke asked, and Bill shrugged.

"That makes you the primary suspect," Zeke stated. "The crossbow used for the shooting belonged to you, you were desperate for the missing money to reclaim the ring, your arrow is in Russ Johnson's back, and you discovered the body."

"Almost everyone touched that crossbow and the arrows during one of the card-playing breaks," Sue said. "It's covered in fingerprints and DNA from many of the guests."

"I'm glad I didn't touch that crossbow or the arrows," Loretta said. "This time, I'm off the hook for the sheriff's investigations."

"I'll be happy to help any of you who want my advice," Zeke said. "Don't answer questions without an attorney."

"Do you think Sheriff Stone will arrest me?" Bill asked, and Zeke replied, "I'll do my best to see to it that he doesn't."

"Will you take me as your client?" Bill asked, and Zeke said he'd be honored to represent him and Lilly, too, if she needed him.

"We need to report the murder," Mia said. "Do you want me to call Sheriff Stone?"

"Please do," Sophie said. "I look forward to getting this behind us."

No one mentioned the marked money, as three of the remaining guests were unaware of it. There would be a paper trail of marked money from the murderer, who was also a thief, and Sheriff Stone was aware of it. I was tired from the activities, but I looked forward to helping Sue search for clues. Zeke was brilliant—one of my favorite two-leggers on the planet. He would defend the innocent only after he had uncovered the truth himself.

Chapter 22
The Sheriff

Sheriff Homer Stone arrived at Luke's house shortly after Artemis and I had breakfast in the kitchen. I was happy that Sue brought my favorite dog kibble, given the increasingly long morning that followed the murder. There was no telling how long the sheriff's questioning would take, but we had full bellies for the encounter. I sampled the kibble that Artemis ate, but decided I preferred my own, and we eagerly finished our breakfasts before the sheriff's arrival.

As everyone knows, Sheriff Stone was a rookie when it came to investigating a murder. His usual cases were speeding, petty theft, and the rare arrests for drunken bar brawls. Sweetwater Springs had very few career criminals; however, the recent influx of people altered the crime dynamics. Thomas Baldwin's housewarming party was the venue for the first murder in twenty years.

I first met Sheriff Stone before the Baldwins' housewarming party. Sue took me to the jail for dog-friendly prisoner visits to boost morale for the inmates. Most of the prisoners liked dogs, and my presence had been a boon for the jail. Sheriff Stone never forgot my good work and granted me jail meet-and-greet privileges whenever he thought it was safe for me and Sue to visit the inmates.

After the first murder, Sue and Mia quickly realized that the sheriff could use some assistance in solving the crime. He had one deputy and no detectives on board. Sue and Mia worked together as sleuths, with me in assistance, as their crime-solving dog. They had the brains, and I had the nose for the details that made a difference.

I liked Sheriff Stone. He gave me tiny dog treats, from his deep pockets, that tasted better than any I'd ever had. I thought he must have a dog at home to be so astute regarding my palate, but I had never met his furry companion. According to Luke, everyone recognized his investigative limits, except—increasingly—Homer, whose head got inflated after solving the recent crime.

Luke opened the door after the bell rang. "Hello, Folks," Homer said, jingling his pocket change while raising his head to reveal his clean, hairless nostrils. "I understand there's been an altercation here."

Sophie stood behind her son. "An altercation!" she screeched. "Is that what you call it when somebody gets murdered?"

Sheriff Stone cleared his throat. "Yes, ma'am," he replied. "At this point, I don't know if there was a murder."

"Well, some Scum Bag didn't just shoot himself in the back with my wayward son's crossbow," Sophie declared, and Luke shushed her. "Mother, please," he said. "Let's give Sheriff Stone a chance to uncover the details."

Bill was practically shaking, but he composed himself quickly. "I thought you promised not to compare me to Luke anymore, Mama," he calmly said. "Now is a perfect time to make improvements."

Sophie shook her head. "You're right," she told Luke. "I'll try to do better," she added, inviting the sheriff inside the mansion. "Please join us in the sunroom," she said. "I'll make some iced coffee while you take a walk."

Artemis and I followed Luke and Bill into the sunroom, where Gio and Val sat at the card table with Mia, Sue, and Thomas. Now, the morning sun shone on the oak trees across the river, casting great shadows behind them. I longed for a romp with Artemis before the scorching heat of midday ruined our dog run.

"Show me the body," Sheriff Stone told Luke and his brother. "We'll talk when we get back. Don't go anywhere," he advised the others at the table.

Luke opened the door for Sheriff Stone and his brother, who would show him Russ Johnson's dead body. Artemis and I escaped in a fast-paced run, three times around the yard. Moments later, we joined them in the surrounding wetlands.

"It looks like the arrow went between his ribs and straight through his heart," Sheriff Stone said.

"He must have died immediately," Luke said.

"At least it didn't take long," Bill, who was shaking, added.

"I'll call my deputy and the coroner," Sheriff Stone said. "Let's go back inside."

As we walked towards the house, the Boggs brothers, who were still fishing, called from their boat. "Hey, Sheriff, we need to talk to you," Frankie said, and Butch added, "Come see us later."

"I'll stop by your house later on," Sheriff Stone said. "I've got some business here, first."

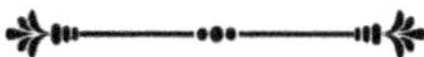

Sophie could compose herself before she returned from the kitchen. According to Luke, cooking calmed his mother's nerves. Sue had no such relief from her kitchen endeavors. My two-legged friends talked while Sophie made iced coffee.

Luke described the long card game and noted the high stakes. The Sheriff was familiar with the card game and the setup with the marked money, but Bill and Sophie weren't aware of the setup.

"Do you know I could arrest you for illegal gambling?" Homer asked them. Bill said he should have known better, but the others kept quiet.

"Where is the money from the card game?" the sheriff asked, and Luke said nobody knew.

"Who found the body?" the sheriff asked, and Bill said, "I did."

"Oh boy," the sheriff replied. "This is beginning to sound familiar."

"What was the murder weapon?" he asked, and Bill said, "A crossbow."

"Where was the crossbow?" Sheriff Stone asked, and Bill replied, "In my truck."

"Anybody could have taken it," Luke added, because his brother said he was feeling ill.

"Where is it now?" the sheriff asked, and Bill weakly replied, "In my truck."

"Anybody could have put the crossbow back in his truck," Luke added.

"Who was at the party?" Sheriff Stone asked.

"Everyone at the card table, plus Lilly Wilson, Shameka, Doug DeLeon, and Andy Lemar."

"Who left the house early?" Sheriff Stone asked, and Gio replied, "All of the above left at least two hours before the rest of us—and we're still here."

"Lilly left early because she was mad at Bill," Luke explained, because Bill was scared speechless.

"She gave him one week to find the money to buy back her ring that he hawked to play poker, or she'd divorce him and get the money for the ring herself," Gio added because he admittedly had no sympathy for the wives of gamblers.

"It sounds like Lilly was rightfully angry," Sheriff Stone replied. "I can understand why Bill is nervous. He lost his money and his wife."

"Bill left later on," Luke explained. "He said he needed some fresh air, then he found the body."

"Who is Shameka?" Sheriff Homer asked, and Mia said she ran the museum.

"She was in love with Russ, but then she found out he had a girlfriend, and a wife—just tonight," Gio added.

"Russ and Doug cheat at poker," Gio said, and Sheriff Stone said he'd heard about it from some of the locals.

Artemis and I lay beside the table while everyone talked. Sue was quiet, which usually meant she was deep in thought. Bill was nervous, shaking, and speechless. Gio and Val seemed like themselves, although I didn't know them well. Mia was disturbed, but calm, while Thomas had been mostly quiet.

"Bill wanted the money to build a golf course," Sophie said, returning with a tray of iced coffee in paper cups and defending her son.

"The locals don't want a golf course on that land," Homer replied. "Haven't you heard?"

"Maybe," Sophie replied, passing cups while Bill poured iced coffee into paper cups. "Maybe not. Everyone doesn't want the same things."

"The old locals want a neighborhood park," Sheriff Stone said, and Sophie mentioned he must have been talking to the Radcliffes and the Boggs Brothers.

"The new locals want their businesses," Mia said. "They want jobs for their children."

"Everyone wants a clean river," Sarah said. "We hear about it at the museum every day."

Thomas said. "I'm working towards the solution to clean up the algae. We will figure this out."

"It looks like I have some figuring out to do myself," the sheriff replied. "If you'll excuse me, my deputy has arrived. "I'll get back to you later, after we talk to the others."

Sue stayed at Luke's house for an hour after the sheriff left. Zeke reminded her that he'd be glad to support the innocent as their attorney. It had been a long day, and we were happy to get home to Toby. I hopped into Sue's car for the ride back home to see my favorite feline.

Chapter 23

Lilly's House with Sue, Luke, and Mia

The following morning, Toby saw the ducks again. Last time, they had looked like an alligator from a distance when they were ducks in a row. This morning, it was more obvious they were ducks when they swam into the cove in a serpentine pattern. Two bigger adult ducks accompanied them, as before, but the family dynamics were different.

Toby moved towards the screen, where I sat, to watch the ensemble. We watched the duck family swim to its usual take-out point, where Sue exited her kayak after we paddled. Recently, Sue had mentioned a stray from a different species had joined the ducks. According to Sue, when a stray animal loses its family, it often joins another family.

Sue, Mia, and Luke sat behind Toby and me at the table. Sue was smiling at the procession, which had also captured the attention of Luke and Mia.

"You have a fabulous view of wildlife from your porch," Mia said. "My house sits too far away from the spring to see ducks, like this."

"Yes, it's a fun perk," Sue agreed. "My house is small, but vibrant with water-life."

"Spring is my favorite time of year," Luke said, as the family marched up the incline to the back yard.

"It's eternal," Sue agreed. "It reminds us that time marches on, but renewal is everlasting."

I did not bark, nor yap at the ducks, as I did with people who came to Sue's house. Toby sat still beside me, with eyes wide open. Toby had no interest in the ducks as prey. The river-to-ground march was something that happened every day to lift our spirits.

Today, the last duck in the row hobbled behind the others. "He's lame," Luke said, and Sue agreed that something must have happened to him since the previous morning. "He's trying hard to keep up, but he can't do it."

"You weren't here yesterday morning," Mia reminded her. "We were at Luke's house."

Everyone knew the lame ducks usually didn't make it, but no one mentioned it. "I hope he makes it," Luke said, and Sue agreed that she'd be cheering for him at every turn.

"Maybe an alligator bit him," Mia said, but Sue mentioned it was unlikely he wouldn't have eaten the duck.

"He's strong in spirit," Sue said, as the ducks marched out of sight, with the lame duck taking up the rear.

"Yes, he is," Luke said, after he sipped his orange juice. "Maybe it will help him heal." Mia agreed.

"You have a remarkable cove," Luke said. "I have to walk from my house down to the river to see the Boggs Brothers try to catch that elusive fish."

Toby found another creature to watch from the corner when the ducks were gone. I wasn't so interested in crickets and lizards. I found a resting spot near Sue and lay beside the table.

"The Boggs brothers must have been fishing when Russ was murdered," Sue said.

"I wonder if they saw anything," Mia added, and Luke suggested it was unlikely because Russ was killed behind the wetlands that separated the river from the land.

"Maybe they heard an argument or something," Sue said. "They want to talk to the sheriff."

"You're right," Mia agreed. "It's unlikely that the killer marched up to Bill's truck, grabbed the crossbow, and shot him in the back."

"Then, put it back in Bill's truck," Sue said.

"Unlikely, but not impossible," Luke said. "Somebody wanted that money bad."

"Russ had been threatened to pay his debts," Sue suggested.

"It shocked Shameka when his wife called, and Lilly was disturbed to discover he was married," Mia added. "Lilly wanted the money as much as anyone else."

"My brother is beside himself that Lilly is gone," Luke said. "He's more worried about her than himself. Bill is afraid he put her in harm's way."

"He should have thought of that before now," Sue said, and everyone agreed.

"I don't know her well, but Lilly seems like a nice girl who got caught up in a mess with Bill's gambling," Mia said.

"None of us knows Lilly well," Luke replied. "My mom was not discreet about her favoritism for me, and it extended to the wives."

"Maybe it's time to get to know Lilly better," Sue said, and Luke suggested we could take a drive to her house.

Sue called Toby inside the house. My feline friend had learned to come when called, but this usually applied to moments when he felt like it. He had done enough porch time because he trotted indoors without a second directive. Now, he could be indoors where it was cooler and comfortable.

I hopped into Luke's truck for the drive to Lilly's house. It was taller than Sue's car, but an easy launch from the ground to the floorboard for a leggy dog like me. Mia sat in the back with me, while Sue sat in the passenger seat.

"As I recall, Daisy was nervous around Lilly's Great Dane," Mia said, putting her arm around me, and Sue concurred. "She was nervous at first, but she got better when she got to know him."

"Sargie is a good old sport," Luke said.

"He's a big Un," Sue agreed. "Daisy doesn't bark much around Sargie. I think she's intimidated."

I had the feeling I wasn't supposed to be afraid, but Sargie was humongous. He towered over my medium-sized frame, like a giant. He was a dog of few words, but when spoken, they were meaningful.

"Does Bill miss Sargie?" Sue asked.

"He is so distraught about Lilly, he hasn't mentioned Sargie," Luke replied. "My brother is an animal person, like me. I'm sure he misses Sargie."

When we arrived, the Great Dane met us at the front door. He barked his awkward, Woooof, Wooooof, Woooof, when Lilly opened the door to greet us. I stepped around the great dog, as did the others, when she invited us inside.

"You might have called first," Lilly said, pulling her robe around her and cinching the tie. "It's been a long night."

"I'm sorry," Luke said. "I should have called, but I didn't think to."

"We're worried about you," Sue said, and Mia offered her assistance if Lilly needed help.

"Bill is worried sick about you," Luke said. "He loves you dearly."

"I'm sorry, I don't want to hear that right now," Lilly said. "The man hawked my wedding ring; he lost the money to a card shark with a bad reputation for cheating people, he got murdered at your card party, and the sheriff acts like he thinks I killed him."

"Has the sheriff talked to you?" Sue asked.

"Yes, he came with a warrant for the crossbow," Lilly replied. "It was in Bill's truck, so I let him take it."

"Did he question you?" Luke asked, and Lilly suggested he had asked some poignant questions, but he didn't have a warrant to arrest her.

"Did you let him inside your house?" Sue asked, and Lilly confirmed that she did.

"You don't have to answer his questions without an attorney," Sue said. "My daughter's husband has generously offered to assist you if you have questions."

"Tell him I said thank you," Lilly replied. "But I didn't kill Russ."

"That's perfect," Sue said. "Zeke won't take a client unless he believes they're innocent."

I sat at Sue's feet facing Lilly and Sargie. She looked a fraction of the woman who confidently shot the crossbow into the target when I first met her. She looked defeated and shrunken.

"I'm sorry my brother sold your ring," Luke said. "Do you mind telling me where he sold it?"

"Why don't you ask him?" Lilly asked, and Luke said Bill rarely left his room since the murder.

"He told me he went to Brian's Pawn Shop," and Sue said she had heard of the place.

"Will you repurchase it for me?" Lilly asked, and Luke said that only she or Bill could repurchase the ring before it went for sale to the public.

"I'll take a loan," Lilly said, and Luke reminded her of a past loan that was never repaid. "I'd love to help where I can," he added. "I'm sorry, but I can't lend you money until the first debt is paid."

Sargie stood beside Lilly while staring at us with interest, but no malice. His mouth was open, and his giant tongue lolled out of his mouth. He shed more than I did. His white fur was scattered all over the dark laminate floor of their house.

"My dog sheds a lot, too," Mia said, without thinking that Lilly might be insulted.

"I would have sent out the robotic vacuum if I knew you were coming," Lilly replied. "Yes, Sargie is a shedder."

"Does the robot pick up his fur?" Mia asked, and Lilly replied, "Most of it."

"How often do you run it?" Sue asked, and Mia said, "Three or four times a week. It's a pet-friendly robot that chops up fur on the roller when it goes home."

"I should get one like that," Sue said. "My roller gets covered in fur. I have to chop it off with the scissors."

"I wish they made a robot for furniture," Lilly said. "I've tried everything—tape rollers, sponges, hand-held vacuums. There's always fur left behind."

"Pet fur is a challenge," Sue agreed. "Next time, I'll try a robot like yours."

Sargie was still standing when Sue stood up to leave with her friends. Although he looked at us with kind eyes, I suspected it wouldn't take much for him to become protective of Lilly. He was a loyal dog with guarding instincts.

"Do you mind if I ask a personal question?" Mia asked before we left.

"Why not?" Lilly asked. "Fire away."

"I noticed you seemed upset when you discovered Shameka was dating Russ," she continued. "Why would you care?"

Lilly blushed deeply before she answered. "I was upset for Shameka," she finally said. "I feel sorry for her."

"You don't know her," Mia replied.

"He won't be faithful, and it will break her heart," Lilly said. "My mother married a cheat. Once a cheat, always a cheat."

"Thanks for talking to us," Luke said as we walked toward the door, and Sue reminded Lilly that Zeke was available for her questions. She handed Lilly a card with his phone number on it. "Call him if you need advice," she said. "He's a dedicated attorney, and he knows the case."

Luke drove to Sue's house with Mia and me in the back seat. When we stepped outside, Sue and her friends were covered in short white dog fur from sitting on the couch. "I want to try something," Sue suggested when they walked inside. "Let's sit on my couch and see if Sargie's fur comes off our clothes and sticks to it."

"Why does that matter?" Luke asked. Sue replied that she wasn't sure yet, but it might come in handy.

Chapter 24
Cat Tails Pub with Andy

The following morning, Sue let me out as she always did, after letting Toby into the bedroom. He arched his back happily while she stroked his soft fur. Toby was very smooth, unlike me, who had kinky fur from my Poodle side. His fur was short, but he shed like Sargie.

I scooched through the door while Toby watched through the glass panes, as he preferred indoor life. It was warm outside—the warmest day of the season. Sue said there was to be record heat in the afternoon. I did my business quickly and returned inside for breakfast of dog kibble, while Toby munched cat food on the counter, where I couldn't reach his delectable dish.

After breakfast, Sue lifted her old robotic vacuum off the base to clean the roller and wheels, which were covered in fur. Sue said my Australian Shepherd's side showed with fur on the wheels. Toby's shorter fur got trapped in the capture base, with the other undesirable goodies, mostly tracked in by Sue and me from the yard.

Toby and I didn't like the robot. It was loud, ratchety, and moved in unpredictable directions. It ate our fur. Toby raced back to the bedroom to avoid it, while I followed nonchalantly and joined him on the bedspread.

Later, I joined Sue for the house cleaning. Sue wore the sleeveless thing she called a cotton tank that she had worn to Lilly's house yesterday to clean the house. She brushed it with a tape roller to remove most of the fur, but not all of it came off.

"Why is it that fur sticks to black?" she joked to herself. Later, she admitted it wasn't about the color, but rather the textile: "Fur sticks to cotton, but not so much to polyester. My polyester tops do not have fur on them. My cotton shirts have fur on them, even after they are washed."

She grabbed a wet sponge to remove the fur from the furniture. "I'm going to experiment," she said aloud. "If I put a cotton sweatshirt with fur on it on the couch, how much fur will come off the sweatshirt and stick to the couch?"

At first, it didn't look like much. Then, she scooched the shirt around a bit, as might happen when a human sat on a couch. Eventually, she proved to herself that a dog doesn't have to visit your house to get fur on your furniture. "Clothes, especially cotton, can be a vessel to carry fur from one couch to another," Sue announced.

"Wallah," she said, scooching on the couch in her tank top. "Sargie's fur is on my couch."

I wasn't sure what the hoopla was about, but I was glad the noisy robotic vacuum had finished its work. Sue seemed pleased with the results of her experiment. She was up to something that might make a difference to someone. Later, all would become clear.

Toby wandered out of the bedroom to join us when all was safe and quiet. He jumped into Sue's lap, purring loudly, while she relaxed and awaited the afternoon activities. Sue was petting Toby while I relaxed on the floor when the phone rang.

"Hi Mia," she said, speaking on the speakerphone so she could pet the cat. "I've got Toby in my lap."

"He's a sweet cat," Mia said. "Very affectionate."

"He's had a stressful morning listening to my noisy old vacuum. It's time for a new one."

"I liked that pet-friendly vacuum of Lilly's," Mia said. "Sargie sure is a shedder."

"His fur is on my couch," Sue replied. "Luke and I brought it home with us."

"Interesting," Mia said. "I suppose Daisy can smell it."

"Daisy can smell his fur on my clothes, but I doubt there's enough on the couch to make a difference unless she was trained to sniff for it."

"Who would train a dog to sniff a dog's fur?" Mia asked.

"If search and rescue can train dogs to follow human scent, they can also train them to follow dog scent."

"Good point," Mia said. "It may come in handy someday."

Toby shifted in Sue's lap and jumped to the floor, making room for my head beside her. I had heard my name and expected something more significant than cleaning to be on the agenda. Averting the robot could be entertaining, but I was ready for an outing.

"Tori called me," Mia said. "Andy Lemar is at Cat Tails Pub."

"Excellent," Sue replied. "We can talk to him about Russ."

"Do you want to meet for lunch in ten minutes?" Mia asked.

"Sounds good," Sue said, "but let's make it fifteen minutes. I need to change clothes."

"I'll call Tori and ask her to have Peter delay Andy's lunch order," Mia said.

"Is Peter working today?" Sue asked, and Mia confirmed it. "Perfect," Sue replied. "He's the best chef at Cat Tails."

Peter Gardener was Sue's neighbor, an ex-chef from Miami, and the cat rescue man, who brought Sue and Luke together. When the spay-neuter program where he worked was on the verge of bankruptcy, he returned to his other love, cooking, and took a job at Cat Tails Pub.

Sue changed clothes and prepared to go to lunch. I followed her like a Velcro dog, unwilling to be left behind. Fortunately, this wasn't one of those days she left me home with Toby. After she dressed, she attached my leash and collar for the lunch date.

I hopped into the car, and Sue drove to Cat Tails Pub. I recognized the pub from the parking lot, although we more often arrived by kayak on the river. Hopefully, Tori, who owned the pub, would be there. She always seemed happy to see me, even before Mia and I helped Sue solve the recent murder.

When we arrived, Mia was talking to Tori, who had left her current position as a bartender to someone else. She joined Mia at a more private table on the verandah. I was happy to see she had a bowl waiting for me at the table.

"Hi Daisy," Tori said, patting me on the head, before she greeted Sue. "I brought your ice water."

The ice was the kicker. I loved to bob for it, with my nose under the cold water. Everyone enjoyed watching me perform this feat. My audience today did not disappoint, as the friends laughed at my ice crunches.

"You know you don't have to bartend anymore," Sue said, smiling at me.

"I love bartending," Tori replied. "It keeps me in touch with my customers and gives me a pulse on the community. As everyone knows, I'm no chef, so I leave the cooking to Peter. I'll take any role other than cooking—server, maitre d', bussing tables, kitchen supervisor."

"Interesting," Sue said, "You know everything about your business."

"I know a lot about my business," Tori said. "The employees are on their best behavior when I'm around. I hired a young lady to bus tables and report to me if something happens when I'm not available."

"She's like a spy," Mia suggested, and Tori agreed. "I don't want tattle tales who throw their fellow employees under the bus and scapegoats who pay the price," she said. "Just honest reporting."

"Good idea," Sue said, and Tori said, "It's been helpful to run a tight ship. She told me when Andy Lemar arrived, and we arranged slow service from the kitchen until you could get here."

"I appreciate it," Sue said, glancing across the verandah to the far end where Andy was seated by the river. "It's cleaning day, and I was just finishing up."

"Everyone is talking about the murder of Russ Johnson at Luke's place," Tori said. "Some of them knew him. He was known as a hustler."

"Yes, we know his reputation," Sue replied. "In a small town like Sweetwater Springs, news of misdoings and murders spreads quickly."

"My dad says Russ cheated at cards," Tori said.

"He cheated on his wife, too," Mia added.

"I'm sorry for Shameka about his philandering at the pub," Tori said. "I mentioned it to my mother, who told Sophie that Russ was flirting with other women."

"She had to find out, somehow," Mia said. "We tried to warn her about Russ, but she didn't believe it."

"She must have been furious when she found out Russ was married," Tori said.

"She was shocked and disgusted," Mia replied. "She left the party early, as did some of the other guests."

"Shameka was in love with Russ, and believed he loved her in return," Sue said. "Now, she's a suspect in his murder."

"He was in love with that silver-plated pistol," Tori grunted, and Mia replied, "It's hard to make a mistake like Russ, but she'll get through it and learn to trust herself again, just like I did."

Tori patted me on the head and subtly signaled the server to bring Andy Lemar his order. I sensed everyone's tension as they avoided looking in his direction. They wanted to talk to Andy, without him thinking they were talking about him. Tori was a friend, and that was all he needed to know.

Sue and Mia ordered chicken salads, which came quickly. They engaged in small talk about the weather and the unusually high temperatures for the season. They watched the kayakers paddle past the restaurant and remarked how refreshing it would be to jump in the water. I recalled the blessed feeling of my belly in the cold river, and longed for a soak.

After I finished my ice water, which was nearly melted, yet still cold, Sue and Mia waved to Andy Lemar. He signaled to them to join him at the table by the river. I followed them to the table and lay in the shade of the big umbrella.

Sue got straight to the point after they greeted him. "I'm sure you heard about Russ Johnson," she said, and Andy confirmed he knew he'd been murdered. "It's the talk of the town," he said. "How does word spread so quickly?"

"People worry about the out-of-towners," Mia replied. "This has been a small town for a long time."

"Everyone knows everyone," Sue said, and Mia added, "They take care of each other."

"In case you're wondering, the sheriff already talked to me," Andy said. "He's a piece of work."

"He's a good man," Sue replied, and Mia added, "He's probably not as suave as the cops in Miami, but he has a perfect record for solving murders."

"Interesting," Andy said. "As you know, I'm a suspect."

"Everyone at the card party who went for a walk before Russ was murdered is a suspect," Sue reminded him. "Someone discovered the body two hours after the game was over."

"I understand Bill Wilson discovered the body," Andy said.

"How would you know?" Sue asked.

Andy smiled. "The river has ears," he said. "And so do the Boggs brothers. I overheard them say Bill looked like he saw a ghost when he came out of the woods before the sheriff arrived."

"You put two and two together," Mia said, and Andy agreed.

"In case you're wondering," he continued, "Russ was a con, but I had no reason to kill him. It was a long shot to play poker at Luke's that night. But the Eco Retreat was a great idea for that beautiful parcel of land. I'm tired of the rat race and ready to leave Miami for good."

"Why did you play?" Mia asked.

"I'm a good card player. I like a little risk. The money would have been a good start for the Eco Retreat."

"A little risk?" Sue asked.

"I like cards," Andy replied. "I've risked more than $100,000 at a card table."

"How long have you known Russ?" Sue asked.

Andy replied, "A few years."

"Did you have other dealings with him?" Mia asked.

Andy replied, "I deal with a lot of people. As you know, I'm a developer. I don't remember Russ specifically, but my staff deals with most of the people."

Sue watched the shimmering river flow gently past the verandah before she spoke, "Why did you say you'd never play poker with those two men—Russ and Doug— again before leaving Luke's house?" she asked.

"Doug DeLeon is a slick one," he said. "People say he lent that farmer money for a card game and put him in the stall with a bull when he lost and was late to pay up."

"Why did you play if you knew?"

"I found out about the bull beating after I agreed to play," Andy replied. "I've had enough of loan sharks like him in Miami. I'm ready for a simpler life."

"The kicking he got from that bull was horrific," Sue agreed.

"Nobody deserves a slaying like that," Mia said. "He was barely alive."

I lay in the shade under that table while they talked. The mention of Doug Deleon's name made Sue tense. He had lived in Sweetwater Springs his entire life. It wouldn't be hard for Sue and Mia to learn more about him.

Chapter 25

Rita's House

Sue tugged at my leash, waking me from my nap, with one eye open, at Andy Lemar's table. Of course, I had been paying attention, as I always did around Sue, but pretending not to. I sensed her concern about Doug Deleon, who had lived in town most of his life. Sue had an excellent contact who would know more about him.

"I think we should talk to Rita," Sue told Mia, after they said goodbye to Andy Lemar. "She most likely had Doug as a student, or knew of him."

Rita was Sue's neighbor, living across the street from her home. According to Sue, Rita spent most of her life teaching elementary school in Sweetwater Springs. She had a remarkable memory for the school children, many of whom never left the riverside town. Rita had insights into their backstories, which often influenced their adulthoods.

"Good idea," Mia said as we walked toward the parking lot. "I haven't seen Rita in ages."

Sue replied, "I'll give her a call and ask her if we can visit. She's off for spring break this week."

After Rita welcomed them, I hopped into Sue's car for the ride. Mia drove separately and parked in Sue's driveway, alerting Toby to a newcomer. I jumped out of Sue's vehicle when she parked in the garage. Most days, Toby would have met us inside the connecting house door, but today we weren't going inside.

"Toby was sitting in the window when I got here," Mia said. "He didn't stay long."

"He'll be back out in the open as soon as you leave," Sue replied. "Don't let it make you feel bad. He's a family guy, but not one for company."

Together, we walked across the street to Rita's house with me in the lead. I pranced across her yard to see our good friend, who has a kind heart, a sweet granddaughter, a community cat, a dog, and a grumpy husband. I sat at the doorstep when Sue rang the bell.

"Hi, ladies," Rita said, opening the door. "I was hoping you'd stop by," she added, offering me a dog treat. "Please come in."

We followed Rita to the sun room, where her husband was watching a golf game. "Hi, Sue, Mia, and Daisy," he said. "Trouble in the river city again?" he asked, knowing the answer.

"You know us too well," Sue replied, smiling at his choice of words for the increasingly popular riverside town. "Yes, there's been a murder in Sweetwater Springs."

"Let me guess…you were there," he said.

"Yes, we were at the home, but not the murder site," Sue replied.

"Luke's estate?" Fred asked, and Sue confirmed.

"Trouble follows money," Fred remarked, of the home of the legendary multi-millionaire. "Where there's a boom, there's a bang."

"It wasn't a bang, Dear," Rita reminded him. "The murder victim was shot with a crossbow."

"I suppose you've been talking to the Boggs Brothers, too," Mia said, because they knew more than they should have about the murder.

"No, I saw Lilly at the grocery store," Rita replied. "She's beside herself about the ring."

Sue and Mia locked eyes without saying a word. I sensed their mutual understanding, yet they were unwilling to reveal it. Finally, Rita broke the knowing stare.

"We'll leave you to your golf game, Honey," she said. "We'll have tea in the dining room."

I followed Sue, Mia, and Rita into the dining room. Rita had steeped a pot of tea, which sat on the table next to her cat, Sparkles, who quickly retreated when I arrived. By that time, I had learned that Toby liked me better than most other cats, who preferred their solitude to my company. That said, there were a few exceptions.

Rita poured tea for Sue and Mia, while I found a resting place near the table. "Did you have Lilly in your class in school?" Mia asked, stirring her tea.

"Yes," Rita replied. "She was in my third-grade class."

"I grew up in Sweetwater Springs, and I don't remember her," Mia said.

"Lilly was a quiet girl," Rita remembered. "She was smart and thoughtful. She helped the other students when she finished her work."

"Interesting," Sue replied. "I wonder how she met Bill Wilson."

"I wouldn't know," Rita said. "The Wilsons came later, as you know. They weren't from Sweetwater Springs. What do you know of Lilly?"

"She has a friendly old Great Dane," Sue said. "He's lived beyond his years."

"She is an exceptional archer," Mia added. "We met her at an archery match at Bill's house."

"She's furious at Bill for hawking that ring," Rita remarked after she sipped her tea. "She says he's a compulsive gambler."

"According to Lilly, it's not the first time Bill has hawked her things to pay for his bids in a card game," Sue said.

"Is Lilly a suspect?" Rita asked, and Mia replied, "She had motive, means, and opportunity."

"She wanted the money, she knew had to shoot a crossbow, and she was there," Sue reiterated.

Where is the money now?" Rita asked, and Sue said, "We don't know."

Rita passed me a dog biscuit and set a plate of tea cookies on the table. I crunched my biscuit into crumbs, licked them up, and lay down again. I took a long, deep breath and awaited their conversation.

"Have you heard about the farmer who was nearly kicked to death by a bull in his stall?" Sue asked.

"No," Rita replied, horrified. "Has it been in the newspaper?"

"I don't know," Sue replied. "It happened last week. A card shark and his accomplice, a local loan shark, hustled the farmer."

"Do you know who they were?" Rita asked.

"The card shark was Russ Johnson, the man murdered at Luke's house," Sue said.

"The loan shark was a local from Sweetwater Springs," Mia added. "Have you heard of Doug DeLeon?"

Rita gasped. "Of course, I've heard of Doug DeLeon," she said. "He was a con long before Sweetwater Springs knew anything of them."

"He is a suspect in the murder of Russ Johnson," Mia said, and Sue added, "Russ owed him money, and he threatened him to pay up."

"What do you know about Doug DeLeon?" Mia asked. "He came after my school years."

Rita sipped her tea while she recalled the details. "Doug DeLeon was a lonely child," she said. "He was a pleaser, seeking the spotlight in sports, but his father couldn't be pleased. Eventually, he acted out."

"Where was his mother?" Sue asked. "She had enough kids by the time Doug came along. She fed him well, washed his clothes, and let him do what he wanted."

"Was Doug a wild child?" Mia asked.

"Yes," Rita said. "I think many people would agree with that. The family had little discipline, and a mother who gave up trying when their father made fun of them."

"Doug was highly competitive," Rita continued. "His parents were done celebrating their children's accomplishments."

"That's sad," Mia said.

"Where did becoming a con fit in?" Sue asked.

"Doug played football in high school," Rita recalled. "He was a star quarterback and received a scholarship to college."

"That's not easy to do," Mia said.

"He lost his college scholarship," Rita continued. "Gambling became more important to Doug than sports. He'd bet on the other team and throw the game."

"Yikes," Sue declared. "That's for shame."

"He threw his teammates under the bus to win money by making his team lose the game," Mia reiterated. "It fits with the man he became."

"Doug was a bad, bad man. He used the money he made from throwing football games to become a loan shark," Sue suggested. "What a waste of incredible talent."

Sparkles passed through the dining room while I lay under the table. I suspected she was trying to get used to me, but she didn't come close. Toby sometimes did the same thing when we had guests. He'd walk down the hall for a peek, then scoot back to the bedroom if they noticed him.

I decided not to disturb her secret mission and stayed in my place near Sue. When I was younger, I might have risen to play, but by now, I knew what cats were up to. It had been enriching to live with Toby. It gave a new dimension to a dog's life to understand the feline motives.

"Has Dr. Loretta met Doug DeLeon and Russ Johnson?" Rita asked after she passed the tea cookies.

"Yes," Sue replied. "Loretta and Zeke went to the card party. Doug brings his German Shepherd to the clinic."

"Does Russ have a dog?" Rita asked.

"Not that I know of," Sue said. "But he and Shameka have kayaked with her dog, a yellow Labrador."

"I heard about Russ and Shameka," Rita said. "She's a nice person. She must be devastated."

"Shameka is a suspect," Mia replied. "She was aware Russ was flirting with other women at Cat Tails Pub, and she discovered he was married at the card party. She could have snapped."

Rita sighed, "Poor Shameka," she said. "She told me she was in love with Russ when I saw her at the museum."

Sue replied, "Some people think he was in love with that pistol she kept in the museum."

"This will be tough on Shameka," Mia said. "But she's a strong person, and she has Sarah to comfort her. They were childhood friends."

"Shameka has the resilience of youth," Rita agreed. "She'll make better choices in men next time. For now, she'll have to get through the sheriff's questioning."

"Are there other suspects?" Rita asked as she poured the last cup of tea.

"Five people top the list for motive, means, and opportunity: Bill Wilson, Lilly Wilson, Doug DeLeon, Andy Lemar, and Shameka."

"Who is Andy Lemar?"

"A wealthy developer from Miami. He says he wants to build an Eco Park on the Green Cove property, but some people think he wants to build a development."

"Did he threaten Russ, too?" Rita asked.

"Not exactly, but he did say he'd never play poker with Russ or Doug again when he left the card game," Sue replied. "They were working together on a hustle when Doug beat up that farmer."

When they finished talking, Sue called me out from under the table. I rose slowly, not to disturb Sparkles, who was watching me from above. She kept her head glued to the table, with eyes wide open, but didn't move. It was progress.

"Thanks for chatting with us," Sue said, "You've shed some light on the subject."

Mia added, "Thanks for the tea and cookies."

When we were out the door and halfway home, they looked at each other, knowingly, and frowned. "Did you hear what I heard?" Sue said.

Mia responded, "Do you mean, how did Lilly Wilson know Russ was killed with a crossbow?"

It was a question neither of them knew the answer to, but both wanted to find out. In time, their investigations would uncover the answer. Tomorrow was another day. They would begin with a visit to Peter and Stanley's house to learn what they could about the Miami boys: Russ Johson and Andy Lemar.

Chapter 26

Peter and Stanley's House with Photo

Shameka met us at Sue's house the following morning. She looked tired from the long nights she had lost sleeping after Russ Johnson's murder. I sniffed her clothes, which were covered in her dog's fur. They smelled like her Yellow Labrador.

"I'm so glad I have Cleo," Shameka said, rubbing some light-colored fur off her clothes with her hand. "She's been my lifesaver through this nightmare."

"Sue said. "Daisy was my rock after my husband passed away. We are lucky to have our loving pets."

I had met Cleo before, but we had never played together. She was a kayaking dog, like me, but we hadn't encountered each other on the river. She was mainly a newcomer to my world.

"Russ and I used to take Cleo kayaking," Shameka said. "I guess it will be up to me to take her on the river now that he's gone."

"It's easy to paddle alone with a dog on the right kayak," Sue said. "You simply need a kayak with some room for her to sit, in front or behind, wherever is best for balance. Since Cleo is a seasoned first mate, she probably won't jump off the boat. You're welcome to join us sometime."

"Thank you," Shameka said. "I appreciate the offer."

"Did you and Russ kayak often?" Sue asked.

"Only a few times," Shameka replied. "Sometimes he paddled without me."

"I don't know why anyone would paddle alone when they could have company," Sue replied, and Shameka agreed.

"Russ had some strange habits: an obsession with the gun at the museum, flirting with other women, and paddling by himself when I could have joined him. I understand them better now that he's gone. I should have known something wasn't right."

"Has Sheriff Stone been by to question you?" Sue asked.

"Yes, but he says he'll be back again," Shameka replied. "I was angry when I found out that Russ was married, and it doesn't look good that I lost my temper just before he was murdered."

"Agreed," Sue replied, but you weren't the only person angry at Russ that night."

I jumped up from my haunches and galloped to the door when the bell rang. At first, I didn't recognize Sarah, but a quick sniff made the difference. Mia and her daughter, Sarah, were joining us to talk to Sue's neighbors from Miami.

"I'm glad you could make it," Sue said when Mia and Sarah popped inside.

"Anything to help my old friend," Sarah replied, picking a Cleo hair off her shirt. "You missed one," she said.

"Cleo's been at my side day and night," Shameka replied. "She's shedding more than usual."

"I've been trying to solve the same problem," Sue remarked. "I ordered a new vacuum, like the one Lilly has. I'm not sure Toby will be happy about it."

"Where is Toby?" Mia asked, and Sue pointed toward the bedroom. "He's in his hiding place under the bed," she said. "He's not a cat for company."

"Thank you for inviting me to join you at Peter's house," Shameka said. "I need to feel part of the loop right now."

"You've suffered a great loss and hopefully learn a great lesson," Mia said. "We're glad to have you along to talk to Sue's Miami friends."

Sue attached my leash to my collar and we walked out the door, with me in the lead. I had never heard Peter referred to as a Miami friend, but I knew where we were headed. The house at the end of the street belonged to Peter and Stanley.

Peter greeted us at the door and led us to the sunroom, facing the river, where Stanley was sitting, reading a book. "Hi, Girls!" he exclaimed, placing the book face down in his lap. "I'm glad you could make it."

"We wouldn't miss a chance to see you," Sue said, introducing him to Shameka and Sarah, whom he remembered from the previous murder. "You're the Miami Call Girl," he announced.

"I used to be a Call Girl," Sarah said. "Now I work with Shameka at the museum."

"I love that museum," Stanley said. "Every town should celebrate its roots and the scams and shams that it had to overcome to succeed."

Stanley was a criminal attorney from Miami, but he had played a role in solving the first murder in twenty years, which put Sweetwater Springs on the map. "Didn't you donate the silver-plated gun?" he asked.

"Yes," Sarah replied. "It was in the family."

"My, such blended roots you have," he said, and Sarah said she had much to celebrate from her mother and some to overcome from her dad.

"Don't we all?" Stanley said, without revealing his demons.

According to Sue, Stanley was morbidly obese, but unready to tackle the roots of his eating disorder. He loved food and had no intention of forgoing his pleasure.

Stanley's cat, OC, watched us from his perch on the bookshelves. I think he was looking at me, as he often did, with a sense of disdain. Today, however, he wasn't jumping off the shelf to join me with the unfamiliar group of people.

"My daughter's husband, Zeke, has offered attorney advice for the Russ Johnson murder," Sue told Stanley. "I hope you don't mind."

"Of course not," Stanley replied, having assisted with law advice for the previous murder, "I'm busy with work at the Miami office."

"Miami has its share of criminals," Sarah agreed. "I worked with enough of them."

"I'll bet you did," Peter said. "I'm glad you got out of the business."

"I was lucky," Sarah said. "I have good friends, a supportive family, and I have learned from my mistakes."

Mia smiled. "She's a forgiving soul," she said. "It takes grit to overcome the obstacles that Sarah has."

I watched the river flow through the glass panes while they talked. Here, there were no alligators or otters to be seen from the sunroom. I liked Sue's view of the ducks and alligators better, but Sue said this was the million-dollar view. I shifted between watching OC's glaring stares and the current in the shimmering river.

"What can I do for you ladies?" Stanley asked. "I'm sure you had something in mind when you called."

Sue said, "We enjoy your company, but we need your input. We were hoping you had information about the Miami boys."

Stanley chuckled. "The Miami boys?" he said. "Is that what you call them?"

"Yes," Mia replied. "My childhood family is from Sweetwater Springs, so we are familiar with many of its residents, but we don't know many people from Miami."

"You know Tori," Peter said of his boss, the pub owner.

"Yes, but she's young and moved away from Miami. Now, she's a Sweetwater Springs lady at heart."

"You know Gio and Val," Stanley said of Tori's somewhat notorious parents, who followed their daughter to the riverside town.

"Yes, and they can be helpful with tips and advice. It's good to collect information from different people."

Mia scrolled through her phone app for the photograph of Russ Johnson, Andy Lemar, and Doug DeLeon. "Do you remember when we showed you this photograph from the Archery Meet at Bill's house?" she asked.

"Yes, of course," Stanley replied. "I've been thinking about that photo, myself."

Peter said, "We've seen the three of them together in Miami at pubs and clubs. This trio of cons know each other."

"They worked together for years," Stanley concurred, pulling up the photo app on his phone. "This photo of Russ Johnson, Andy Lemar, and Doug DeLeon is from ten years ago."

"They have a history," Peter said. "A Card shark, aka stockbroker, a developer turned Ecopark aficionado, and a Loan shark, aka football player, gambler, game rigger, and street fighter, in cahoots for at least ten years."

"Where did you take the photo?" Mia asked.

Stanley said. "This is the only photo I could find. It's from a lunch and learn for investors."

"Interesting," Mia said. "Can you text me a copy?"

"Absolutely," Stanley replied. "I'll text a copy of the photograph to all of you."

I turned away from the shimmering river, where I had focused my attention on a tall white bird in the wetlands across the river. It was almost time to go. No one, but me, had noticed the orange cat who didn't seem any friendlier.

"Thanks for everything," Sue said, and Mia mentioned Peter's chicken salad was delicious at the pub.

"Tell Zeke Good luck with the case," Stanley said. "I hear he's done well with dog cases and evidence."

"We're learning," Sue said. "There are plenty of dogs for evidence in this case."

Sarah and Shameka bid farewell to the attorney and pub chef. I swallowed my intimidation and trotted past the snarly cat on a shelf. We had been to the same place, but we had seen and learned many different things. Somehow, somewhere, it would all pull together in the end.

Chapter 27

Val and Giovanni's House with Photos

"I think we should pay a visit to Gio and Val," Sue said when we were walking back to her house. The women were walking in a row, with Sue and me at the end. I stayed near Sue, who held me on a short leash so I could walk on the grass.

"That's a good idea," Mia replied, "Gio knows people from everywhere, but especially from Miami."

"I met Gio and Val at the card party," Shameka replied. "He didn't approve of my dating Russ, and had no mercy about telling me so."

"You didn't know he was married," Mia replied, and Shameka said, "I don't think he cared about that."

"Probably not," Sarah agreed. "He cared that you were my young, naive friend who was getting used by a con and a womanizer."

"I've heard rumors about Gio's career, but I don't know him well."

"No one can prove Gio's profession," Sarah said. "Men like him can be secretive about their work."

"Russ says he was a mob boss," Shameka said. "It made me nervous."

"Tori and I were friends," Sarah said. "Gio helped me get out of the profession."

"We couldn't have solved the first murder without his help," Sue added.

Sue did not mention that Gio had masterminded the use of marked bills in the card game. His tips could be invaluable in solving crimes, but his dog was much too short and serious for my taste. Gio and Val had a fabulous yard for running, but I needed a playmate.

I enjoyed sinking my feet into the neighbor's cool grass on the walk back home. The road was scorching, but the grass felt good on my pads and between my toes. Sue allows me to walk on the grass on hot days so I don't burn my feet. If she has any concerns, she tests the pavement herself, with her own bare feet.

"Daisy is loving the grass," Shameka said. "I wish I had brought Cleo."

"You can bring her another time," Sue said. "Friendly dogs are always welcome at my house."

"It would be a bit much to ask Gio and Val if we can bring another dog to their house," Mia remarked. "They love dogs, but they can be aloof about company."

"They expect Daisy, but another dog might be overwhelming them," Sue agreed, as she placed the call to the Miami folks.

After Val welcomed us for the visit, everyone piled into Mia's car for the short drive to their house. The route was familiar. Sue knew most of their neighbors on the Green Cove. I had played with some of their dogs.

Sue drove past the actor's house, the mayor's house, the teahouse owner's house, the dog trainer's house, the snowbird's house, and the house that belonged to the lady who worked at the pub. She drove past Bill's house. None of them had a fenced yard for doggie playtime.

While the dogs were lively, options for play in a fenced yard were limited. I enjoyed running freely, but I had to visit my cousin's house to find a yard where I could do so. Although we didn't go to Loretta's house every day, I would have cherished the opportunity for a daily run.

"This land is the perfect place for a dog park," Shameka announced when we passed the parcel that everyone wanted for different reasons. Bill wanted to purchase it for a golf course, Doug for a steakhouse, and Andy Lemar for an Eco Park.

"Who can afford it?" Sue asked. "I'd be honored to donate the fence, but the land is too much."

"Bill hawked his wife's ring and staged a high-stakes card game to buy this land," Mia reminded them.

"I can envision a grand dog park here," Sue said. "The beauty of this parcel is enchanting. It's a lovely place for dogs to play and their people to get inspired for their work and hobbies."

"It could be a community dog park," Shameka said. "We could charge a small fee for a yearly pass and staff it with the proceeds. All dogs would have to be neutered, healthy, and vaccinated."

"A portion of land could surely be fenced for a dog park," Mia agreed. "The Radcliffe family owns it. They'd love to keep it, but it's too costly."

"Where would the dog owners park their cars?" Sue asked. Mia replied, "Upriver and walk the path."

The Boggs brothers drove past in their old two-tone truck with their Coonhound, while we admired the land. I had not met the Coonhound before, but enjoyed playing with Artemis, who was also a hound dog.

"What are you girls up to?" Frank Boggs asked, stopping the truck beside us.

"Shameka suggested using part of the land for a dog park," Sue said. "We were admiring the land and thinking it's a great idea."

"Who's Shameka?" Butch asked.

"I am," Shameka replied, shifting down in her seat.

"What do you know about Sweetwater Springs, young lady?" he asked.

"I manage the museum," Shameka said. "My friend, Sarah, donated the silver-plated gun used in the first murder in twenty years."

"This town is about more important things than murder mysteries," Frank Boggs said, and his brother, Butch, added, "It is a historical microcosm of human existence, mutual love and respect, and the value of community over global pursuits."

Mia slunk into her seat and whispered. "Does that mean he wants a dog park?", making Sue cover her mouth and try not to laugh.

"By the way, I recognize you," Frank told Shameka. "You were at Luke Wilson's house the night Russ Johnson was murdered."

"How do you know that?" Shameka asked.

"I saw you walk into the wetlands where they found the body," Frank said, and Doug added, "That makes two of us who saw you walk into the woods the morning that man got killed."

It wasn't the right time to pursue the matter of the dog park, although the idea was good. I stuck my head out of the car window to get a better look at the Hound Dog, who was looking at me. He was indeed a fine dog in his prime, with plenty of energy to run off.

Sue was changing the subject when Butch said, "That's Daisy, ain't it?"

"Yes, it's Daisy," she replied. "What's your dog's name?"

"Hank," Frank replied.

"I'll bet Hank loves to run," Sue said, before she mentioned that I did, too.

"Hank would put that Poodle-thing of yours to shame," Frank gloated, and Sue replied, "Daisy would love to challenge Hank to a play date one day. My Poodle-thing can run circles around your hound."

It wasn't like Sue to brag about anyone or anything, but sometimes it was important. I had no doubt I could beat Hank at any match they chose. He was only a tad better than old Sargie, who lived next door.

"Good to see you, Sue," Frank said, smiling as he drove away. "See you soon."

I felt tension in Sue's car from everyone, but especially Shameka. It seemed their voices were muffled by a strange, inaudible silence. It felt as though someone was about to explode.

"That was weird," Shameka finally said, as Sue puttered down the road towards Gio and Val's house. "Frank made me feel guilty," she muttered, and Sarah added, "It didn't sound good."

"I'm sure he told the sheriff he saw me walking into the woods," Shameka said, and Sue reminded her to contact Zeke if she needed the advice of an attorney.

"Loretta must have been horrified when she was arrested," Shameka said, and Sue reminded her that everything turned out all right in the end.

Val greeted us warmly and invited everyone inside their lovely home overlooking the sparkling river. Their expansive sloping backyard led to the waterfront. It was a fine place for a dog to play, but it required a playful dog to truly enjoy it. Jelly Bean was not that dog.

Gio sat in his recliner with Jelly Bean in his lap. "Excuse me if I don't get up," he said. "Jelly Bean is comfortable, and I don't want to disturb him."

I could not imagine Sue using such an excuse to avoid standing to greet her guests, but he was Gio, and that was Jelly Bean. Spoiled. Looked down his nose at others. A snob dog.

"Please, don't disturb Jelly Bean on our account. Stay seated," Sue replied.

"Is your Border Collie here?" Mia asked Val, who explained the dog had escaped the yard to chase deer who emerged from the wetlands, and the Boggs Brothers weren't happy about it."

"Of course," Sue replied. "The Boggs Brothers."

"They are a piece of work," Gio said. "We weren't expecting the remnants of the old Radcliffe guard for neighbors."

"My Border Collie is living with my sister until we get a proper fence," Val said. "She would love to run and play with Daisy."

"The feeling is mutual," Sue replied. "Daisy would love to play, too."

Jelly Bean stood on his short legs to tower over me as much as possible for a dog less than half my size. "What can I do for you ladies today?"Gio asked, still holding the dog in his lap.

"We're gathering information about Russ Johnson's murder," Sue said. "Since you're from Miami, we thought you might know something about Russ and Andy."

"I can tell you Russ and Doug were cheaters in cahoots at that poker game," Gio said. "They were slick, but it was apparent."

"Do you think they split the profits?" Sue asked, and Gio said there were many ways to divvy it up.

"Has someone found the money Russ won at the game?" Gio asked, since he knew it was marked, but Sarah and Shameka had no idea.

"Not that I know of," Sue replied, and Mia agreed she hadn't heard of it.

Mia took her phone and showed Gio the photo of Russ, Doug, and Andy that Stanley had shared with us. "It seems our newcomers have known each other for a long time," she said. "This photo was taken ten years ago."

Gio studied the photo, which struck a chord. "Russ Johnson started an investment scam about ten years ago," he said. "I'll dig into it for you. I know people who may remember it."

I stared at the glorious backyard, longing for a romp to stretch my legs. Val's Border Collie would have been a great playmate, but I was stuck with Jelly Bean, who lived to do nothing. I couldn't imagine such a lazy life, but that was just me. Jelly Bean was content with his life.

While I was thinking about a dog's life, Val produced a photo of Russ Johnson and his wife from her phone app and passed it around for everyone to see.

"She's beautiful," Shameka said while gaping at the photo. "What on earth was he doing with me?"

"Her name is Kate," Val said. "My friends say she was as sassy and smart as she is beautiful."

"Maybe she got wind of me and his other female conquests and killed Russ, herself," Shameka said.

"She took her sick son to the emergency room that night," Val replied. "She spent the night with him."

"She has a good alibi," Sarah said.

"That must be why she called Russ at the poker game," Mia said, and everyone agreed he was the worst kind of bad dad, boyfriend, and husband on the planet.

"Be glad he's out of your life," Sarah said, and Shameka reminded her it wasn't over until they found Russ Johnson's killer. "Sheriff Stone will be back to talk to me," she said.

"Can you give us a copy of the photograph of Russ and his wife?" Sue asked Val, and she shared it with the group, just before Tori called.

"Doug DeLeon is at Cat Tails Pub," she said when she finished the call with her daughter. "Tori thought you'd want to talk to him."

"We appreciate your help," Sue said, and everyone thanked Gio for digging up details and Val for the photograph. "We'll be back," Sue said, as they departed for the next destination.

I hopped into the car for the drive to Cat Tails Pub. I had missed a romp in Gio's great big beautiful yard, but I looked forward to bobbing for ice cubes. We passed through the parcel where Shameka suggested a dog park, and past Lilly's house, where Sue and her friends waved to Lilly and Sargie on the drive back to the pub.

Chapter 28
Cat Tails Pub with Doug

Sargie barked his awkward old dog, Wo-oof, Wo-oof, as we drove past his house. I looked at him standing there, so old and frail that barking made his whole body quiver. It was hard to believe I was once afraid to meet him. He was well past his prime, yet still loving and protective of Lilly.

Sue recalled that Sargie barked at strangers, but not at people he knew. He had met Sue and her friends, but probably didn't recognize them in the car.

"Sargie barked at everyone he met at the archery match," Mia recalled, smiling at the determined dog.

"Everyone except Russ Johnson," Sue remarked.

Mia was surprised. "You never told me that he didn't bark at Russ," she said.

"I didn't think much of it," Sue said. "Lilly and Russ were putting ribbons around the turtle nests when we first saw them."

"Did anyone see how Sargie reacted when Russ first arrived?" Shameka asked.

"Not that I know of," Sue said. "They were already together."

"If Sargie knew Russ well, he wouldn't bark at him," Mia said.

"Maybe Russ and Lilly knew each other better than we realized," Sarah replied.

"Maybe Lilly was one of his conquests, like I was," Shameka grunted.

"Lilly was a married woman," Sue said.

"That wouldn't have mattered to a man like Russ Johnson," Sarah declared.

When we arrived at the pub, Tori was behind the bar making cocktails, just like she had been when we talked to Andy Lemar. Today, she didn't join us at a table, but went about her job, as usual. She didn't want Doug DeLeon to think she had tipped Sue off about his presence at the pub. The friends waved to each other, but didn't stop for a chat.

Sue grabbed a dog bowl and filled it with ice for me as we passed the table with the complimentary service. I was disappointed that Tori wouldn't serve me herself, but I looked forward to the ice. I wondered if other dogs liked ice as much as I did.

Mia was the first to see Doug DeLeon, who was seated at a corner table by the river. "Hi Doug," she said, waving, while Sue collected the ice.

"Hello, ladies," he said as everyone drew closer to greet him.

Sue held me tighter on the leash as we approached Doug DeLeon's table. He sat at a picnic bench with a dog near his feet, under the table. According to Sue, it was a German Shepherd, and she appeared to be friendly.

"Hi Doug," Sue said, as the dog emerged from underneath the table to rub noses with me. "Do you remember Daisy?" she asked.

"Of course," he replied. "You brought her to the card party."

"I haven't met your dog," Sue said, and Shameka added, "She's a beautiful German Shepherd."

"Thank you," Doug replied, rubbing her behind the ears.

"What's her name?" Sarah asked, and Doug said, "Greta. She's from an old German line."

A tattered briefcase sat next to him. It was closed, and he didn't divulge its contents. The handle was covered in teeth marks. "Greta carries my briefcase for me," Doug explained when he saw Sarah looking at the marks.

"Interesting," Sarah replied, frowning at Shameka, who said she had never heard of a dog carrying a briefcase before. "I guess you can train a dog to do just about anything."

"I have a yellow Labrador," Shameka said. "She likes to play fetch."

"Greta likes fetch, too," Doug replied. "We play every morning before I go to work."

"What do you do for work?" Sue asked, without divulging her knowledge of his profession.

"I lend money to people who have bad credit," Doug replied.

"What do you do if they can't pay it back?" Shameka asked, although everyone knew the answer.

"Whatever it takes," Doug replied, without elaboration.

Sue set my bowl of ice water beside Greta. It wasn't the first time she shared my ice with other dogs, but today I was excited to crunch it. I hoped she saved me some ice.

"Does Greta like ice?" Sue asked, and Doug confirmed it. "As you can see, hers is melted," he added, pointing to her bowl.

"You take good care of your dog," Sue said, and Doug agreed it was important. "Loretta is my veterinarian," he replied. "Greta loves to see her."

"You played cards with her husband at the party," Sue said. "Loretta is married to Zeke."

Doug smiled. "I remember Zeke. He seemed like a Newbie to the game, but he did alright for himself."

"He's a quick learner," Sue said, and Doug replied that it was unusual for new players to join high-stakes games. "They usually start small," he said, and Sue reminded him that Zeke only bet half as much as the others. "It's my fault," she said. "Luke is one of my best friends, and I suggested Zeke for the game. I hope he doesn't make it a habit."

"A man being murdered at his first high-stakes tournament may be a deterrent," Mia said. "He may never play again," she added, and Sue said it would be for the best.

"Sheriff Stone has been questioning me about Russ Johnson's murder," Doug said, and Mia added that he questioned everyone who left the party after Russ was murdered and before they found his body.

"I didn't kill Russ," Doug declared. "I hold people accountable for their debts, but killing is not my style."

No one mentioned hearing about the farmer in the bull's stall. "You did say he owed you money," Sarah reminded him. "You threatened him to pay you back right here at Cat Tails Pub. A lot of people heard you say it!"

"I had no reason to kill Russ Johnson," Doug thundered.

"Whoever killed him took all the money he won in the poker match," Sarah argued. "It was much more than you said he owed you!"

Doug quickly shifted the blame to Shameka. "You had a better reason to kill Russ than I did," he told Shameka. "Russ Johson was a snake. I have no clue why women don't see through his pretentious facade."

"It's more evident to me now," Shameka replied. "He was so nice to me, but it wasn't for real."

"He already bagged you," Doug growled, without remorse or apology. "Russ wanted Lilly Wilson."

Shameka gasped. "I had no idea Russ felt that way about Lilly."

Sarah embraced her old friend, who had started to shudder. "I should have known," Shameka said. "Everyone tried to warn me."

By now, Greta had eaten all of the ice from my water bowl. I had nothing to chew, crackle, or crunch to calm my nerves. The scene at Cat Tails Pub was making me nervous. If it escalated further, Tori might call the bouncer or the sheriff to escort us out of the pub.

Everyone around us seemed to be watching. The whole town knew about Russ Johnson's murder, whether or not they had met the players. They understood it involved a lot of money and were upset that Sheriff Stone had not stopped the card game.

“He should have arrested all of them,” a random customer said.

“This is exactly why high-stakes poker is illegal,” a second customer replied.

“It’s just like drug dealing,” a third added. “Somebody is going to get killed.”

“Luke Wilson probably gave the sheriff a cut to let them off the hook for playing,” the second man said.

Tori left her position as a bartender to speak to Sue and her friends. “You need to keep your voices down,” she said. “People are talking, and it’s not a good thing,” she continued, adding a handful of cubes to my water bowl. “They are all mixed up.”

“About Me!” Doug asked, and Tori, who knew about the setup with the marked bills, didn’t respond. “Just pipe down,” she said.

Doug DeLeon knew of her father’s reputation and didn’t oppose Tori. “Yes, Ma'am,” he said. “I’ll be leaving shortly.”

I crunched the ice that Tori had left for me. This time, I left none for Greta, who didn’t seem to care as much about the commotion as I did. She wasn’t a bad dog, but she had taken the first bowl for herself, and I didn’t feel like sharing at the moment.

Doug picked up his briefcase and prepared to leave. “I thought Greta carried that for you,” Sarah said.

“She does when I ask her to,” Doug said. “Not always.”

Sue observed the tattered briefcase. "Just one more thing before you leave," she said, and Doug waited. "How long have you known Russel Johnson?"

"I don't keep track of long-term acquaintances," he said. "Ten years or so."

"And how long have you known Andy Lemar?" she asked.

"I met him last year," he said. "Andy was at the jobsite for a house he was building in Miami."

"Interesting," Sue said as Mia retrieved her phone from her purse. "Are you sure you just met Andy last year?"

"Yes, as a matter of fact, I remember the meeting, exactly," Doug said. "We met at a beautiful home he was building for a friend."

"I'm afraid you have a bad memory, Mr. Deleon," Sue said, as Mia pulled up the photograph of the Three Amigos on her phone.

"This photograph was taken ten years ago," Mia said, pointing to Doug, Russ, and Andy. "The three of you have known each other for a long time."

"Who cares?" Doug asked. "What difference does it make?"

"You lied about how long you knew Mr. Lemar," Sue replied. "We'll see how that turns out for you."

The meeting was productive, filled with many unexpected insights and valuable tips. For now, Sue needed to separate the truth from the lies. I jumped into the car to ride back home to see Toby. Tomorrow, we would revisit Lilly, who had been implicated more than anyone anticipated.

Chapter 29

Lilly's House with Sargie

When we returned home, Sue's new robotic vacuum cleaner was waiting for her on her front doorstep. It came in a square box with a picture on the side. The vacuum appeared to be significantly larger than the one she had used for years. As it turned out, the size was determined mainly by the recharging base.

"Yay, it's my new vacuum," Sue said aloud when she saw the package. "Toby won't be thrilled about it, but it's time for an improvement."

The old vacuum had gone on a circling rampage the last time Sue used it, leaving Toby and me running for cover in the bedroom. I was typically braver than Toby about the ratchety thing, but the circling had been the last straw. Sue pulled the hair out of the wheels, dumped the container for the last time, and ordered a new pet-friendly version, like Lilly had.

When we stepped inside the garage door to the kitchen, Toby was waiting for us. He ambled towards Sue, rubbed her leg, and purred with happiness for the reunion. Sue scratched his head behind his ears after he jumped on the countertop. He arched his back and danced for the attention.

It was much the same as every other reunion when we came home. Toby greeted us at the door and nudged Sue, while I waited for him to finish the cat dance. Sue gave us water and refilled our food bowls as needed. Then she changed clothes to something comfortable for relaxation.

A walk through the house gave Sue a good idea of where Toby had been while they were away. If the back of the loveseat had an indented nest, he would have spent his day there. Otherwise, she might find cat fur on the bed or the ottoman. Today, she found most of his fur on the loveseat. She picked it off by hand before she retrieved her new toy from the front porch.

"I'm sorry, Toby," she said, as he jumped on the table where she opened the box and unveiled her robot. "You may not like this as much as I do, but it's time for an update."

We hadn't liked the old robot with a mind of its own. Still, it had a small base and stayed hidden most of the time—until Sue released it from captivity. This one would have to be out in the wide-open all the time for it to find its way home.

Toby enjoyed exploring the empty box. He watched Sue remove the components from the box, leaving him a den. When Toby explored the box, Sue assembled the base and placed the round robot, which resembled the last one, on the big charger.

The base, however, looked much different than the older robot. It was tall, dark, and ominous. Sue found the one place the robot could find its way home and plugged it into the wall, where everyone would see it.

"This is where the new robot will live," Sue said, while Toby crept over to sniff it. He quickly backed away, unimpressed. Then, he summoned the courage for a second sniff and repeated the process: creep and sniff, promptly retreat.

I had no interest in the base, the plug, or the round robot when it was quietly sitting there. Sue often brought strange new objects into the house for her pleasure. This one had no particular charm, but it did not inspire my curiosity, as it did Toby.

The following morning, after it was fully charged, Sue ran the robot for the first time. By now, Toby had chased the beetles on the back porch and crept past the undesirably suspicious object on his way back inside. He kept a distance as he crept past it. Then, he circled back to touch it before making a rapid retreat.

Sue pulled the object off the base and pushed the button to start the vacuum. It said something, started its engine, and purred around the house for the first time. By now, we both knew what it was doing and scampered off to our hiding places in the bedroom.

It was not as loud as the older one, but not quiet, either. Finally, when it was finished puttering around the house for what seemed like eternity, it found its way back to the base, like it was supposed to.

"Yay," Sue said when it landed on the charger. "Mission accomplished."

The loudest part was yet to come, when it cut the fur that had become wrapped around the roller. "Eureka," Sue said, looking at the empty roller. "It works."

Now that the fur was gone, it was safe for Toby and me to return to the living room. “I don’t know whose fur was whose,” Sue said. “But, I don’t have to cut fur off the roller every time I run the robot anymore.”

Mia arrived at Sue’s house shortly after the robot finished its work. “You bought a pet-friendly vacuum,” she said, looking at the base against the wall. “How do you like it?”

“It does a good job,” Sue replied. “Toby and Daisy will need time to appreciate it as much as I do.”

“Toby isn’t the bravest cat in the den,” Mia said.

“He’ll have to get used to it,” Sue said. “For Daisy, it’s the same as the last one, but Toby is more intimidated by the bigger base. He doesn’t trust anything new until he gets used to it.”

“Are you ready to visit Lilly?” Mia asked, and Sue grabbed her purse and my leash for the drive to her house. “Yes, ma'am,” she said, recalling the questions from the previous visits. “She has some explaining to do.”

When we arrived at Lilly’s house, she and Sargie were standing in the front yard. Sargie barked, awkwardly, as he always did, when he saw us. I stood calmly and quietly, now that I knew him.

“It looks like Sargie still doesn’t remember us,” Mia said, and Lilly agreed he was slow to recall newcomers. “He’ll lick you to death when he knows you," she added. "His memory is slower in his older age."

Lilly invited us indoors, where it was cooler. "Is it hotter earlier than usual this year?" she asked, as we followed her into the living room, and Sue agreed it seemed like an early summer, although it was still spring.

Sargie stood beside Lilly, who sat in a chair in her living room, and I lay at Sue's feet while they talked. I looked at the base for her robot, the same as Sue's new one. Some of Sargie's fur lay in short white hairs on the dark hardwood floor.

"I'm sorry I haven't run my vacuum yet today," Lilly said, brushing stray hairs off the couch onto the floor. "I usually have Sargie's fur picked up by now."

"I bought the same robot," Sue said, looking at the base. "I used it today for the first time. How often do you change your bag?" she asked of the paper container where the chopped-up fur was stored.

"I change the bag every other week on Thursday—the day the garbage collectors come," Lilly replied. "How do you like your robot?"

"I'm impressed, but my cat isn't," Sue said, and Mia suggested that Toby wasn't a fan of new things.

"I don't have a cat—yet," Lilly replied. "One day, I'll adopt a stray from the neighborhood."

"Sweetwater Springs has many sweet stray cats," Sue replied. "I've adopted two of them, but my friend's daughter took one of them when she moved out of my house."

"Are you referring to Jessie?" Lilly asked, to which Sue affirmed. "She's writing a cookbook."

"I'd love to meet her," Lilly said. "I've been so busy with Bill's shenanigans since we moved here, I haven't had time to make friends."

"We're visiting Jessie today, if you'd like to join us," Mia said, and Sue agreed she'd love a new contributor for her CHEWS: for healthy living cookbook.

"I'd be delighted to join you," Lilly said. "I need to get out of the house."

Sargie had moved very little since we arrived. It was hard to imagine what life would be like for one so stiff, but he seemed happy. He was a young dog at heart who loved his family.

"Does Sargie miss Bill?" Mia asked, and Lilly frowned. "He was happy to see him when Bill came by the house to pick up his clothes," she said.

"If you don't mind my asking, how did you know Russ was killed with a crossbow?" Mia asked since they had ventured into tougher topics.

"Bill told me about the crossbow when he picked up his clothes," Lilly replied. "As you must know, my husband found Russ Johnson's body."

"Yes, we were still at Luke's house when Bill found the body," Mia said. "He looked horrified."

Sue added, "The Boggs Brothers said your husband looked like he saw a ghost."

Lilly took a deep breath. "Awwwww, the Bogg's Brothers," she said. "Peas in a pod, if you ask me."

"They know a little about everything," Mia said. "Their grandparents were security guards for the Radcliffes, who were one of the original families."

Sue kept eyeing the vacuum base with interest. I'd seen the look before. She was thinking of something important, but had to keep it private, for now.

"We saw Doug DeLeon at Cat Tails Pub yesterday," Mia said. "He was talking about you and Russ Johnson."

"Russ Johnson and I?" Lilly said. "What about us?"

"According to Doug, Russ Johnson was putting the moves on you," Mia said. "I'm sorry to be the purveyor of street gossip."

"I am a married woman," Lilly said. "He helped me with the turtles."

"Mia is telling you the word on the street," Sue said. "We thought you should know what's out there."

"Russ was a married man," Lilly said, and Mia mentioned she could learn more about Russ at Jessie's house.

"I'd like to change clothes before we go, if you don't mind," Lilly said, and Sue replied, "Of course, we can wait for you outside at the car."

Sue peeked into the container for the vacuum bag before they went outdoors. "It's full," she whispered to Mia, who shrugged.

"Russ was murdered on Friday," Sue explained, after they reached the car. "The robot vacuumed on the day Russ Johnson was murdered, a week ago. If he were inside the house, we might find evidence inside the bag."

"What kind of evidence?" Mia asked, and Sue replied, "Cleo's fur."

"Why didn't you take the bag?" Mia asked, and Sue suggested it was better to be discreet."

Sue started the car's engine to kickstart the air conditioner. I hopped into the backseat for the drive to Jessie's house, followed by Sue, Mia, and Lilly. We passed through town and turned into the subdivision where Chris and Jessie lived in the home upriver, across from Mia's run.

Chapter 30

Chris and Jessie's house with a Photo

Jessie greeted us warmly, as she always did, when we walked into her house. The kitchen smelled delightful. I breathed in whiffs of home-baked dog cookies along with lunch, of uncertain lineage, for the human guests. Jessie was a nurse who loved to cook; it had to be bold and healthy.

"Hi friends," she said, tossing me and her dog, Redman, dog biscuits. We sat politely, prepared for the ritual of the biscuits. Sue said we were conditioned: the sooner we sat, the sooner we received our treats.

Redman was an older dog, like Sargie, but he looked nothing like him. According to Sue, he was a red Doberman. Sargie was a white Great Dane with black spots, she called Harlequin, and was much taller.

They were both old, short-haired, stiff, and creaky seniors, living on love. Neither was a good playmate for a dog in her prime, but it was nice to see them, nonetheless.

"Lilly," Sue said, introducing them. "Meet Jessie and Chris."

"I've heard good things about you," Lilly said. "It's nice to finally meet you."

"And you as well," Jessie said. "You're the latest talk of the town."

"Your introduction to Sweetwater Springs has been eventful," Chris added without commenting whether it was good or bad.

"Trouble follows my husband," Lilly said. "I'm sure you heard he hawked my wedding ring for money for the card game."

"And lost the game," Jessie said. "You must have been devastated."

"This isn't the first time Bill hawked my things," Lilly said. "I gave him a week to repurchase my ring, or else…"

"Is he a good man?" Chris asked, and Lilly answered. "I want my ring back."

Chris was chopping vegetables. According to Sue, he had exceptional knife skills and could shred and dice fruits and vegetables into perfectly matched pieces in the colors of the rainbow.

"You're an expert with that knife," Lilly said, glancing at bowls of shredded carrots, diced onions, cubed mangos, sliced green avocados, tiny diced jalapenos, raisins, chickpeas, shredded cilantro, and cut limes.

"I like building and woodworking," Chris said. "Jessie translates my hobbies into me as her sous chef."

"That's a terrific idea," Lilly said. "Women appreciate help from their husbands in the kitchen."

"Jessie plans the meals," Chris said. "I cut the vegetables."

"I write healthy eating cookbooks," Jessie said. "My first cookbook is called "CHEWS One": Recipes for Healthy Eating. Now, I'm working on CHEWS Two: Healthy Recipes for Couples Cooking.

CHEWS stands for Cheap, healthy, easy, wholesome, spicy," Chris explained.

"I love your hobbies," Lilly said. "They're so much better than gambling away my priceless, expensive jewelry."

"Healthy eating is simple with whole foods," Jessie said. "We eat the colors of the rainbow in fruits and vegetables at lunch and dinner."

"Today, we're having fish tacos with mango salsa and carrot salad with raisins and chickpeas," Jessie said. "The fruits and veggies are nutritious and the chickpeas are a good source of fibre and magnesium."

"I made the dog biscuits with carrots, peanut butter, and flour," she added.

"She used to make the dog biscuits with fish, but the house got too stinky," Chris said. "Sometimes we cook them outside."

I gobbled down my second peanut butter and carrot biscuit with Redman. All of Jessie's dog biscuits were tasty. We licked up the crumbs before Chris tossed us another biscuit.

"Chris helped Zeke build a chicken coop at my daughter's house," Sue said.

"Zeke and Loretta are nice people," Lilly said. "I remember them from the card party."

"Zeke isn't much of a card player," Sue explained. "Chris helped him improve his game."

"Why didn't you play?" Lilly asked Chris.

"Too rich for my blood," Chris replied. "I'm not a high-stakes guy."

"Zeke isn't either," Sue said. "We had to twist his arm to join the game."

I suggest you untwist it," Lilly said. "It's a dangerous hobby."

"I hear you knew the man who was murdered," Chris said.

"We were friends," Lilly said, "Or at least I thought so. He helped me build demarcations for the turtle nests with ribbons."

"You have unusual tastes in friends," Jessie said. "Most married women don't take up with strangers who call themselves stockbrokers, then turn out to be card sharks at the poker table."

"I was stupid to trust Russ," Lilly said. "I know that now."

Mia pulled a photograph of Russ Johnson up from her phone. "Have you seen this man paddling on the river?" she asked, and Chris and Jessie agreed they had seen him with Shameka a few times.

"Shameka is a nice girl," Jessie said. "I met her at the museum. Her heart must be broken to have fallen for a Ladies' Man and lost at love."

"Shameka is smart," Mia said. "She's hurting now, but she will learn her lesson."

"Did Shameka know Russ was married?" Jessie asked, and Chris replied, "No one, except his buddies, knew Russ was married until his wife called at the poker party.

Mia pulled up a photograph of the couple on her phone and passed it to Lilly, causing her jaw to drop. "She's drop-dead gorgeous," Lilly gasped.

"Shameka thought so, too," Mia said.

Loretta blackened the fish, making my mouth water. I had loved the fish-flavored dog biscuits. The scent was strong from the pan-fry, but Sue said that baking them as dog biscuits was stronger. Redman and I would stick with peanut butter and carrots for dog biscuits today.

Lilly was still staring at the photograph of Russ Johnson and his fabulously beautiful wife while we chomped our dog biscuits. "Did Russ say anything about the phone call with his wife?" she asked Chris.

"According to Zeke, he was short with her. Their son was in the Emergency Room at the hospital, but he didn't want to hear about it."

Lilly was stunned. "Their son was in the hospital, and Russ didn't care?"

"He told her not to bother him when he was working."

"Russ said that playing cards was working?" Lilly asked, and Chris confirmed. "After the third phone call, Russ ghosted her."

"That's despicable," Lilly said. "He's an evil man!"

Everyone agreed that Russ Johnson was an evil man and a worse husband. "I can't believe he didn't tell Shameka he was married," Lilly said.

Sue reminded Lilly that Russ hadn't told her he was married either, and according to Doug DeLeon, he had wanted to make a move on her, too.

"I'm sick of this whole mess," Lilly said. "I'm getting my ring back, whatever it takes!"

Everyone agreed the fish tacos were delicious and full of bold flavors. "Jessie has convinced me that healthy food can taste as delicious as the junk I ate before I met her," Chris said. "I'm honored to be her sous chef."

Lilly replied that she'd be delighted to contribute a recipe to Jessie's cookbook, but first, she had to help solve a murder and recover a ring. "I've been an idiot," she said, "I should have known better than to trust a Miami stockbroker with a soft spot for turtles."

Sue drove Lilly back home to formulate her plans. No one knew for sure what to make of the conversation, but Sue and Mia knew where to stop next. I was excited for a trip to Luke's house to romp with my friend, Artemis, while they talked to Sophie. I had eaten too many dog biscuits, and it was time to work off the menu.

Chapter 31
Sophie's House

My stomach was full of dog biscuits, and my spirits were high when we reached Sophie's house. Artemis stood at the grand, beautiful gate, waiting for me as Sophie pressed the button to open it from inside the home. I had enjoyed the dog biscuits at Jessie's house, but they were talking back at me on the drive. A run with Artemis would clear the air and settle my stomach.

Artemis was wagging his tail when Sue drove through the open gate. I stood at the car window, excited for his companionship after visits with two senior dogs. I was excited about having a playmate who loved running in the yard, just as I did. Three times around the big backyard should be perfect for both of us.

Sue and Mia stepped out of the car and set me free. The soft grass felt incredible between my toes after spending so much time indoors. Artemis gave me a quick sniff, and we were off to the races. We ran down the borders of the yard to the river and back again, in a quick circle.

Sue and Mia were smiling as we passed them after the first loop around the enormous lawn. We barely slowed down by the river, as we often did. It was the perfect day for a swim, but we stayed on track on the loop.

"Daisy has so much fun playing with Artemis," Sue said. "She'd come more often if we could make it."

"Big dogs need to run," Mia agreed. "It's fun to watch them have a good time."

"Daisy is lucky to have Artemis and Loretta's dogs to play with," Sue said. "She can work off her energy in their backyard, since mine is too small."

"What did you think of Shameka's idea for a dog park on the Green Cove property?" Mia asked.

"I'm for it," Sue replied, "Daisy would love to attend with her old friends and make new ones."

Mia suggested, "Cleo could be her first playdate," and Sue agreed that Shameka would be excited to have a place where her Labrador could run free.

"She's an excellent museum manager," Mia said. "It's a shame she got tangled up in this mess with Russ Johnson."

"Do you think she'll learn her lesson?" Sue asked.

"If Sarah has any say in this, and I know she will, Russ Johnson will be her one and only man friend with a string of red flags, like he did."

Artemis and I ran slower on the second loop around the yard. Sue and Mia followed our tracks around the perimeter towards the river. The wetlands bordered the yard on both sides. We stayed on the plush grass for the run and avoided the swamps, although a path led through the marsh.

"Russ Johnson was killed twenty yards south of us down that path," Sue said, pointing in that direction.

"He made some enemies in his love life and his scams," Mia replied. "It's hard to say which got the better of him."

"He lied to everyone," Sue said. "It was all a game for Russ to see if he could get away with it."

"It caught up with him," Mia replied.

"Someone got away with a lot of money," Sue said.

"Someone who can shoot a crossbow," Mia declared, looking down the path.

"The money will turn up," Sue suggested. "When it does, we'll get some answers."

By our third loop around the yard, Sue and Mia had walked to the river. Artemis was ready to drop, and I was tired from the exercise. When we stopped beside Sue, we saw the Johnboat across the river. The Boggs brothers called out to us.

"By Golly, I think that's Daisy been racing around the yard like a blue streak with Artemis," Frank, the big man, said.

His brother, Butch, said, "I believe you're right, Big Bro. Sue and Mia are here, too."

"It's good to see you," Sue said, and Mia added, "Did you catch that bass you've been after yet?"

"We wouldn't be here if we did, now would we?" Frank asked, and neither woman responded.

Butch remarked, "We're still working at hooking him. He's a smart old guy."

"Some of the old ones get so smart, they're hard to catch," Frank agreed. "They've been caught so many times before, it's hard to hook them."

"Doug DeLeon is just like that old bass," Butch said. "He's been scamming folks for so long with his loan sharking and beatings, it's hard for the sheriff to catch him, and people are afraid to talk."

Mia recalled that Doug had orchestrated a beating of their friend with a bull after a poker match with him and Russ. "Did the sheriff ever pin that beating on Doug?" she asked.

"He never could prove it," Frank said, "Like I said, the old ones can be hard to catch. Nobody talks about a beating from Doug. They're afraid he'll go after them again."

"Didn't you go to high school with Doug?" Mia asked, and Frank said he'd been the same his whole life: A gambler, cheater, scammer, and a thug.

"My Big Bro thinks Doug killed that card shark, Russ Johnson," Butch said, "but I think it's more likely that woman."

"What woman?" Sue asked.

"The woman who was screaming at Russ in the woods the morning he was killed," Butch said.

"We haven't heard about a woman screaming at him," Sue said. "Who was she?"

"Let's just say, she was white, at the card party, and related to the Wilsons," Butch replied, and Sue gasped. "Do you mean Lilly Wilson?" she asked.

"The same," Butch said.

"What did Lilly scream at Russ?" Mia asked.

"We heard bits and pieces," Butch said. "She called him a married snake and told him never to come to her house again."

"Russ went to Lilly's house?" Mia asked.

"I'm just telling you what she said," Butch replied. "I wasn't there with them."

"What did Russ say?" Sue asked.

"He laughed at her. He called her a fool. He said nobody in Sweetwater Springs could hold a candle to his wife in Miami."

"She's a beauty," Sue said.

"Have you told Sheriff Stone?" Mia asked, and Butch replied they had told the sheriff everything they knew about Lilly Wilson and Russ Johnson. "Yes, Ma'am," he said. "We told the sheriff."

Sue and Mia waved goodbye to the Boggs brothers. "I hope you catch that bass soon," Sue said as they walked toward the mansion with Artemis and me ahead of them. "He's been trouble enough for your dinner table."

Artemis and I were the first to arrive at the doorstep, where Sophie was waiting. She looked impatient and grumpy, even for Sophie, who was always bold and outspoken. Although she was usually friendly to Artemis and me, today she shooed us past like dogs.

"What took you so long to get here?" she thundered at Sue and Mia when she let them inside the home.

Sue pointed toward the river. "We were talking to the Boggs brothers," she said.

"Those two again?" Sophie screeched. "Can't they quit pretending they're trying to catch a big fish and admit they're snooping on us?"

"It does seem that way," Mia agreed. "I had the same thought myself."

"It was a revealing conversation," Sue remarked. "I'm not sure you'll want to hear about it."

"Of course I want to hear about it!" Sophie said. "My son is a suspect, and he's living at this house with me and his brother, who doesn't approve of his ways and means."

"Is Bill here?" Sue asked, and Sophie said they had both gone out for the morning.

"Did they go out together?" Sue asked, and Sophie affirmed; they left together.

"Are you the only person here?" Mia asked, and Sophie reaffirmed she was alone. "Shall I pour us a shot of limoncello to celebrate?" she asked, sarcastically, and Sue said, "No, but you may want to sit down with a cup of soothing tea."

"Can we help you make it?" Mia asked, and Sophie declined the offer.

"I prefer to work in my kitchen, alone," she said, ambling away. "Make yourselves comfortable."

Artemis and I lay on his huge, oversized dog bed while Sophie went to the kitchen. I had wanted one just like it, but it would fill a bedroom at Sue's house. I could admire it at a distance and share it with Artemis when we visited. It was unlikely I'd have one of my own.

"Do you think Russ Johnson put the move on Lilly?" Mia asked while Sophie was in the kitchen.

"It's hard to say," Sue replied, nodding her head. "Consider the source."

"Doug DeLeon," Mia said. "He may have been deflecting the guilt."

"It's hard to say," Sue responded. "I was beginning to feel like I knew Lilly, but those words between her and Russ on the day he was murdered carried a certain implication."

"Maybe the Boggs brothers misunderstood something," Mia said, and Sue mentioned they needed to get to know Lilly better.

Sophie returned with a teapot, cups, dog biscuits, and tea biscuits. She poured tea for everyone and passed Artemis and me a dog biscuit, which I declined due to overdistension from our previous visit. Artemis eagerly consumed the extra biscuit and licked up the crumbs.

"How well do you know your daughter-in-law?" Sue asked after they sipped tea.

"As you know, we don't see each other often," Sophie said. "Bill and Lilly moved away for years to manage their golf courses."

"Do they have a good marriage?" Mia asked, and Sophie returned, "What are you getting at?"

"It can't be easy to live with a compulsive gambler who hawks your treasures for bid money," Sue said, and Mia added, "Lilly has reasons to be angry with Bill."

"Don't most women have reasons to be angry with their husbands?" Sophie asked.

"I don't have many arguments with Thomas," Mia said, and Sue agreed that she and Wade hadn't argued much before her husband passed away. "I'm not a good person to ask."

"I think most wives would be livid if their husband blew their fortune on a card game," Sue said.

"Maybe they'd want to leave him if someone else, who they thought shared their dreams, came into their lives," Mia added.

"What are you getting at?" Sophie flared again. "Do you think Lilly found another man?"

"Do you think Lilly was shocked when she discovered Russ was married at the card party?" Sue answered.

Sophie was stumped. "She seemed surprised."

"Why would she care?" Mia asked, and Sophie replied, "Shameka was dating Russ. No one knew Russ was married. Everyone was surprised to learn he was married."

"You're keeping something from me," Sophie insisted, and Sue recounted the stories of Doug DeLeon, who said Russ made a move on Lilly, and the Boggs brothers, who overheard her conversation with Russ, calling him a married snake the morning he was murdered.

"Doug is a suspect," Sue retorted. "He's scapegoating Lilly."

Sue and Mia agreed Doug's words were tainted by his role as a suspect. "The sheriff will be questioning Lilly," Sue said. "The

Boggs brothers shared their story of the argument between Lilly and Russ with him, too."

"Sheriff Stone may need your help," Sophie said, and Sue reminded her that Zeke had offered his services as an attorney for Bill and Lilly.

"I'll keep that in mind," Sophie said. "Bill has been talking to Zeke already."

"Mia and I will talk to Bill and Lilly's neighbors tomorrow," Sue said. "We want to learn everything we can about Lilly and Russ."

I rose from sharing the big dog bed with Artemis when Sue and Mia were ready to leave. It had been a comfortable rest after a needed run in the big yard for me. The Boggs brothers had provided new and incriminating information about Lilly. Tomorrow, Sue and Mia could investigate the details of their story.

Chapter 32
Neighbors on the Cove

Toby and I sat side by side on the back porch watching the ducks waddle out of the cove. It wasn't often we had the same mission. Today was one of those days. We watched them file up the kayak launch in a row, just like they had when they were swimming, and the procession looked like a giant alligator from a distance.

The ducks were growing bigger. According to Sue, it was hard to tell the mother from her baby ducks. She counted seven ducks instead of nine, and the last duck was still limping.

"Do you think the lame duck is getting better?" Mia asked after she sipped her coffee.

"Yes, I do think he's improving."

"I hope he makes it," Mia said, and Sue agreed. "Swimming has been good for him," she said.

"We should swim, too," Mia said, and Sue agreed, as swimming had many benefits. "We should add it to our list of summer activities," Sue replied.

Toby was the first to lose interest in the ducks, as he was more alert to the fast-moving life, such as bugs. "I miss having a cat," Mia said, watching Toby's curious nature as he zoned in on a moving blade of grass outside the screen.

"There are many great adoptable strays in Sweetwater Springs," Sue said. "We could easily set you and Thomas up with your cat."

"I'll talk to Thomas about that," Mia said. "He'd enjoy a feline friend to keep us company."

"I certainly enjoy Toby's company," Sue said, picking up the coffee cups to take them to the kitchen. "You should feel honored," she added. "He trusts you with his company."

"I am blessed to be one of his chosen people," Mia said, and Sue offered that he hid under the bed until he got familiar with people, and then chose those worthy of his trust.

"We should be going," Sue said, calling Toby indoors, as Mia and I followed her. "It will be too hot to walk the cove before too long."

"Lilly wants a cat, too," Mia recalled, placing the cups in the dishwasher, and Sue offered that they had much to learn about Lilly.

"She may not be so sweet as she seems," Mia agreed. "I wouldn't be happy if Thomas blew his family fortune on gambling and sold my jewelry to pay for his bids when it ran out."

Toby was lying on the couch when we left for the morning walk around the Green Cove. I hopped into the back seat, excited for a shady walk, when Sue grabbed my leash. There were many shady areas in Sweetwater Springs, but the Green Cove neighborhood where we were headed was one of my favorites.

Today, we will see some of my old friends. Sue and Mia will discuss Russ Johnson and Lilly's strange and evolving partnership with Lilly's neighbors. Was it more than it seemed on the surface? Or was Lilly another woman duped by Russ Johnson's charm into believing he wanted to save turtles when he made a move on her?

I had met Russ Johnson, sniffed him, and wasn't sure about his intentions, despite my superior abilities in detecting good and evil. If a dog can be deceived, anyone— man or woman—could fall for his charms.

Mia carried the photograph of the three amigos—Russ, Doug, and Andy— who wanted to buy the beautiful property on her phone. By now, most people in Sweetwater Springs knew about Russ Johnson's murder. Residents wanted to get to the bottom of it. Sheriff Stone had warned them about the scams and the increasing accidents that didn't seem accidental, but felt more like threats.

Sue parked on a berm to take a walk through the neighborhood, which led to the exclusive property. Most people knew Sue because of her sleuth work on solving the first murder in twenty years. They recognized Mia as her partner and the wife of the local billionaire, who had spent lavishly at local businesses for her housewarming party and had continued to do so ever since. At the same time, her husband had the dubious goal of building a luxury hotel in Sweetwater Springs.

Mostly, they knew about me. I was the cute kayaking dog, with a nose for solving crime. Thanks to my renowned ability, Sweetwater Springs was a safer place for everyone.

Sue attached my leash, and we began the walk of discovery on the cove. First, we stopped at the home of a retired country songwriter, who enjoyed her privacy and was predominantly incognito when paddling on the river. After introductions, Mia showed her the photograph, and they dove into conversation and questions for the only celebrity cove dweller.

"Isn't this Daisy?" the songwriter asked, ruffling my fur. "I've seen this Cute Dog paddling on the river before."

"Yes, Daisy is the Captain of the kayak," Sue said.

"She's a beautiful dog," the toned woman said. "I wish my dog would learn to kayak."

"You can teach her," Sue said, but the actress insisted she would jump in and it would be impossible for her to reboard.

Sue agreed that reboarding could be a challenge, but suggested a harness with a handle and keeping her nails trimmed.

Mia produced the photograph and pointed to Russ Johnson. "Have you seen this man paddling a kayak on the Green Cove?" she asked.

"Many times," she said. "He paddled to that house at the end of the road, where the newcomers live, and met a woman by the water."

"Lilly's house," Sue said, and the songwriter didn't know her name.

"How long would you say he's been coming here?" Mia asked, and the songwriter replied, "More than a month," before becoming elusive. "I'm sorry, I don't know any more than that."

We walked up her driveway from the cove, visiting four homes along the way, and headed towards the Doc's house. Most of the conversations were similar, but the clues varied in each one. The Doc concurred with the songwriter and provided new information.

"Hi Daisy," Doc said, fluffing my fur. "Do you want a dog biscuit?" he asked, shuffling through his kitchen for the treat.

When Mia showed him the photograph, Doc agreed that the kayaker, Russ Johnson, had been paddling to the cove for about a month and had met Lilly by the water's edge.

"How often did he paddle here to meet her?" Mia asked.

"Three or four times a week," he said. "Recently, he came more often."

We left the Doc's house, and next, we walked to several homes where no clues were forthcoming, before visiting the mayor's house. I knew the mayor and his daughter, who played with Jessie's daughter, who loved to see me.

"It's Daisy," she yelped after she opened the door. "Please come in," she suggested to Sue and Mia.

The mayor agreed that Russ Johnson had been paddling to the cove three to four times a week for approximately a month. His wife said a woman met them at the water's edge, and their daughter noted that Lilly's Great Dane never barked at Russ.

"That dog barks at everyone," she said. "He's huge, but his bark is tiny and awkward, like this, "Wo…of, Wo…of."

"He didn't bark at Russ?" Mia asked.

"Nope, never," the young girl replied. "I'd know Sargie's bark anywhere. I never heard a dog bark like him before."

"Thank you," Sue said, "You've been very helpful."

"Are you going to the Colemans' house?" she asked, and Sue mentioned it was their next stop. "Say hello from me," she called, as they walked away, and Sue assured her she would relay the message to her friend, who had been most helpful with tips in the past.

When we reached the Coleman house, Nella, who had repurchased the local teahouse, was hanging freshly washed clothing on the line. "Hi, Ladies, and Daisy," she said. "Would you like to come inside for tea?"

"We'd love to," Mia said, speaking for both of them. "We've been talking to your neighbors about Russ Johnson's murder, and your house is our last stop on the cove."

"Tea would be delightful," Sue agreed. "I recommend your tea shop to everyone, and each cup reminds me why I like it best."

We followed Nella inside the house, where she had water simmering in a kettle. She poured the hot water into a teapot filled with loose-leaf tea, which she had sourced from the country of origin. Today's tea was Indian Darjeeling.

While the tea steeped, Nella passed me a dog biscuit. Sue remembered to relay her friend's message, but Nella's daughter wasn't home. "She's at Beth's house today," Nella said, and Sue replied, "It's a perfect day to spend on the river with Jessie's daughter. We took Lilly to Chris and Jessie's house yesterday."

"Have you met your new neighbor?" Mia asked when Nella poured tea.

"Yes, of course," Nella replied. "Lilly and Bill. I took them a welcome basket with tea and fresh scones two weeks ago today."

"Sweet," Mia said. "I'm sure you heard about Russ Johnson's murder," Sue added, and Nella affirmed her suggestion. "Russ was murdered on a Friday—eight days after I took them the welcome basket."

"Did Russ visit often?" Mia asked, and Nella affirmed the same schedule as the other neighbors. "About three times a week for a month," she said. "It seemed odd because she's married," Nella added. "He helped her with the turtles. I don't know what else they did."

"Some people seem to be wondering," Sue said, without mentioning flirting at Cat Tails Pub, a girlfriend, and a wife. "Russ had a reputation for being a scammer and a ladies' man."

"Are you sure about the day you took Lilly the welcome basket?" Mia asked.

"Yes, it was a Thursday—the day the garbage is picked up—like today."

"Interesting," Sue said. "Russ was murdered on a Friday, eight days later."

"Lilly washes her sheets every two weeks, like I do," Nella said. "She washed them on Thursday, last week—the day before Russ was killed."

"She washed her sheets the day before Russ was murdered," Sue repeated.

"Lilly was running her robotic vacuum for eight days without changing the bag when Russ was killed," Mia said.

"She's been running her robot for two weeks without changing the bag," Sue remarked. "Today is bag-changing day."

"I'm not sure what you ladies are getting at," Nella said. "But the sheriff couldn't have done it without you last time."

"Thank you for the tea, Nella," Sue said, and Mia added, "You've been more helpful than you realize."

Sue attached my leash to my collar, and we departed Nella's house for our next destination—Lilly's garbage can.

"Are you thinking what I'm thinking?" Sue asked, as they plodded ahead of the garbage service to take the vacuum bag, and Mia replied, "Most certainly."

"If Russ were inside Lilly's house, there would be remnants of something left behind," Sue said. The sheriff could test for Russ Johnson's DNA if needed later on. For now, they had a preliminary test that could be useful—a search for Cleo's fur.

"The sheriff will have a primary suspect when somebody spends the marked money," Mia reminded Sue.

Sue reminded Mia that Zeke had offered his services as Lilly's attorney, and he would appreciate reassurance that Lilly was innocent if she was not guilty of Russ Johnson's murder.

The garbage truck was five houses behind us when Sue retrieved the vacuum bag from Lilly's garbage can. Sue and Mia had learned a great deal about Lilly and Russ today. I enjoyed seeing our old friends, but was excited for wherever we would go tomorrow. Sue and Mia were hot on the trail, and I was right there beside them.

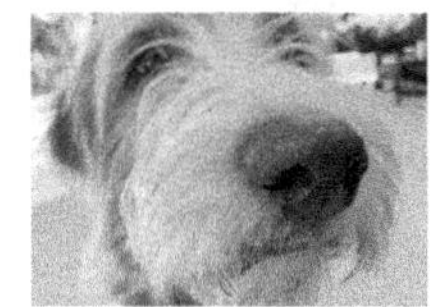

Chapter 33
Sue's House re Thugs

Early the next morning, Mia burst into Sue's house, saying, "Sheriff Stone arrested Doug DeLeon last night! He's in jail!"

Sue sat in her recliner, with me by her side, relaxing on the tile floor and Toby in her lap. Mia's boisterous announcement caused Toby to dart down the hall to the bedroom. I stayed with Sue in the living room, immediately sensing Sue was unsettled.

"What on earth happened?" Sue asked, stunned by the unexpected news.

"Doug got in a fight in the parking lot at Magic Manatee Pub," Mia said. "He beat a man up and put him in the hospital."

"How did you find out about it?" Sue asked, and Mia said the pub was buzzing with lights, sirens, and emergency vehicles. "Seven of them came to the incident, including Sheriff Stone and Deputy Livingston."

"That's the biggest emergency response since…" Sue glanced at Mia, as if reconsidering, but then continued, "Your housewarming party."

Mia frowned, and Sue asked, "I'm sorry, Mia. How did you find out about the fight?"

"The mayor called this morning," Mia replied. "He wanted to talk to Thomas, but he wasn't home, so he passed the message on to me."

"Thomas?" Sue asked, and Mia explained that her husband and the mayor had built a rapport to tackle the rising crime problem in Sweetwater Springs.

"Excellent," Sue said, and Mia reminded her that the hotel had been approved and that everyone wanted a safe place to enjoy nature.

"Absolutely!" Sue said. "We should take a drive to Magic Manatee and find out what happened."

"It's a rowdy pub," Mia said, and Sue mentioned it should be fine in the daytime before the bands of bandits shuffle in for the nightly brawls.

"Thomas wouldn't approve," Mia said, and Sue agreed it might not sit well with Luke, either.

Toby peeked around the corner, now that the news had settled. I rose off the floor and met him as he padded into the living room, then sat on my haunches beside Sue. I sniffed her apprehension, but it was short-lived.

"Did you ever tell Thomas about the note in my mailbox?" Sue asked about the threat, and Mia said, "I didn't want to worry him."

"Did you tell Luke about it?" Mia asked, and Sue said, "No, I didn't want to worry him or be followed by his investigator, again."

"We promised them we'd be careful," Sue said, and Mia mentioned they were snooping around a seedy pub with a long history of brawls where a guy got his leg broken last night.

"Doug DeLeon broke his leg?" Sue asked, and Mia said, "Yes, with a baseball bat."

"We're not dealing with nice people," Sue said bluntly, but we can handle it. We need to find out what went down."

I followed Sue to the bedroom, where she rummaged through her closet for inconspicuous bar clothes. She chose musty old T-shirts for herself and Mia, which made my nose twitch. She also picked a printed headband with a similar smell for Mia. Sue wore blue jeans and leather boots, which I had never seen before. The leather smelled nice.

"Did you ever ride a motorcycle?" Mia asked when Sue was done.

"Not for long," Sue replied. "I still have my license."

"You look like a Motorcycle Mama," Mia said, and Sue reminded her she drove it. "Some stuff you keep for the parts," she added. "Magic Manatee is no place for bathing suits, coverups, and sunhats."

"Do you think we'll see anyone we know?" Mia asked, and Sue replied that everyone needs a place to hang out. "Doug Deleon was there," she said, and Mia reminded her he was a loan shark and a card cheat.

"Doug DeLeon and who else?" Mia asked, and Sue replied that they would find out.

Sue grabbed my leash, and I hopped into her car for the drive to Magic Manatee Pub. I had never been there before, as we usually went to Cat Tails Pub, where the crowd was mainly friendly locals and tourists, who were unlikely to get in a brawl. According to Sue, today's destination was the hangout for rough types. It was doubtful they brought their dogs to such establishments.

Sue brought me along for the ride, since it was early. The pub was down an alley from the main drag through town.

"Do you think they'll let Daisy inside the pub?" Mia asked, and Sue wasn't sure. Still, having me along might break the ice with a hardened server or bartender. "It's worth a try," Sue said.

Sue turned left onto Manatee Street, where the pub was located, on the other side of the railroad tracks. The parking lot was nearly empty. Three cars, a motorcycle, and a bicycle were parked near a dumpster.

I sat on my haunches and gazed out the window at the ghostly lot. When Sue opened the door, I inhaled the damp air. It was a muggy morning, with lingering scents of last night's sordid activities.

"That's where the fight took place," Mia said, pointing toward the garbage bin. "You can still see the tire tracks from the rescue in the clay.

"It was a bad fight to break the guy's legs," Sue replied, and Mia reminded her that Doug DeLeon had a reputation for rough and dirty fights. "Sheriff Stone is eager to take him down."

"That must put his skivvies in a twist," Sue said, and Mia agreed Doug had been pointing the finger at Lilly, who was increasingly suspicious, to deflect blame.

"How long until Doug's out on the street?" Sue asked, but Mia wasn't sure. "He'll surely post bail and be out of jail shortly."

I followed Sue and Mia up some wooden steps to the pub, sticking my nose inside the open door. "Hello….." Sue said, "Anybody home?"

A darkly tanned woman stood behind the bar, arranging mugs and glasses. "Yes," she replied. "I'm here. The bar doesn't open for another hour."

"We're not here to drink," Sue replied, and Mia added, "We're here to talk to you about the bar fight last night."

"I've been talking to Deputy Livingston all morning," the bartender said. "I'm talked out about the fight."

"We only have a few questions," Mia said, as a pretty blonde cook emerged from the kitchen, visibly astonished. "Do you know who that is?" she asked the bartender as Mia dropped $20.00 on the table, and the bartender shrugged.

"She's Mia Baldwin," the blonde said. "The wealthiest woman in Sweetwater Springs."

"How about $100.00 for our thoughts, then?" the bartender asked, and Mia agreed, placing two $50.00 bills on the bar.

"Is that Daisy?" the cook asked, and I walked closer.

"Yes, can she come inside?" Sue asked, and the women agreed because the bar wasn't open for an hour.

I leaned against the cook, who rubbed my chest affectionately. "I've seen Daisy on the river," she said. "She's an exceptional kayaker."

The bartender ignored the small talk. "What can we do for you?" she asked. "You have ten minutes to ask anything you want about last night."

"Can you tell us what happened?" Sue asked. "Did you hear any arguments that may have precipitated that fight?"

"A woman named Lilly came to the bar," the bartender said, and Mia produced a photograph. "Is this Lilly?" she asked, and both women affirmed it was Lilly Wilson.

"She wanted money," the bartender said, and the cook added, "At first, Doug wouldn't give it to her."

"There was another man," the cook said. "I remember him because he insisted his burger was well done."

"Most of the regulars don't want their burgers burnt," the bartender explained. "This guy did."

"Is this the other man?" Sue asked, showing a photo of Andy Lemar. "He's a developer from Miami, but he wants an EcoPark in Sweetwater Springs."

"I'd like to buy the Brooklyn Bridge," the chef snorted.

"Yes, that's him," the cook said. "He probably thought he'd get food poisoning at Magic Manatee."

"He's more likely to get poisoned from fish in Miami," Sue said, and the women chuckled.

"He and the first guy, Doug, argued about money for an hour," the bartender said. "Then Lilly came, and wanted in on some money, too."

"Did they give it to her?" Sue asked, and both women affirmed that some money had changed hands with Lilly.

"I was too caught up behind the bar to notice," the bartender said. "It didn't seem to matter at the time. Money changes hands here, a lot."

"Interesting," Sue said, not delving into the matter. "How did the fight start?"

"It happened fast," the bartender said, and the cook agreed. "Our customers love a good fight."

"The farm boys were here by then," the cook said, and Mia asked, "Which farm boys?"

"They work at the farm where Doug Deleon put that guy who owed him money in a stall with a bull," the cook explained.

"I think the sheriff wanted to pin it on Doug," the bartender said, "It's pretty evident that the farmer had more of a grudge against Doug than anybody else."

"The farm boys came to the pub and discovered Doug was here," the cook announced. They pried open his trunk and took his baseball bat, but it didn't work out so well when he took it back from them. The bartender agreed, "It was self-defense, but the sheriff had to arrest him. Doug Deleon will get out of jail and be the premier loan shark and card shark in no time."

"After the first guy went down, the second farm boy didn't bother to fight," the cook said. "Everyone knows Doug's reputation as a street fighter."

"Did it take seven emergency cars to arrest Doug and take that guy to the hospital?" Sue asked.

"We've had more," the bartender said. "You should join us sometime for an evening."

Sue chuckled and ignored the invitation. "Thanks for your help," she said, and Mia passed each of them a $50.00 bill.

"Anytime," the bartender said, and the cook added, "Don't worry about dressing in your better blacks and leather for us. We appreciate your tipping policy."

The cook gave me one last rub on the chest before we left the pub. It was a lovely massage and it felt great. I hoped that a lovable dog softened her rough life. Both women enjoyed the drama of the hard-boiled pub, but who doesn't like the warm and the fuzzy?

The Boggs Brothers—Frankie and Butch awaited us outside the bar. "You need to be careful," they warned us. "Alligators are dangerous, and sharks are skilled. You're playing in infested waters!"

"We'll be careful," Mia replied, and Sue added, "Thanks for swimming beside us. I wasn't sure about you at first, but we know who our friends are."

I launched into the back seat of Sue's car, and we were off on our next adventure. Sue and Mia were confident that Lilly would take the money to Brian's Pawn Shop. No one wanted a ring back more than Lilly. Now, she had the ways and means to pursue it.

Chapter 34

Lilly at the Pawn Shop

Doug DeLeon was leaning against his dark green antique muscle car with the busted trunk when we arrived at Brian's Pawn Shop. His legs were crossed, and he looked annoyed. I hadn't seen Doug often, but his body language spoke volumes. He was perturbed.

I jumped out of Sue's car and leapt over to sniff at the man who had been arrested for the beating he did not commit. "Get away from me, Dog," he said without recognizing our past encounters.

"Her name is Daisy," Sue said. "You've met her before."

"I'm not impressed by fluffy dogs," Doug replied, as I sat beside him. "I'm a Shepherd man."

"Your Shepherd carries your suitcase," Sue recalled, and Mia asked if he had gotten a Get Out of Jail Free card.

"Aren't you the funny one?" Doug asked sarcastically. "Your sheriff has it in for me," he announced.

"Imagine that?" Sue said. "Where there is a card cheat or a beating, you can count on a Doug DeLeon."

"That guy stole a bat out of my car and tried to beat me with it," Doug said. "I retrieved it and returned the favor."

"It sounds like you've pissed off a few people in this town," Mia said. "What did you do to that one?"

"I've never met him before in my life," Doug said. "He was way too scrawny to mess with the likes of me."

"Why did he steal your bat?" Mia asked, and Doug replied that his fingerprints were on it, and it was unclear what they had intended to use it for—perhaps for future fights. The parking lot was full of spectators who would confirm my story. "Best fight they've seen all season," Doug said. "They'll look forward to the next one."

I was mainly fixated on Doug, but a parked car caught my attention. I stood on four legs to observe it from a distance. From here, I couldn't smell anything predictable, but I recognized something.

"Isn't that Lilly's car?" Sue asked, pointing toward the edge of the lot.

"Yes, I think so," Mia replied. "It has a lot of bumper stickers."

"Lilly is opinionated, like Sophie," Sue replied, and Mia said they'd get along as long as they agreed, but be prepared for a conflict if they didn't.

"She's been here for over an hour," Doug said, noting it was afternoon. "What do you think I'm doing here?"

"Guarding your precious antique sports car?" Mia asked, and Sue mentioned he might have done a better job last night.

"I'll give you Ladies credit for your guts over brains," Doug said, shaking his head. "Too bad about your clothes."

"You fight like a girl," Sue replied, and Doug said he didn't think so. "You're lucky not to know better," he said. "By the way, I admire your spunk."

"We heard you had an argument with Lilly and Andy in the pub last night," Mia said. "Do you mind telling us what it was about?"

"Money," Doug said. "Lilly wanted money to repurchase her ring."

"Did you give it to her?" Mia asked, and Doug said nothing.

"Can you blame her?" Sue asked, and Doug said it was between her and Bill. "I'm not married to him. The fact is, I'm not married to either one of them. From what I know, Lilly was too close to Russ for her good."

"Russ spent a lot of time at Lilly's house," Sue agreed, and Mia admitted it was too much time.

"Russ believed every woman was his to conquer—Shameka, Lilly, and even his own wife," Doug said. "It was only a matter of time before it all came back to haunt him."

I looked at the entrance to the parking lot when a two-tone truck rumbled in. By then, I recognized Frankie Boggs, the driver, and his brother, Butch. The big man, Frankie, was protective of his city, and the river, and increasingly, Sue and Mia.

"I'd think you'd get tired of gambling," Frankie told Doug. "You've been rigging games and betting on the wrong team since high school."

Doug agreed that he had experience, but in his case, it was beneficial. "I know my trades," he said.

"I'll bet you do," Butch said.

"You lost your college scholarship over those scams," Frankie said. "You should have learned something from your mistakes."

"Instead, you invested in a loan shark business, and linked up with a card shark to fund it," Butch said. "A card shark who owed you money."

Doug shrugged and changed the subject. "Some guy took a baseball bat out of my trunk last night and tried to beat me with it," he said. "How did he know where I was?"

"Somebody must have heard you arguing with people at the pub and tipped him off," Frankie said. "You have plenty of enemies in Sweetwater Springs."

"It seems to me one of them is the sheriff," Doug said. "He wants me gone."

Lilly walked out of the pawn shop while they talked. She paused at the top of the steps to admire the ring on her finger. Then, she looked across the parking lot where I stood and leaned against Sue. I could feel Sue's tension escalating as the players arrived at the pawn shop.

Lilly met everyone's gaze and walked towards us across the parking lot. "I got my ring," she announced, displaying the stone.

Sue and Mia complimented her success. "That's wonderful, Lilly," Sue said, and Lilly agreed it hadn't been easy, but it was worth it. "I love this ring," she said. "Now I can forgive Bill, and we can get on with our lives."

"I hope it's that easy," Mia said, expecting more hurdles.

Doug Deleon marched forward with his threats. "The sheriff is on my back and I'm sick of it," he bellowed. "Russ was coming on to you, and I knew it!"

"Russ didn't come on to me," Lilly retorted. "He helped me section off the turtle nests, so nobody tripped on their digs and the turtles could be safe."

Doug was sarcastic. "That sounds like Russ," he said. "A real empath."

"He liked turtles," Lilly droned.

"He liked you!" Doug thundered.

"He liked Shameka," Lilly replied, and Doug said briefly. "You were another notch on his belt."

"That's a lie!" Lilly hollered. "Russ and I were never intimate. We were teammates for a cause."

"Wake up, Lady!" Doug replied. "The only cause Russ had was to scam the innocent, the gullible, and the unsuspecting. You're it!"

Doug turned the key and revved the deep engine of his sports car. He shifted into first gear and spun the tires as he exited the parking lot. I could smell a burning smell, like one I had not sniffed before. It was the smell of rubber from a man taking his fury out on his car.

After Doug was gone, Sue and Mia spoke to the Boggs brothers before entering the pawn shop. First, they discussed the evidence they had shared with Sheriff Stone.

"We heard you yelling at Russ the morning he was murdered," Frankie told Lilly. "You're not off the hook."

"He means you're a suspect," Butch said. "You accused him of betraying his wife and told him not to come to your house again."

Lilly took a deep breath and sighed. "He was betraying her with Shameka."

"Some of your neighbors think Russ came to your home more often than he should have," Sue said.

Lilly was indignant. "Russ Johnson was never inside my house."

"How would anyone know?" Mia asked, and Sue already had a plan to figure it out. She needed to talk to Zeke before she could confirm her idea. "I'll let you know," Sue said.

Lilly and the Boggs brothers departed the pawn shop for their homes. "You're playing with rough stock, but we have your back," Frankie said as they drove away. "Be careful!"

I followed Sue and Mia to the pawn shop. Sue had me on a tight leash as we climbed the steps to the building. I had never been inside the pawn shop before. I suspected it was a more respectable establishment than a seedy bar.

Sue opened the squeaky door and stuck her head inside. "Hello," she said, seeing no one in the shop. "Is anyone here?"

A red-headed man stepped out from behind a draped-off cubicle. "I'll be with you in a moment," he said, and Sue asked if I could come inside with her and Mia.

"I guess so," the man replied. "I like dogs, and no one else is here at the moment."

"Thank you," Sue said, as the man disappeared behind the curtain.

We walked through a series of shelves with a variety of odds and ends and knick-knacks. I was careful not to wag my tail and knock something off a shelf. Finally, Sue and Mia surveyed the glass cases containing the jewelry.

"Lilly had the most beautiful ring of all," Sue said, while they looked.

"It was lovely," Mia agreed.

"No wonder she wanted to repurchase it," Sue said, and Mia mentioned it was harder than ever to believe he sold it.

"I don't know much about gambling addiction," Sue said, "but I hope Bill can conquer it."

In time, the red-headed man returned from behind the curtain. "I'm Brian," he said. "I'm the owner of this shop."

Sue and Mia introduced themselves to him on his return.

"I've heard of you," he said. "Sheriff Stone said I could expect to see you."

"I'm glad to hear that," Mia said. "He's got a lot on his plate with solving this murder. We were hoping we could help him."

"What can I do for you?" Brian asked.

"Did Lilly Wilson repurchase her wedding ring from you just now?" Sue asked, and the man affirmed it. "It was a beautiful ring," he said. "She had a hard time coming up with the cash, or she would have gotten it sooner."

"Can we have a look at the money Lilly used to buy the ring?" Mia asked, and the man produced a stack of twenties that weren't marked.

She passed it back to him. "Can we see more?" she asked, and he produced a stack of hundreds that weren't marked.

Finally, they hit the jackpot on the third stack of bills. "This is what we're looking for," Sue exclaimed. "We need to call Sheriff Stone."

"He'll be here shortly to retrieve them." Mia added, "Don't worry. He'll replace them with normal money."

"Normal money?" the owner asked, and Mia said, he'd know more later.

We waited for the sheriff to arrive at the pawn shop before leaving for home. Sue and Mia didn't want any possible interference with the plan for the sheriff to confiscate the marked bills, which was proceeding nicely. Tomorrow, we will visit Zeke and Loretta. It was easier to prove some things than others. I could smell a difference in dogs, but Zeke was more likely to observe their fur color and interpret test results.

Chapter 35
Zeke and Lilly

The following morning, Toby was exceptionally loving with Sue. He jumped into her lap on the recliner while she drank her coffee, purring loudly, while he rubbed his face on her chin. Sue rubbed faces with him before he rested comfortably in her lap. He didn't want to be petted. He just wanted to be there with her.

When Toby became affectionate, it didn't leave much time for me. I lay on the couch, basking in the love and listening to his purr. You could have heard him down the hallway and probably into the bedroom. It was a moment that Sue didn't want to interrupt.

I spent a lot of time visiting neighbors and exploring with Sue, so I wasn't jealous of Toby. At times, I wished he'd come with us, but that was never going to happen. He loved his home life and had no interest in travel. He had a nice travel crate, but when Sue opened it, he scurried down the hall to avoid it.

Eventually, Sue stopped trying to make him a traveling cat. Today, we will be visiting Loretta and Zeke, who would have welcomed him, but he didn't want to leave his comfortable nest. Honestly, Toby didn't want to leave the porch, much less explore the joys and nuances of life on the road with family and good friends.

For me, Loretta's yard was one of the best places ever. It was hard to choose between her big yard and Luke's riverfront yard as my favorite. Still, I loved seeing my sister and my two cousins who lived with Loretta and Zeke. They were more playful than Artemis, especially mischievous Luna.

Today, we will watch the chickens explore their new coop, on the other side of the dog fence. First, we will run races in the yard, then settle into our new pastime. I am a fan of bird-watching, but until the chickens arrived, I had only seen wild birds. Water birds are much taller than chickens, while song birds are smaller.

I was thinking about birds just before I closed my eyes when Lilly called. "Hi Lilly," Sue said, "What's up?"

"I've been thinking about Zeke's offer to be my attorney," Lilly said. "I need his advice."

Sue did not mention that she needed Zeke's advice more than ever now that she had spent marked money to repurchase her ring at Brian's pawn shop. "Mia and I will be going to Loretta's house today," she said. "I'll be happy to relay a message to Zeke."

"Doug DeLeon is trying to pin Russ Johnson's murder on me," Lilly said. "I didn't kill him."

"Has the sheriff been by to talk to you again?" Sue asked, recalling that he had picked up the crossbow with a search warrant.

"No, but he will be back," Lilly said. "He has evidence against me. Doug insists Russ was making a move on me, and the neighbors know how often he came to my house."

"Doug DeLeon is a suspect," Sue reminded her. "His word doesn't mean much to Sheriff Stone."

"Probably not," Lilly replied. "But the Boggs Brothers heard me yelling at Russ the morning he was murdered," she added. "It didn't sound good."

"True," Sue said. "But, you weren't the only one to lose your temper with Russ."

"I was the only one to yell at him just before he was killed," Lilly said. "The money was missing and I wanted it to repurchase my ring."

"You had a clear motive to kill Russ," Sue agreed. "But, I think we can help you."

"I hope so," Lilly said. "I'm getting worried. I shouldn't have cared so much about that ring."

"Nobody blames you for that," Sue said. "It wasn't the first time Bill sold your jewelry without your consent to gamble."

"Are you sure you can help me?" Lilly asked, and Sue reassured her that Zeke was the best attorney around. "He's especially good with dog evidence," she said.

"Do I have dog evidence?" Lilly asked, and Sue explained she had been doing some experiments with dog fur herself and had taken the vacuum bag out of her garbage can before the garbage service picked it up.

Lilly was stunned. "You scrounged through my garbage?" she asked, and Sue affirmed. "I had an instinct it may come in handy."

"How so?" Lilly asked.

"When I was at your house the other day, I noticed you wiped off your couch with your hand before you ran the vacuum cleaner," Sue said. "The fur went on the floor."

"So…."

"Was Russ Johnson ever inside your house?" Sue asked, and Lilly repeated, "Never. Russ and I worked together outside, but he never came indoors."

"Russ Johnson had been visiting your house for a week before you ran that vacuum," Sue said. "He was there the day he was murdered."

"Yes," Lilly agreed.

"Russ had been spending weekends with Shameka," Sue explained. "She has a dog named Cleo, a Yellow Labrador who sheds a lot."

"And…"

"If Russ came inside your house, surely some of Cleo's fur would have been on his clothes. It would have come off on your furniture, and you would have wiped it to the floor before you vacuumed."

"What does that mean?" Lilly asked, and Sue explained that Cleo's fur would have been mixed with Sargie's fur in the vacuum bag. "I'm taking the vacuum bag to Zeke's with me this afternoon," she added. "Cleo's fur is yellow, and Sargie's fur is white or black," she said. "If there's no yellow fur in the bag, it helps to show Russ was never inside your house."

"It's better than my word against my neighbor's observations," Lilly said, and Sue agreed. "It helps."

Toby jumped out of Sue's lap and scooted towards the bedroom when Mia arrived. He would have stayed for Mia, but didn't know it was her when the bell rang. "Come in, Mia," Sue said. "Are you ready to go to Loretta's house?"

"You betcha," Mia replied, and Sue explained that Lilly had agreed to ask Zeke for advice.

"She needs it," Mia said, noting that he already knew that she bought the ring with marked money. "He has probable cause for another search warrant."

"Lilly insists Russ was never inside her house," Sue said. "I want to believe her, but Doug and her neighbors suggest otherwise. I'm taking the vacuum bag to ponder the contents with Zeke and Loretta."

I jumped into Sue's car for the cross-country drive to Loretta's farm. When we arrived, I raced towards the house, full speed ahead, to join my four-legged friends. It was exciting to play with my besties. Artemis was a joy, but the trio of Doodles stole my heart.

Sue opened the back door for the dog races, which ended at the fence line, across from the chicken coop. We were watching the chickens when Sue and Mia joined Zeke and Loretta at the coop. "We have another rooster," Loretta said, as a robust black bird stood atop the coop and crowed to his heart's content.

"We were hoping for one rooster, not two," Zeke said.

"This one seems to control the hen house," Loretta said of the black rooster. "The other black and white rooster never fully developed his voice, and cackled a bit. Now he gave up trying to learn to crow."

"That could be good," Sue said. "If he doesn't challenge the bigger black rooster, they may not fight for control."

"They may get along," Loretta agreed, watching the bird, which looked like a statue atop the henhouse. "How are the fights at Sweetwater Springs?" she asked, and Sue described the man with the broken leg at Magic Manatee.

"There are some unresolved conflicts," Mia said. "Lilly repurchased her ring with marked money, but she doesn't know it yet."

"Sheriff Stone is aware of it," Sue added. "We followed her to Brian's Pawn Shop and checked the money ourselves."

"Where did Lilly get the marked money?" Zeke asked, and Sue said that was the sixty-million-dollar question. "She had been arguing with Andy and Doug at the pub. The staff didn't witness the money change hands, and the pub is a local hangout for brawlers, who enjoy watching the fights."

"It's not exactly a family place," Mia said. "Sue had some black shirts and leather garb from her motorcycle days, so we tried to fit in."

"Did it work?" Zeke asked, and Mia suggested that the fifty-dollar bills she paid for information were more impressive.

"Lilly is worried the evidence is stacking up against her," Sue said. "She asked for your advice as her attorney."

Zeke suggested they go inside, where it was cooler, to reflect on the evidence. My cousins and I followed them. Three of us lay on the tile floor near the dining table. Stevie sat beside Sue with her head on Sue's thigh, enjoying attention, like Toby.

"Sheriff Stone will get a search warrant for DNA evidence to determine whether or not Russ Johnson may have been inside her house, if the evidence keeps mounting," Zeke said. "The forensics team will look for skin cells and body fluids to test for DNA."

"Lilly swears he never went inside her house," Sue said, and Zeke suggested proof. "The forensics team will thoroughly search the house," he said. "Unfortunately, Lilly is a prime suspect."

"Meanwhile, I have a vacuum bag full of dog fur," Sue said, producing the scavenged bag. "We can not test for DNA from shed fur, but we can observe the color of the hair."

"Cleo has yellow fur," Mia explained.

"Sargie's fur is black and white," Sue said.

"If Russ was inside Lilly's house, he should have carried some of Cleo's fur with him, left it behind on the furniture, and the bag would contain yellow fur too."

The group thoroughly searched through the contents. The vacuum bag was filled with Sargie's white and black shed hairs, none of which had a root bulb, which could be a source of DNA. There wasn't a single, solitary yellow hair in the bunch.

"There is no sign of Cleo's fur in this vacuum bag," Sue said. "It's a start."

Zeke replied, "We need to visit Shameka's house to see if Russ Johnson left any clothes behind. We can check for Cleo's fur on his clothes."

"The sheriff probably took them," Zeke said, but no one knew for sure.

Tomorrow we will visit Shameka, who remains a suspect. I looked forward to seeing the museum manager, who was becoming a friend. I jumped into the back seat for the drive back home for an evening with Toby and Sue before our next adventures.

Chapter 36

Shameka and Lilly

The following morning, I was particularly hungry. This doesn't happen to me often, but occasionally I feel the urge to indulge in extra food. Most mornings, I barely finish my morning meal, which Sue leaves available to me at all times. According to Sue, I am a free-choice eater, unlike my cousins, who can't control their appetites.

I went outside to do my morning duty and barked for Sue to let me back inside the house for breakfast. It wasn't ready yet. Looking through the window, I could see Toby on the countertop, rubbing heads with Sue, which was part of the early morning ritual before eating. I was ahead of schedule, but hunger can do that to you.

Toby was hungry for love, and I was hungry for breakfast. We had a big day ahead of us. I lapped up a bowl of water while Sue added two cups of kibble to my bowl. When my belly was full, I lay on the floor. Toby followed Sue around the house, getting stuck in her closet while she repeatedly changed her attire.

Zeke and Loretta arrived shortly after Sue finished getting dressed. They let themselves in, and Loretta called out to Sue. "Hi, Mom," she said. "We're here."

"I'll be right there," Sue replied, departing the bedroom to greet them.

"I like your outfit," Loretta said, referring to the pink camp shirt paired with a tank and white shorts.

Loretta was wearing a floral skirt with a matching tank. "I like yours, too," Sue replied. "I'm ready for a day of casual fashion over black grub or gym clothes."

"You and Mia dressed the parts for the pub," Loretta said, of the motorcycle garb.

"How did you know Lilly had been at Magic Manatee Pub?" Zeke asked. Sue explained that the mayor had called Thomas, but he wasn't home, so he relayed the message about the bar fight to Mia instead. "Mia told me about Doug breaking the farmer's leg with his own stolen and recovered baseball bat. We went to the pub to investigate and found out Lilly had been arguing with Doug and Andy about money."

"Interesting," Zeke said. "After that, you went to the pawn shop and discovered the marked money from the poker game Lilly paid for her ring?"

"That sums it up," Sue replied. "Neither Lilly nor Shameka knows about the marked money."

"Of course," Zeke said. "I'm aware of that."

"Sheriff Stone recovered the money after we left the pawn shop."

"He's been busy," Zeke said. "I hope he's keeping up with it," Loretta added, and Sue said he was better than he used to be, but could use some help."That's what we're here for."

We loaded into Loretta's truck, with Sue and me in the backseat. I gazed out the window during the short drive to Shameka's house on Cypress Street. This was our first visit to the place, as we had usually met Shameka at the museum. When we arrived, Mia and her daughter Sarah were already there.

"What a cute house," Loretta said of the tiny white wooden home with a front porch and red trim. "It looks like it's been restored from the fifties."

"Shameka's doing a nice job of maintaining it," Sue agreed. "The lawn is mowed and the house is freshly painted."

"There she is," Zeke said, as Shameka came out of the house and waved. "Come in," she called from the porch. "I have coffee, dog biscuits, and donuts inside."

I jumped out of the truck and trotted to the front door, a short distance away. Cleo was waiting to greet us. I had not spent much time with Cleo, as she had never joined us for walks at the Green Cove. This was a new experience and hopefully the start of a friendship for future adventures.

Cleo was a happy dog with a fluffy tail that wagged as much as she wiggled. She had a hard time keeping still. I wondered how she managed on a kayak with so much energy. Even so, it didn't take more than one or two hops in the cold river to relax.

"I love your house," Loretta said. "What a comfortable place to live!"

"Now that I'm a single woman, it feels different without Russ around, but it's growing on me," Shameka replied. "It's a good size for me."

"Did Russ help you with the work?" Zeke asked, and Shameka mentioned he mowed. "I've never had to mow before," she said, and Zeke offered to help her start the mower if she needed it.

Sarah went to the kitchen to retrieve the coffee pot, while Mia passed around the donuts that she and Sue had given up. "You don't know what you're missing," Sarah said, and Loretta agreed that Sweetwater Springs had the best donut makers.

"You seem like you're adjusting to single life," Loretta said. "Breaking up is hard to do, but you move on."

Everyone agreed that Shameka had a lot going for her. "I should have listened to you when you warned me about Russ," she said. "I wasn't ready to hear it."

"You'll know better next time," Mia replied. "Russ was a bad boyfriend, but you'll find the right person."

Zeke pulled a mass of yellow fur off the couch and rolled it between his fingers. "Has the sheriff contacted you lately?" he asked.

Shameka apologized for the yellow fur, which was also scattered in pieces on the dark wooden floor. "I haven't seen him for two days," Shameka replied. "He must have other suspects on his mind."

"For good reason," Zeke said.

"I'm sorry about Cleo's fur," Shameka reiterated. "She's in a massive molt right now."

"Don't be sorry," Sue said. "Cleo's fur is something we need to talk to you about."

Shameka frowned. "What about Cleo's fur?" she asked, and Sue described the contents of Lilly's vacuum cleaner bag, which contained only Sargie's fur.

"I like Sargie," Shameka said. "He's weird, but I like him."

Sue smiled. "His bark is creaky, but it's allowed. Sargie is an old man."

"I didn't mean to judge," Shameka said. "He's different. I'd love to walk with Cleo, Daisy, and Sargie on the Green Cove property someday."

"I hope that can be arranged," Zeke said.

"Lilly is on Sheriff Stone's short list," Sue added, "With good reason."

"Lilly asked me to advise her as her attorney," Zeke explained.

Shameka was surprised Lilly thought she needed an attorney. "Has Lilly been arrested?" she asked.

Zeke said, "No, but you don't have to be arrested to hire an attorney."

Cleo and I chomped dog biscuits while they talked. I imagined she'd be a good running partner at Luke's big yard or Loretta's farm. I wanted to get to know her better, but that could come later. For now, Zeke had work to do.

Zeke observed the furniture and floor in the living room. "Cleo sheds a lot," he said bluntly. "Do you have any of Russ Johnson's clothing left from the weekends he spent here?"

"I found a pair of his shorts in the dirty clothes hamper, just today," Shameka said. "I also found a dirty T-shirt and a bathing suit under the bed in the guest room."

"Is it black?"Sue teased, but Shameka didn't catch her drift, and Sue didn't explain. "I'm sorry. It's a bad joke," she said.

Shameka retrieved the articles of clothing, which were covered in Cleo's yellow fur, with traces of Sargie's fur, as expected. "I experimented with fur at my house," Sue said. "Clothing can be a vehicle to move fur from one place to another."

"You mentioned you didn't find any of Cleo's fur in the vacuum cleaner bag," Shameka said, and Sue agreed it suggested, but did not prove, that Russ was not inside Lilly's house.

"It's a start," Mia said.

"Sheriff Stone can get a warrant to search Lilly's house, and forensics will perform more specific tests if he needs them," Zeke said.

"You should hold onto Russ Johnson's clothes," Mia said. "He may want them."

"Thank you so much for talking to us," Sue continued. "Let us know if there's anything we can do to help you."

"Please give my best to Lilly," Shameka said as we departed her house for our next destination. Mia replied, we'd keep in touch.

I hopped into the back seat of Loretta's truck for the drive to Lilly's house. I gazed out the rear window while Mia followed behind in her car. I was looking at Mia, but thinking about Cleo and the fun we could have. By the time we reached Sargie's house, she was still on my mind.

"Please come in!" Lilly said when Loretta and Mia parked in her driveway. "I've been expecting you."

We followed her into the waterfront fixer-upper, where she offered chairs and iced tea for the two-leggers. I was left with Sargie, who spent all of his time and effort standing.

"It's good to see you, Lilly," Zeke said. "This has been quite a ride for you."

"You can say that again," Lilly replied. "Thank you for offering to represent me."

"I'll represent you if Sheriff Stone arrests you," Zeke said. "For now, I'll advise you."

"Do you think I'll be arrested?" Lilly asked nervously.

No one mentioned she had spent marked money, which Lilly knew nothing about, to repurchase her ring. "The good news is that the only fur in your vacuum bag belonged to Sargie," Sue said.

"We just came from Shameka's house," Mia explained. "Russ Johnson left some clothes behind, and they were covered in Cleo's yellow fur—enough to come off on your furniture."

"It's a primitive observation compared to the DNA tests Sheriff Livingston will order from forensics, if he has probable cause for a warrant," Zeke added. "He'll test for Johnson's skin cells and body fluids."

"Russ Johnson was never inside my house!" Lilly insisted, and Zeke said it was easy to say and harder to prove. "Do you believe me?' she asked, and Zeke explained that it mattered more that a jury believed her if the case went to court.

Something drew my attention to Lilly's bathroom. I'm not sure what it was—a smell? I trotted off to the master bath, leaving Sargie standing by the fireplace, to see what I could see. Something unusual was in the trash basket.

I grabbed the cigar-shaped stick between my teeth and trotted back to the living room. "Daisy….What do you have?" Sue asked, pulling the object from my mouth.

"It's a pregnancy test!" she announced, handing the object to Zeke, who announced it was positive. "You're pregnant," Mia said, and no one offered congratulations, as seemed to be the usual course in such matters.

"Wow!" Sue said, with jaw agape. "How far along?"

Lilly replied I'm eight weeks late, and Zeke suggested that she could have a paternity test. "I know who the father is," Lilly said. "He needs to believe it."

It was an interesting turn of events with news to follow. Later, we would visit Bill, who is still living at Luke's house. I looked forward to a romp with Artemis, like always. I wasn't sure where this was going for Lilly and Bill, but it would be a good day for me.

Chapter 37

Bill at Luke's House

"I knew that woman was no good!" Sophie shrieked after Sue drove through the gate to Luke's estate and parked in front of the house.

"What are you talking about?" Sue asked, frowning at Luke's mother, as she stepped out of the car. "What woman?"

"Do you think I don't hear what's going on in this town?" Sophie thundered. "I may be an old homebody, but people still talk to me."

"Sophie, you're one of the wisest people I know," Sue said, trying to hug her before she released me to run with Artemis, but Sophie pushed her away.

Mia scowled at Sophie as she stepped out of the car. "We need to know what you heard," she said, and Sophie hurled into a rant about Lilly.

"I heard that Russ was pursuing Lilly," Sophie said. "It all makes sense now. The whole kit and caboodle. Lilly was having an affair with Russ Johnson while he was dating Shameka and married to his wife. He kayaked to her house and romanced her, while pretending to care about turtles."

"Where did you hear this?" Zeke asked, and Sophie mentioned the Boggs brothers. "They said all the neighbors know about it, too."

"How would the neighbors know what went on between Lilly and Russ?" Sue asked. "Were they there, too?"

"Listen to me, Young Lady," Sophie said, although Sue was nearly a senior citizen. "It doesn't take Einstein to figure this out."

I was happy for a chance to fly the coop and race around the yard with Artemis, who wagged his tail when he saw me. I am not a nervous dog, but Sophie made me anxious when she was loud. Her voice was more audible than usual, even for Sophie. I wasn't sure how Artemis managed her rants, but he seemed thrilled to run the big yard, too.

When we returned, Sophie was still screeching. "The Boggs brothers heard Lilly arguing with Russ about being married that morning, and then he was killed. They said Lilly was at the pub asking for money that night Doug DeLeon beat up that farmer. They said she got the money and took it to Brian's Pawn Shop to repurchase her ring."

"Circumstantial," Sue said. "You might have missed something."

"Missed something?" Sophie spat. "What am I missing?"

"For one thing, why would Lilly need to get the money from Doug DeLeon if she killed Russ and took the briefcase with Russ Johnson's winnings from the poker match in it?"

"Maybe Lilly left the briefcase behind," Sophie retorted. "Maybe she didn't see it."

"I'll beg your pardon, but the briefcase was in his hand," Sue said. "Whoever killed Russ couldn't miss it."

"How do you know Lilly got money from Doug DeLeon?" Mia asked, and Sophie replied, "Everyone knows it. The bartender told the Boggs brothers that she'd overheard Lilly and Doug arguing about money before he got arrested for beating up that farmer in the parking lot of the pub."

"You should let the experts handle the investigation," Zeke suggested. "It's more complicated than you know."

"The Boggs Brothers aren't the sheriff," Mia added, and Sophie reminded her it was Homer Stone's second homicide investigation since Sweetwater Springs had had minor crime before the recent murder.

"He's improving at his job," Sue said. "He has experienced his first murder investigation. He's less likely to rush into things than he used to be."

"He'll do better at this investigation," Zeke said. "I'm sure of it."

Artemis and I followed our two-legged friends indoors for refreshments. It didn't take long to get thirsty in the current heat wave. A romp around the yard was nearly crippling, compared to the milder spring weather just weeks ago. It was going to be a hot summer.

Sophie provided us with two bowls of ice water. Artemis recognized the ice as a perk of our friendship. After Sue suggested it, he seemed to enjoy the cubes as much as I did.

"Is Bill here?" Sue asked while we crunched our cubes. "We'd like to talk to him."

Sophie guided them to seats in the sunroom while she continued to talk. "Yes, I'll tell him you're here."

"Great, we appreciate it," Sue said.

"He's in Luke's shed working on his new hobby," Sophie said, walking toward the doorway.

Sue shrugged after she left. "I'm glad Bill is keeping busy," Sue said, then added, "Luke won't like this. He doesn't like anyone working in his shed."

"I wouldn't want my brother messing with my tools," Zeke chuckled. "I may be just a newbie at building chicken coops with Chris, but every man wants to know where his tools are."

As they talked, Bill entered the sunroom to join them. "I'm glad you're here," he said, asking his mother for iced tea for a moment alone with his guests. "Mother insists Lilly killed Russ, and I'm sick of listening to her rants."

"We heard," Sue said. "We're here to help you."

Zeke did not mention that he had taken Lilly's case as her attorney. "We have some questions," he said, and Bill replied to fire away. "I'm going to need some honest answers in case this goes to court."

"You're that attorney who can't play poker," Bill said, studying his face. "I remember you."

Zeke chuckled. "I'm learning," he said. "Loretta thinks I should stick with chicken coops."

"I thought it was strange you were at the poker game," Bill said, and Zeke replied he had hoped to be discreet, but it must have been obvious.

Bill added, "I thought it was strange that Giovanni was at the game, too. Everyone knows his reputation."

Zeke avoided the implication. "Did Sargie have a favorite?" he asked.

Bill was surprised. "You're asking me about my dog?" he asked.

"We'll explain later," Zeke said. "Just answer the questions."

"Sargie loved both of us," Bill said. "He didn't have a favorite."

"Did he like strangers?" Zeke asked.

"Not especially. He was protective."

"What did he do if a stranger came to your house?" Zeke asked.

"He barked, an awkward woof now that he's older," Bill replied. "Sargie was an alarm dog. He was never aggressive towards anyone."

"That's the best kind of guard dog," Zeke said. "Did you notice he never barked at Russ Johnson?" he asked.

"Come to think of it, I never heard him bark at Russ," Bill said. "I hope this doesn't mean you're agreeing with my mother about Lilly."

"No judgment," Zeke replied. "Just a few questions to clear things up."

Artemis and I raised our heads as Sophie returned to the sunroom with dog biscuits. We sat politely at her feet, waiting for our treats. I was happy she had calmed down from her previous outburst and hoped it would continue. I chomped my biscuit into bits while she poured tea for the two-legged guests.

"How long have you been a gambler?" Zeke asked, and Bill replied, "Long enough to know better."

"Did Lilly ever ask you to stop gambling?" Zeke continued.

"Yes, many times," Bill said, after taking a swig of iced tea. "I quit counting."

"Did Lilly ever threaten to leave you if you didn't stop gambling?" Zeke asked.

"Yes," Bill replied softly, setting the glass on the counter. "She threatened to leave me."

"What did you think would happen when you lost the money for Lilly's ring at the poker game?" Zeke asked, searching his face.

Bill whispered. "I thought she'd leave me."

"For how long?" Zeke asked.

Bill replied, "I was afraid it might be forever this time."

"This time?" Zeke asked. "Has Lilly left you for gambling before?"

"Yes, Lilly left me twice before we returned to Sweetwater Springs," Bill said. "It was excruciating for me while she was gone."

"You must have wanted to buy Lilly that ring back," Zeke said, glancing at Sophie and then boring into Bill's eyes. "I imagine losing that money has been eating at you real good."

"Do you think I killed Russ Johnson?" Bill asked, and no one answered.

Finally, Sophie rose from her chair to defend her least favorite son. "What do you mean Bill killed Russ Johnson?" she asked, in a huff, and Zeke suggested he didn't say that. "I'm suggesting Bill had motive, means, and opportunity to kill Russ," he said.

"He wanted money to repurchase Lilly's ring, Russ was killed with an arrow from Bill's crossbow, and Bill found the body after the murder."

"Lilly was having an affair with Russ Johnson," Sophie spat.

"If so, that doesn't improve Bill's case," Zeke said. "It wouldn't be hard to convince a jury that Bill killed Russ Johnson with the evidence we already have."

"I hope there's a big piece missing," Sophie said, and Zeke assured her they were looking into it with all their might.

"Do you think I killed Russ Johnson?" Bill asked, and Zeke replied, "No, we don't think you killed him."

"Do you think you know who killed him?" Bill asked, and Zeke didn't answer.

Sue replied, "Yes, we think we know who killed Russ Johnson."

"I hope it's not my wife," Bill said. "Not Lilly. I'd never forgive myself for what I've put her through."

Artemis and I were lying on his enormous, comfy dog bed when we noticed a change of tone. Sophie was no longer sure of her false convictions. It made me happy that she would stop yelling, as she did so often.

"Maybe I need to rethink this," Sophie said, and everyone agreed it was better not to jump to conclusions. "We're getting close to figuring it out," Sue said, and Mia suggested they needed the evidence to prove it.

"What are you making in Luke's shed?" Sue asked Bill.

"Some flower pots for under the window sills of our fixer-upper," Bill said. "I can't wait to move back home again if Lilly will have me."

"Oh, I think she will," Sue said, and Mia agreed. "Lilly's more worried that you won't have her back," she said.

"We'll keep in touch," Sue said, as they bid Sophie and Bill farewell.

I hopped into the back seat of Sue's car for a ride back to Lilly's house. They could revisit Lilly with new hope for the future. I felt better for her and Sargie already.

Chapter 38
Lilly's House for Advice

When we arrived at Lilly's house, I saw Sargie standing next to Lilly down by the waterfront. I trotted down the long slope of sparse grass towards the cove with Sue and her friends. Unlike the lush feel of the Radcliffes' family property that made me want to lie down and roll, I could feel patches of sand between my toes at Sargie's house. According to Sue, the yard, like everything else about Bill and Lilly's property, needed tender loving care.

I planned to be careful not to bump into Sargie, who wasn't very steady on his feet in his senior years. He watched us closely, mouth open, as it often was, as he stood on the rickety dock. I wondered if he could see well enough to recognize who we were, but surely he would have recognized me. If nothing else, he could smell me at a distance.

By now, Sargie knew Sue and Mia well enough not to bark his awkward woof that sounded an alarm for strangers. I wasn't sure if he would bark at Zeke, who had been inside his house for the first time earlier today. It hadn't been so long ago that Sargie would have forgotten Zeke, and it had been a friendly visit. Still, one had to wonder—how long did a dog consider someone a stranger?

As it turned out, everyone walked onto the dock without a peep from Sargie. His enormous, teetering body was glued to Lilly's leg. I suspected it helped him with balance, but he was affectionate with his family, like I was. Bill's prolonged absence couldn't be easy for anyone.

Lilly greeted her friends, then gazed at her wedding ring and back again before she spoke. "If my husband thinks I slept with Russ Johnson, my marriage is over," she said. "I've been a fool to trust that womanizer."

Sue reminded her, "You didn't have an affair with Russ."

"How do you know?" Lilly asked.

"I believe you," Sue replied, and Mia said, "Sometimes a healthy relationship is about trust as much as love."

"I need to prove I didn't have an affair with Russ," Lilly replied. "How am I supposed to prove it?"

"That can be tough," Zeke said. "As I told you before, if Sheriff Stone has probable cause to search your house, he will have the forensics team search for DNA evidence of Russ Johnson's body fluids and cells."

"The sheriff is coming to talk to me later today," Lilly said. "He says he has more evidence against me."

Zeke replied, "I'll be here to represent you."

"I wish that man had never helped me with those turtles," Lilly said. "I should have known he had other things on his mind."

"Did he flirt with you?" Mia asked, and Lilly replied, "No, he didn't flirt. We talked about turtles being on the property, making it less desirable for developers, like Andy Lemar, to buy it."

Mia replied that the turtles had been a deterrent for Thomas to purchase the land, but not everyone would be deterred by them.

"Did you talk about anything else?" Zeke asked.

"Russ insisted the turtle nests lowered the property value," Lilly said.

"Maybe Russ had an ulterior motive for one of his friends to purchase it," Mia suggested, and Zeke agreed that the turtles could be relocated. "It lowered the price of the land for a golf course, development, or a steakhouse."

"What about an EcoLodge?" Lilly asked because no one believed the scammers wanted it anymore. Her friends shook their heads and scowled at the preposterous thought.

Lilly glanced at her illustrious ring once again, and then at her watch. "It's lunchtime," she said. "You've been busy all morning. How about we go back up to the house and I'll make us some sandwiches?"

Sargie trudged up the slope, stopping every so often to rest along the journey. The yard seemed bigger with Sargie in it. It was a much bigger space for a romp in the yard than my tiny enclosure, but not as big as the yard Luke had for Artemis, but big enough for a four-legged playdate. With a fence, it could be a remarkable dog park for Cleo, Artemis, and me to run and play.

Sargie would enjoy watching us from a distance. It would take him outside, as he had loved to do during his youth. Eventually, Lilly could make friends with the neighbors, and they could enjoy it, too. It had been a rough start for Lilly and Bill, but things could improve.

"Would you prefer turkey and cheese or tuna fish sandwiches?" Mia asked. Everyone agreed on the turkey, and they assembled the toppings.

Zeke sliced tomatoes while Mia and Sue gathered spinach, cucumbers, and black olives. "I rarely do this with Sophie," Sue said, "It's fun to help."

"Sophie must be furious with me," Lilly said, and Sue admitted her mother-in-law's first thoughts hadn't been the best. "She's coming around," she replied.

"What changed her mind?" Lilly asked.

Mia said, "Zeke pointed out that Bill had motive, as you did, to want money to repurchase your ring, it was his crossbow and arrow, and he found the body."

"I left him with Sophie and told him not to come home until he got my ring," Lilly admitted.

"Yes, you did," Sue replied.

"I've never met a more opinionated woman in my life!" Lilly continued. "Nothing is good enough for her unless she does it herself. If I did anything, she'd redo it."

"A very good reason to let her do it, in the first place," Mia said. "Sophie appreciates her work in the kitchen."

"I see it as a break for me," Sue replied. "If Sophie enjoys cooking, it's her space."

"I feel guilty not helping her," Lilly said. "She's 94 years old."

"She's proud of being able to do it at her age," Mia reminded her. "Let her have her kitchen glory."

"She's proud to be her age," Sue added. "Sometimes it seems like bad behavior when she screeches at us, but she's a pillar for all of us."

Sargie stood by the table to avoid lying down, as getting up hurt. I hadn't spent much time thinking about old age and its many variables, but he was a pillar for me, too. He was fortunate to have someone care so much about him during his golden years. I was kind and gentle with Sargie and Redman, but I promised myself to appreciate them more.

I had a bad habit of sulking—to myself—when Sue mentioned visiting the older dogs. I was never self-pitying, as dogs don't feel that way about themselves. I considered it one of the significant characteristics that dogs had over people. Life was better without pity, but I wasn't looking forward to seeing them, either. I could do better.

Sue passed a dog biscuit to Sargie and me when we sat at the table. "This is a good sandwich," she said after the first bite.

"I love that it's part sandwich and part salad," Mia added, and everyone thought of Jessie, who was working on the healthy cooking cookbook. "I enjoyed meeting them," Lilly said, and Zeke agreed he couldn't build a chicken coop or play poker without Chris.

"He's good at building fences, too," Sue said. "You might want to fence your backyard someday."

"Chris enjoys a project that brings people together," Zeke said. "If you ever want to make a dog park out of your yard, he'll be here for you."

"Sargie doesn't wander much anymore," Lilly said. Zeke replied, "Neither does Redman, but he still loves to watch the younger dogs play."

I watched Sargie joyfully chew his biscuit while Sue and her friends enjoyed their sandwiches. After he swallowed the last bite of his sandwich, Zeke asked, "When is the sheriff coming?"

"Soon," Lilly replied. "He's probably on his way."

"Before he gets here, there's something I'd like to clear up," Zeke continued. "I need to know exactly what happened at Magic Manatee Pub when you got into that argument about the money with Doug DeLeon."

Lilly was perplexed, yet stern. "I didn't argue with Doug DeLeon about money," she said. "Doug DeLeon and Andy Lemar were arguing about money when I got to the pub."

Sue and Mia locked eyes and frowned. "What were they saying?" Zeke asked.

"Doug insisted Russ owed him money, and he didn't pay up," Lilly said.

"Money for what?" Zeke asked, and Lilly said she had no idea.

Sue recalled that Doug had insisted Russ owed him $100,000.00 when she first met them at Cat Tails Pub. "It was a public argument," she said. "Doug wanted the money and threatened Russ to pay up."

Zeke turned the subject back to the argument at Magic Manatee Pub. "What were Doug and Andy saying about money?" he asked.

"Doug insisted that Andy Lemar could repay the $100,000.00 since Russ was dead."

"Why would Andy repay the money to Doug?" Zeke asked. Lilly replied, "I have no idea."

Mia recalled the three men had known each other for about ten years, although not everyone admitted it. "I have a photograph," she said, producing the image from her phone and showing it to Lilly.

"They've been playing cards for a long time," Lilly declared.

"Maybe," Zeke replied. "Or maybe they've been up to some other scam, and the card games were a way to pay off the debt."

"Interesting thoughts," Sue said. "What is the other scam?"

"I don't know," Zeke said, "But I intend to find out."

Zeke looked at Lilly to pose the ultimate question. "Did Doug DeLeon give you the money to repurchase your ring from the pawn shop?" he asked.

"No, he did not," Lilly replied. "According to Doug, he didn't have the money. I got the money from Andy Lemar."

"Interesting," he said. "I have a feeling we'll solve this case shortly after the week is over."

When Sheriff Stone arrived at Lilly's house, Sue and Mia waited outside with Sargie and me. It was a short visit, shorter than expected. Everyone looked confident and happy when he left, without planning to obtain a search warrant. Lilly was no longer a prime suspect in the murder of Russ Johnson, but it would take time to assemble the pieces.

I was happy to see Toby when we got back home. He was waiting at the back door as he often did. But something was different. His nemesis, the new robotic vacuum, had released itself from the charging station and found the bedroom where Sue had left the door open. It ran out of charge beneath the bed near Toby's secret hiding place inside the cloth.

His eyes were big, but his heart was whole. Toby was happy to have us back home as well.

Chapter 39

A Week Later

Sue was enjoying her morning coffee while Toby and I watched the ducks swim around the cove through the glass door. He usually had his mind on other small things, but today he joined me in watching the ducks. They had grown much larger. The ducklings were as big as their mama.

The greater change was in their ascent up the slope. They no longer walked single file up the slope, but spread their wings to flutter up the slope. I couldn't call it flying because the ascent was so short, but it was something new. Once they arrived, they walked around the yard, as always.

It all happened so quickly. I recalled a time when we could barely see them walking the slope from the porch. I remembered when they resembled an alligator swimming into the cove, in a straight line behind Mama Duck. Birds grow to adult size much more quickly than dogs and cats.

Toby was sitting quietly, intensely focused on the ducks, when Gio called. I left Toby watching the ducks to sit next to Sue as she spoke to Gio.

"I'll come as soon as I can," Sue said. "I'll call Mia. I'm sure she wants to join us," she added before ending the call.

I followed Sue to the bedroom to dress for the meeting. Gio had played an essential role in arranging the setup to catch the scammers. He knew that Russ Johnson and Doug DeLeon were in cahoots at the poker match. Andy Lemar had said he never wanted to play cards with them again, but neglected to admit the original reason for their acquaintance.

I waited for Sue to signal me to join her, joyfully accepting the invitation for the upcoming mission. I hopped into Sue's car and we drove to Gio's house. He met us at the door and ushered us to the living room, where Val was serving coffee and tea biscuits to Mia.

"Hi Sue," Val said, massaging me under the ear. "Gio has news about the marked money," she added, pouring coffee for her.

"Mia has been telling us about your excursions around town," Gio remarked. "She says Lilly spent marked money to retrieve her ring from the pawn shop."

"Yes, she did," Sue replied. "She doesn't know it was marked money, but Sheriff Stone confiscated it as evidence."

"I understand Lilly got the marked money from Andy Lemar at the pub," Gio continued, and Sue affirmed it was true.

"My friends say Andy Lemar was spending marked money at their shops in Miami this week," Gio proceeded. "I've got people on the lookout for the marked bills."

"Fabulous!" Sue replied. "We're getting closer."

"Do you think Andy killed Russ Johnson and stole the winnings from the poker game?" Mia asked, and Gio said he was sure of it.

"What brought the trio together in the first place?" Sue asked.

Gio replied. "Russ Johnson. If you'll recall, he was a stockbroker."

"Yes, I remember," Sue replied. "A stockbroker and a womanizer."

Gio continued. "Russ Johnson scammed some of the wrong people as a stockbroker," he said. "He sold a housing fund a few years back. It was a scam to sell short when the banks were lending excessively and their debtors defaulted. Investors lost a lot of money, while he profited."

"I heard about that," Sue said. "What happened?"

"He took advantage of a few of my friends. They remember Andy Lemar. He lost a million dollars in Russ Johnson's investment scam. He agreed to play poker with Russ to get the money back, but he wanted out of the games."

"That's a lot of money," Sue said.

"Russ still owed Andy $600,000.00," Gio continued. "The winnings from the poker match paid off his debt."

"Interesting," Sue said. "That explains why he never wanted to play with Doug or Andy again."

"What about Doug DeLeon?"

Gio replied, "Doug also fell for the housing fund scam. $100,00 0.00. Mostly, he just liked to play poker and beat up non-payers."

"Weird," Mia said. "Did Doug get any of his investment money from the housing fund back?"

"I wouldn't know," Gio said. "He claims Russ still owed him $100,000.00."

"The money he's been trying to get from Andy, now that Russ is dead," Sue agreed.

"You've been very helpful," Mia said. "We appreciate your effort."

"There's one more thing," Gio continued, and Sue and Mia leaned forward to listen. "Andy Lemar rented a house from a friend of mine in Sweetwater Springs two days ago. He paid with marked money."

"Where?" Sue asked.

Gio described the location next to Chris and Jessie's house. "Wow," Sue said. "That hits close to the home of one of my best friends. Jessie used to be my roommate."

I jumped into Sue's car and we drove to Andy Lemar's rental house, next to Jessie's house. It was surrounded by more law enforcement cars than I could remember. Sue counted eight of them—more than at the recent arrest at Magic Mantee Pub. Moments later, Sheriff Stone led Andy Lemar out of the house, handcuffed.

Deputy Livingston carried the briefcase out of the house, containing marked money from the poker match, and placed it in his vehicle. Another deputy, unknown to anyone, led Andy's Golden Retriever out of the house. Sue later learned that the briefcase contained significantly less than the winnings that Andy Lemar had stolen from Russ Johnson after the poker match—the original quantity, minus the money that Andy had spent.

While we were watching the sheriff arrest Andy Lemar, Loretta called. "Mom, you need to come to the clinic," she urged. Doug DeLeon brought his German Shepherd to the clinic for injuries sustained in an accident. He paid a deposit in marked bills."

"Where is Doug now?" Sue asked, and Loretta replied he'd be back shortly. "I told him it would take about two hours to clean his dog's wounds and pull his dangling tooth."

"What happened to his tooth?" Sue asked, and Loretta said the German Shepherd had broken it loose while carrying Doug's briefcase back to his house from the car the night before.

"Interesting," Sue replied, "But I don't think his dog was carrying Doug's briefcase. Sheriff Stone just arrested Andy Lemar. I think he was carrying Andy Lemar's briefcase."

"How so?" Loretta asked. Sue replied that she intended to find out. "Mia and I will be there shortly," she said.

I recognized the familiar sights on the drive to Haywood Veterinary Clinic. It was the same drive through farm country as the drive to Loretta's house. Still, it seemed like Sue was in more of a hurry than usual. She seemed nervous, as if she were thinking about something important, but needed the answer.

Mia sat in companionable silence while Sue was lost in thought. She didn't want to disrupt the scenario in her head. Now and then, Sue mumbled something. "That dog must have taken Andy's briefcase and put it back," she said aloud. "He knew how to carry a briefcase, and Doug was working with him at retrieval."

"How are you going to get Doug to admit his dog stole Andy's briefcase?" Mia asked, and Sue replied that she might not have to get Doug to admit anything. "Maybe somebody saw him take the briefcase," Sue said.

Sue called Chris, who admitted to having observed the strange scenario the previous night. "It was weird," he said. "I didn't know what it meant, but something didn't seem right."

"What happened?" Sue asked.

"Andy got home around 8 PM," he said. "He went inside his house without the briefcase, then emerged a few minutes later and retrieved it."

"What's weird about that?" Sue asked.

"That's not weird," Chris replied. "What happened in between is weird."

"Go on…"

Chris explained, "A dog, about the size of a Golden Retriever, emerged from the hedge between our lots. It jumped into Andy's truck and took the briefcase somewhere."

"What happened next?" Mia asked.

"The dog put the briefcase back inside the truck and disappeared into the hedges. It seemed odd, but people do train their dogs to retrieve certain things."

"Could the dog have been a German Shepherd, not a Golden Retriever?" Sue asked. Chris replied, "Absolutely. I think it was a German Shepherd."

"You're a lifesaver," Sue said. "I'll explain later."

Sue drove into the clinic parking lot and got out of the vehicle with me on a leash. Mia followed behind her. They walked to the recovery ward, where Loretta examined the results of her surgical care.

"The tooth was badly fractured," Loretta said. "I had to extract it and suture the gums where it left a gaping hole."

"Excellent job!" Sue remarked, explaining her theory about how the accident occurred. "I expect it will heal quickly."

"Doug's story was similar, except it happened at his house, and it was his briefcase," Loretta said. "He says his dog was in a hurry when he jumped in his truck and must have grabbed the handle just right to fracture his tooth."

"Chris saw otherwise," Sue replied. "It happened at Andy's house next door, and it was Andy's briefcase he took out of the truck."

"That's quite a story," Loretta replied. "Doug must have taken the money he believed was rightly his, and his dog put the briefcase back in the truck."

"You got that right!" Mia said. "He paid you with marked money, and I just received a text message from Tori that he paid for lunch at Cat Tails Pub with marked money, too."

"He must have gone to Cat Tails for lunch after he left his dog at the clinic," Loretta said.

"Forensics can match the German Shepherd's DNA from the saliva when he carried the briefcase," Sue said. "There may be some blood on the handle from the fractured tooth."

"It should be easy to prove Doug's dog retrieved the briefcase, and he took the money," Loretta said. "Zeke would love to prosecute a case like this."

"Zeke isn't a prosecutor," Sue reminded her. "He's a defense attorney. With evidence like this, Lilly is off the hook."

"Why didn't Andy see the blood and saliva on his briefcase's handle when he carried the briefcase into his house?" Mia asked, and Sue replied that the leather was dark brown, and he probably hadn't noticed it.

Sue called Sheriff Homer Stone to inform him of the latest evidence. When Doug came to pick up his dog at the veterinary hospital, he was there to arrest him. Everyone believed he'd be going to prison for a very long time. Doug was an accessory to one of the biggest scams in the history of Sweetwater Springs and a perpetrator of aggravated assault.

Chapter 40
Sheriff to Lilly

Two days later, Lilly invited Sue and her friends to lunch at her house. Bill was back home, and she wanted to show her appreciation for their help in solving the murder of Russ Johnson. It had been touch-and-go for a while, but the evidence began to pour in. Zeke insisted it would be open-and-shut for the prosecution, but it would take time to go to court.

When we arrived at Lilly's house, I hurried inside to join Sargie in the living room. I was growing fond of his speckled self after spending so much time with the big boy dog. Today, he was lying on his big green bed, which Lilly had bought for him, similar to the bed Artemis had. Usually, he was standing when I saw him, but he looked comfortable lying on the bed.

"That's a great bed," Sue said, admiring the firm mattress where he reclined.

"Sargie loves it," Lilly replied. "His old one was worn out, and it needed replacing."

"It's just the right size for him," Mia added.

"He can stand up much more easily from his bed than the floor," Bill said.

"It's better for traction," Lilly said. "Sargie's not as strong as he used to be, and the arthritis makes him hurt when he moves."

"He feels better after his medicine," Bill continued, "Dr. Loretta made a difference to his mobility with the prescription for Sargie's arthritis."

"She'll be glad to hear it," Sue said.

"I hear she treated Doug DeLeon's German Shepherd for a broken tooth." Bill said, and Sue concurred, that he had been a patient at the clinic. "As you know, I don't talk about Loretta's patients."

Bill was seated on the couch, close to Lilly, with his arm around her shoulder. Lilly squeezed his thigh with her hand while they talked. They looked happy to be together after the unfortunate intermission.

"Thank you for coming," Lilly said, leaning forward to pass a tray of hors d'oeuvres. "I don't know where we might be without you," Bill added. "We must be the strangest newcomers to Sweetwater Springs on record."

"Maybe not," Mia said, mentioning the silver-plated gun at the museum. "Sweetwater Springs has its share of wiseguys, thugs, cons, and outlaws."

"I hope we don't fit into the museum," Bill said. "I don't want to be a relic."

"You're one of the lucky ones," Sue said. "You met up with the wrong people, but you found your way out of the woods."

"My brother is right about me," Bill said. "I'm attracted to the wrong people, except for Lilly, of course. She's my best friend and my saving grace."

"I was afraid I lost you," Lilly said, and Bill agreed it had been devastating when she left him. "I thought I lost you," he said. "I'm so sorry for putting you through this ordeal."

"I don't need more money," Lilly said, smiling at him. "I need you."

Sargie lay on the bed, gazing at Lilly, Bill, and their guests. He seemed happy to be there. Lilly and Bill were excited to learn home hacks and prescriptions for arthritis, but they wanted to know about the arrests. "How did you figure it out?" Bill asked.

Zeke replied, "We can't tell you everything because the case hasn't gone to court, but neither of you is a suspect."

Sue added, "The evidence is stacked against Andy Lemar."

No one mentioned the marked bills that had appeared in Miami, at the pub, the rental house, the pawn shop, Cat Tails Pub, and Loretta's veterinary clinic.

Mia said, "This trio of gangsters has known each other for a long time. They left a trail."

"I shouldn't have cared so much about that ring," Lilly said, locking eyes with Bill, who said, "I shouldn't have cared so much about opening a golf course on that priceless land. It was a bad idea for the town, and you didn't want another course."

Sue disagreed about the ring, "It opened up a whole new world of evidence when you repurchased your wedding ring. It was the beginning of the end for Andy Lemar."

"I don't know what you mean, but I believe you," Lilly replied.

Sue and Mia had graduated from being small-town sleuths to forming a friendship with Lilly and Bill. I was enjoying Sargie's company, too. Now that the crisis had passed, everyone seemed friendly.

"Do you think Andy Lemar would have developed that land?" Lilly asked.

"Yes, of course," Mia said. "If he wasn't going to prison for life."

"Andy is a special kind of con man," Sue added. "He'd do whatever it takes to make the most money."

Zeke agreed that he'd build forty houses on the property if he could, and showed them the blueprints. "Butch Boggs made a copy of this before he passed it over to the sheriff," he said. "It's a blueprint for forty houses on the cove."

Mia nodded her head in disgust. "Andy Lemar was a man with a plan," she said. "Honestly, I wish Thomas would buy that land and save it for perpetuity. We could make it part of a walking tour of Sweetwater Springs for the museum."

"That's a great idea," Lilly said. "I like Shameka," she added. "It would be fun for her to lead a walking tour."

"Shameka would enjoy that," Sue agreed. "Anything for the museum."

"I can't believe how much Sargie fur and Cleo fur was on Russ Johnson's clothes," she said.

"There was none of Cleo's fur at your house," Sue said, and Zeke admitted it was another turning point for the case.

"It's just a rough test," Mia said. "Nothing like DNA testing for concrete evidence."

Sargie and I followed the guests to the dining table, where Lilly served lunch of fruit salad, carrot salad, chips, and finger sandwiches. Everyone filled their plates, dropping a salty potato chip to the floor for Sargie and me.

"Sheriff Stone didn't search the house for DNA evidence of Ruff Johson's cells or body fluids," Lilly said.

Zeke replied, "You could have asked him to search the house. He wouldn't need a warrant if you requested the search."

"By then, he had a hunch who the killer was," Sue said. "It didn't take much to prove it after that."

"I would like the search to prove to Bill that Russ Johnson never came inside my house."

"Honey, I didn't care about DNA proof," Bill said. "I have your word."

"I promise Russ Johnson was never inside our house," Lilly replied. "I was stupid to let him come here so often, but we worked on turtles. We were never intimate."

"I believe you," Bill said. "The only reason you were stupid was because I was stupid."

Sargie and I hurried to the front door when the bell rang. We looked out the window at the big man, Sheriff Homer Stone, who was carrying something to the house. On closer look, it was a bouquet.

"Hello Lilly," the sheriff said, passing her the flowers. "Can I come in?"

Lilly accepted the flowers and led him to the table to join them for lunch. "Please join us," she said, ushering him to a seat at the table.

"I don't mind if I do," the sheriff said. "I'm nearly famished."

"It's just something simple," Lilly replied, passing him the finger sandwiches. "We are so thankful for your diligence in solving the murder," Bill added.

"I have those two cons in custody, as we speak," Sheriff Stone said. "It's up to the courts now," he added.

"Sweetwater Springs is safer without them," Mia said.

Zeke said, "I offered to represent Lilly if she needed my assistance."

Lilly squeezed his arm. "That was kind of you," she said. "I'm happier not to need it."

"I think life will be okay for you here," Sheriff Stone continued. "I understand congratulations are in order."

Lilly furrowed her brow in confusion. "I hear Daisy found something in your garbage," he said, and Bill smiled. "Sue found dog fur from my vacuum cleaner," Lilly said.

"None of it was Cleo's."

"I heard that, too," the sheriff said.

Lilly started to babble. "I'd love to have a play date with Cleo, Daisy, and Artemis," she said. "Everyone can get to know each other. It's such a friendly little town, but we had a strange start. Chris can help Bill put up a fence so the dogs can play. We are good people."

"Sheriff Stone means you're going to be a mama and I'm going to be a daddy," Bill said. "I told him Daisy found the pregnancy test."

"Do you want to have a paternity test?" Lilly asked, and Bill replied, "Never. I know who the Daddy is—and so do you."

"You're the baby's daddy," Lilly said, hugging her husband. Bill replied, "There was never a shadow of a doubt in my mind. I love you, Sweetie."

"You two need to settle down and act like adults now," Sheriff Stone said. "No more get-rich-quick schemes."

Bill promised never to gamble again, and Lilly promised to behave more like a new mama. "I'll read everything I can about children," she said. "I'm going to be the best baby mama I can be."

Bill replied, "I'm going to be the best baby daddy I can be, too."

It took months for the cases to go to court, but when they did, Andy Lemar got a life sentence for murder, and Doug Deleon got a lesser punishment for grand theft and aggravated assault. Soon after the trials, Sue hosted a party to thank everyone for their roles in the arrests. I looked forward to the tidbits and the drippings.

Chapter 41
Sue's House

I was excited about the drippings from Sue's outdoor griddle when she hosted the dinner party for friends who helped solve the cases of the scammers. I had almost forgotten about the tasty delicacies that emerged from the cooking beast that could easily fry twenty burgers at once. It was perfect for a feast to celebrate the verdicts from the trials. It was perfect for me to squeeze a few tidbits from the guests.

I lay on the kitchen floor watching Toby. Sue and Luke prepared sides and appetizers, which Toby found most interesting. He enjoyed watching Sue collect ingredients for guacamole, which he didn't eat, but was content to study the process. Luke sliced and diced while Sue combined ingredients and mashed the mixture.

Luke left Artemis at home so Toby could enjoy the preparations. Artemis was not on Toby's list of trusted souls, which included only those closest to his inner circle. Unless I missed my guess, Toby would vanish to the bedroom at party time. For now, he was in his heyday, exploring the kitchen with two of his favorite people.

Luke diced tomatoes, onions, and fresh jalapeños from Sue's garden into small pieces for homemade salsa. Sue combined the ingredients with lime and cilantro. Toby stayed on the sidelines, curious like a cat. It was the most activity he had seen in Sue's kitchen in months.

"I usually bring chicken wings to parties," Sue said. "This is more than I expected."

"We'll get it done," Luke replied as he chopped. "We'll have more than we need."

"Everyone will bring something," Sue agreed, pulling plastic containers off the shelf to send food home with the guests.

"This is going to be a shindig to celebrate for Sweetwater Springs," Luke said. "Justice is served."

"No more card shark, shady developer, and loan shark," Sue said, and Luke added, "Don't forget shady stockbroker."

"I didn't expect someone to be murdered at the card party," Sue replied, and Luke said, "Russ Johnson had the wrong people mad at him. Something was bound to happen someday."

Some of the ingredients went into hummus, which required the use of a noisy processor to mash the chick peas that Toby didn't like. He left the process for a catnap in the living room, returning after the noise subsided.

Sue boiled macaroni on the stove for a pasta salad, while Luke diced sausage. "I wasn't sure about your brother at first," Sue said, "But I like him now."

"I've never been sure about Bill either," Luke replied. "He's growing on me."

"He's sweet to Lilly," Sue continued. "He's been rolling out the red carpet while she's pregnant."

"I hope fatherhood keeps him honest," Luke said.

Sue replied. "He promised not to go back to gambling again. I think he learned his lesson."

"It could have been Bill or Lilly in that prison if we hadn't discovered and proven the truth," Luke said.

"I hope it's all right to expose the details of the setup now that the trial is over," Sue said. Luke replied, "It's coming out one way or another. It might as well come from us."

The party began promptly at 4:00, with guests arriving shortly thereafter. Everyone was aware of the guilty verdicts for the killer, Andy Lemar, and the loan shark, Doug DeLeon, who stole money from Andy, preyed on the town, and beat up non-payers after he lent them money. Few were aware of the card game and the setup with marked money that proved their guilt.

When everyone had arrived, the group assembled on the back porch for a question-and-answer session, followed by an evening of mingling and fellowship. "Most of you invited today had a role in solving the scammer caper," Sue said. "Thank you so much for your information, tips, and clues. We couldn't have done it without you."

Bill and Lilly stepped forward with his arm around her shoulders and her hands resting on her enlarging belly. At eight months pregnant, Lilly was round and glowing. "Meet Bill and Lilly," Sue said. "Bill is Luke's brother. He invited the scammers to Sweetwater

Springs, thinking he could make money playing cards and quickly profit to build a golf course. He has learned a lesson about gambling and no longer wants to build a golf course on the Green Cove."

When the applause died down, Luke continued. "My brother and his wife, Lilly, were both suspects in Russ Johnson's murder," he said. "Sue and Mia asked the right questions, and you provided useful answers to prove their innocence."

"Praise the Lord," Shameka said. "I was worried when Lilly spent so much time with Russ and those turtles," she said. "At first, I was jealous because Russ was my boyfriend, but then I realized he was a bad boyfriend when I found out he was married with children."

Some of the guests were unaware of the museum manager's relationship with the murder victim, let alone his marital status. A few people gasped. Sarah, who had the most experience with men of any kind, put her arm around her best friend. "Shameka will be all right," she said. "She learned a lesson the hard way, but her friends will help her through it."

"Thank you, Sarah," Shameka said, hugging her friend. "I'll always be there for you, too."

Peter and Stanley had supplied the photographs that proved their long-term liaison. Gio had used the photographs to identify the stockbroker, Russ Johnson, and suggested using marked money to follow his scams. Yet, they had never met each other.

"I have a question," Stanley told Luke, since he was a Miami attorney. "Why did Sheriff Stone let you get away with high-stakes gambling?"

Peter, who was head chef at Cat Tails Pub, added, "Some of the customers at the pub think you paid him off to play the poker game."

"I did not pay the sheriff off," Luke replied. "Sheriff Stone wanted to catch the card shark before he scammed more people. He asked me to host the game at my place and later, had it on good authority, to use marked bills to follow a money trail."

Gio grimaced, but said nothing. Although some people suspected his mafia ties, no one could prove it. He was a valuable source of information for tracking criminals, especially when his people were affected by the scam.

Lilly had taken the marked money to Brian's Pawn Shop to repurchase her ring. By then, Gio knew that Andy Lemar was spending marked money in Miami. But it was Lilly who first spent marked money in Sweetwater Springs, and later admitted she borrowed it from Andy Lemar.

"It never occurred to me that the briefcase containing the money was the one he stole off Russ Johnson's dead body," she said.

"We talked to the owner of Magic Manatee Pub," Mia said. "She told us that Andy and Doug had been arguing about money, but it wasn't unusual for arguments at the pub. She didn't know the details."

"It was the same night Doug was arrested for fighting with the farmer they had scammed in another card game," Sue said. "After Mia found out about the fight, we went to the pub to ask questions."

“Next, we followed your trail to Brian’s Pawn Shop, and alerted the sheriff when we realized you repurchased your ring with marked money.”

“That’s why you said, I helped solve the case by repurchasing my ring,” Lilly said. “I understand now.”

The Boggs brothers had been involved in the investigation ever since they thought Sue was a developer when she first took me to the lush grass of the Green Cove property. They knew the history of the Radcliffes and their land because of their grandparents' role as security guards. They had seen the changes at Sweetwater Springs over several generations and wanted the best for the local community. Frank Boggs knew more about Doug DeLeon than most, since he had played football with him in high school.

“I’m sorry I threw you off track about Lilly,” Butch said, tipping his hat to the pregnant lady. “You’re not the person I thought you were when I heard you yelling at Russ before he was murdered. Please accept my apology.”

“Apology accepted,” Lilly replied. “I was upset for Shameka when I found out Russ was married. He didn’t care about his sick child and turned off his phone.”

“You said what you overheard,” Sue replied. Mia agreed they had to investigate the tip, which might have been important.

You told us about his reputation in high school, and Rita warned us about Doug DeLeon betting on the opposite team and rigging the game so his team would lose in college. He’s always been a gambler.

"People can change," Frank said. "But Doug DeLeon is the same old gambler and cheat he ever was."

"What are you going to do with that land now that Doug and Andy aren't going to buy it?" Butch asked.

"We're talking about that," Luke said. "Maybe buy it and hold it so it doesn't get developed."

"The last time you bought land, you sold it to Thomas Baldwin to develop," Frank reminded him. Luke didn't answer.

"My husband cares about Sweetwater Springs," Mia said. "He doesn't want to overdevelop the land, and he's working towards cleaning up the river."

"I believe you," Butch said, before he turned to Sue. "We sent you that note in your mailbox," he admitted. "Frank and I weren't sure about you at first, but now we know you're good people."

Sue replied, "I appreciate that, and believe me, I shall choose my Friends carefully."

Zeke and Loretta had played essential roles as an attorney for Lilly and a veterinarian for Doug DeLeon's German Shepherd. Loretta had reported the marked money Doug paid for services for the broken tooth, implicating him in the crime of stealing Andy's briefcase. Zeke had suggested that DNA sampling could be done on the briefcase to prove Doug's dog had carried it from Andy's truck to Doug, who was hiding in the bushes where he took the money, before the dog carried it back again.

"That was some trick," Sue said, and Loretta agreed it had taken time for Doug to perfect the retrieval and replacement.

"He carried Doug's briefcase. It was a matter of teaching him to retrieve Andy's briefcase, aka Russ Johnson's briefcase, from the truck and return it."

"He didn't have much time to get back the $100,000.00 Russ owed him," Loretta said. Sue reminded her that they had been playing together for a while in Miami.

"Doug's German Shepherd carried lots of briefcases in Miami," Gio vouched. "He was a regular thief and a return dog."

When everyone was finished talking, I received the drippings and hamburger bites I had been waiting for. The afterparty was a success. Sue had cleared up some loose ends, and everyone enjoyed meeting the newcomers and sharing conversation. Bill and Chris decided to build a fence for a dog yard at Lilly and Bill's house. I looked forward to a romp with their first four-legged guests.

Chapter 42

Bill's house

Sue walked me to Sargie's house every day to check on the progress of the new fence. Bill and Chris spent two weeks building the fence for Sargie's dog yard. The fence enclosed half an acre of sloped land that led down to the waterfront. The rear fence had a large gate that led to a dock, but dogs weren't allowed to swim due to the alligators, so it was kept shut.

Sargie watched the fence progress with interest. His backyard was impressive. He followed Bill and Chris with stiff resolve, while they toiled on the project. Sometimes Lilly served iced tea when they took a break from their work.

"The fence looks great!" Sue said, admiring it while I stood beside her.

"It's almost finished," Chris replied, wiping the sweat off his brow.

"You've been a big help for the do-it-yourselfers," Sue said, recalling his work on the chicken coop. Chris replied he was good at keeping it straight. "Bill is good with tools," he added, mentioning his woodworking hobby.

"We're a good team!" Bill said, and Chris agreed.

Lilly waddled down the slope with a plate of sliced watermelon. "Honey, you should rest," Bill said, offering her a lawn chair.

"Thank you, Sweetie," Lilly replied. "I don't want to get up again, so I'll stand."

"Lilly is due in two weeks," Bill said proudly.

Sue smiled at her. "You must be ready to have this baby," she said, and Lilly replied, "I can't wait."

Sargie walked over and stood beside Lilly, putting his head against her thigh. He had always been an affectionate dog with his family, but Lilly's current growing condition made him feel even closer. His senior years made him slower, but didn't diminish his spirit.

"I want to have a dog party this Saturday," Lilly said. "I won't feel like company after I have the baby, so it's a perfect time to invite our four-legged friends for a playdate."

"The fence will be finished," Bill said. "It will be our private dog park, until we can collect opinions for a community dog park."

"Jessie will come, but not Redman," Chris said. "He doesn't go in the car anymore."

"I understand," Lilly replied. "Sargie will love watching the dogs play, but he doesn't participate anymore."

"Do you think Loretta and Zeke will bring their three Doodles?" Lilly asked.

"I'm sure they'd love to join us," Sue replied. "I'll let her know and have her call you."

"How about Shameka and Cleo?" Lilly asked, and Sue affirmed. "Shameka has been excited for a playdate with Cleo."

"If you don't mind, I'll ask Mia and Thomas, but they won't bring a dog," Sue said, and Lilly said, "Absolutely."

Bill said, "I'll invite Luke and Artemis."

Sue smiled. "It sounds like a perfect group for a dog party."

On Saturday, Luke picked us up for the dog party. I had been to the groomer and sported a new summer haircut for the event. It wasn't often that I got to run in a big dog yard with all of my best friends in Sweetwater Springs. I looked forward to playing with Cleo for the first time.

Sue spent a long time choosing her clothes for the party, although everything looked much the same to me. Worse, she changed her earrings four times. Dogs don't care about such things, but it made a difference to Sue, who was becoming more picky about what she wore around Luke. Still, she insisted they were only friends.

"You look beautiful," Luke said, admiring the pink dotted camp shirt over white shorts.

Sue smiled. "Thanks, you look nice too," she replied.

"Daisy had a haircut," he mentioned, of my shortened locks. "I'm sure she feels better."

"In time," Sue said. "She's still a bit itchy."

Luke patted me on the head. "I remember those days," he said. "Daisy will be better shortly."

I jumped into the back seat of Luke's truck for the short drive to Bill's house. Artemis and I rarely rode anywhere together, so I knew this was something special. He jumped over me to greet the guests when we arrived at Bill's house. It was unusual since I was usually the more excitable dog.

We raced to the backyard, where Leela, Luna, and Stevie were waiting for our arrival with Cleo. "This is terrific," Loretta said. "We can watch them play without worrying about anyone jumping in the river or running across the street."

"I was worried about that the first time we walked on the Green Cove Property," Shameka said. "Cleo would have chased those deer that came out of the woods."

"What's going to happen to that property now that the scammers are in prison?" Sarah asked.

"It will never be developed into a housing project or a golf course," Thomas said.

Luke continued, "I bought it."

"He has no plans to develop it," Sue said. "He wants to give the land to the city and turn it into a community bike park."

"Can we set aside a section for a dog park?" Shameka asked.

"We've been discussing it," Luke said. "We'd need a neighborhood petition and a plan."

"It's complicated because there is no parking lot for cars, and we want to keep it local," Thomas added. "A bike park is better for keeping it small and undeveloped for the neighborhood."

"Feel free to bring Cleo over to our place anytime you'd like," Lilly said. "We'd love to have her. The rest of the dogs are welcome, too."

Loretta brought a bucket full of toys for the dogs to share. Luna pushed a big ball with her nose, while Sargie watched the activity. Eventually, Luna tired of the ball and played tug of war with me, while Sargie chewed on a dog toy.

"Sargie loves the company," Lilly said. "Our big backyard is a perfect dog park for our furry friends that belong to you and the new neighbors we befriend."

"You have a lovely place," Loretta said. "You're welcome to bring Sargie to our farmhouse, too."

Jessie added, "We have a big backyard where the dogs can jump in the river."

"That would be fun," Lilly said. "For now, I'm thankful that Chris helped Bill put up the fence so that Sargie doesn't fall in the cove."

"I'm going to like it here on the cove," Bill said. "We've made good friends already, and I've never felt closer to my brother."

"Maybe we can get together and build something," Luke replied. "Maybe a swingset for my nephew."

"Or your niece," Lilly said. "We don't know our baby's gender."

"Whichever gender suits me fine," Luke said. "I can't wait to be an uncle."

Lilly sat down in a lawn chair with Sargie at her side. He lay his head across her lap, and she rubbed his ears. I lay beside Sue on the sand that would one day be as soft as the beautiful grass on the property that would one day be a park.

"It's hard to believe that only seven months ago, I was a suspect in a murder case, and Sue and Mia were trying to establish my innocence with dog fur color from my vacuum cleaner," Lilly said.

"It was a long shot," Sue said. Mia added, "It was a good idea for a starting point."

"Don't forget about Russ Johnson's DNA," Zeke said. "Sheriff Stone would have searched your house with your permission."

"I was afraid Bill might not believe me about Russ," Lilly said. "I almost asked him for the search for his sake."

Bill said, "I trust you, Sweetie. You had nothing to prove to me, but I'll spend the rest of my life proving to you I'll never gamble again."

"I hear you're the dog lover's attorney," Bill said to Zeke, who replied, "Dog DNA from blood and saliva is trustworthy evidence in court. It was a dealbreaker when forensics discovered Doug's German Shepherd's saliva was on Andy's briefcase, which had belonged to Russ Johnson before he was murdered."

"When Doug spent the marked money, it cinched the case," Sue said.

"The prosecution had an airtight case against Doug because of evidence from his dog's saliva," Zeke said. "I enjoy dog evidence as a hobby for now. One day, I might devote my whole practice to canines and crimes."

I lay in the grass beside Sue, with my four-legged friends. We were tired from our adventures in the new dog yard. Everyone was sleepy, but it was a good tiredness from friendly playtime with a senior who stood watch over us. I enjoyed Sargie and Cleo as much as Artemis and my cousins.

We made friends and outsmarted the scammers. I looked forward to spending time with my growing group of four-legged friends, wherever it might take us in the future. If anything could happen, it could happen in Sweetwater Springs. Make no bones about it—we'd be ready for the next adventure.

Chapter 43

About the Author

Dr. Stacey is a veterinarian and author of animal fiction, a memoir of the Cross-Florida Greenway, and a children's book.

After nearly thirty years of veterinary practice and teaching, Stacey decided to write books as a hobby. As a veterinarian, she was inspired by how pets uplifted people. She was encouraged by stories of people who served the community better with pets, such as school counselors, librarians, teachers, and veterans. Pets gave people purpose, loyalty, trust, and unconditional love.

Stacey takes her Doodle on weekend adventures with her family and friends. Penny is the ambassador for meet-and-greets. You may find them on the trails, kayaking the river, or walking the neighborhood. Penny is a magnet for connection with dog lovers everywhere.

Stacey lives in Homosassa, Florida, where she enjoys spending time with friends, family, Penny, and her cat, Andy— rescued during a summer storm at her previous home in Dunnellon. When she's not loafing with her pets, she writes books, reads cookbooks, practices yard work, or rides her horse on the greenway. Her secret dream is to reimagine recipes that are easy, bold, and delicious with healthy fats and little sugar.

Her cozy mysteries are narrated by a canine companion for a lighter look at crime-solving in Sweetwater Springs. Daisy, the Doodle, is perceptive, insightful, and eager to lend a sniff to the subject. Her crime-solving skills bring justice to the residents of the scenic small town. The perpetrators face accountability for their crimes through the results of her canine cognitions.

If you enjoyed her book, Stacey asks you to leave a review on Amazon. If you borrowed her book from a friend or a Little Free Library, where she donates free copies, please mention it in your review. You don't have to buy the book to review it.

Stacey writes books as Stacey Bonner Gerhart and under her maiden name, Stacey Bonner.

Chapter 44

Other Books by Stacey Bonner, DVM

Pooches and Pubs: A Doc and Daisy Mystery for Dog Lovers, by Stacey Bonner, DVM

Pippin and the River of Wonders: A Voice for Wildlife for Children 9-12, by Stacey Bonner Gerhart, DVM

Paws to Walk in the Woods: Dogs, Horses and Kindred Spirits on the Trails of the Cross-Florida Greenway, A Memoir By Stacey Bonner, DVM

Pets and the Miracles of Love: A Veterinary Novel to Enrich the Head and the Heart— from Dr. Penny's Notebook, by Stacey Bonner Gerhart, DVM

Alley Cats, Alligators, and All Spice: The Dog Walkers Discover Stray Cats, Food, and Friendship in Everyone's Favorite Riverside Town—From Doc and the Dog Walkers by Stacey Bonner, DVM

Stacey writes books under her maiden name, Stacey Bonner, DVM, and as Stacey (Bonner) Gerhart, DVM.

Chapter 45

Dedication

This book is dedicated to my daughter, Dr. Laura Gerhart, who kindly took a lovely senior Great Dane named Poe, pictured on the cover, into her home after his owner, who had worked at the clinic for almost forty years, passed away. Laura took the photograph during playtime in her backyard, where my dog, Penny, loved to visit her cousins. Poe fit in beautifully with her family's trio of Doodles, enjoying the rest of his life to the fullest. May Poe and his loyal owner rest in peace.

www.ingramcontent.com/pod-product-compliance
Lightning Source LLC
LaVergne TN
LVHW010601100826
845148LV00014B/2794

* 9 7 9 8 9 8 6 4 9 4 1 4 2 *